What wo

...in a soft dr__ ____ ____ __ nothing at all? Ian swallowed and spread his hands on his thighs. All his life he'd been surrounded by money and power and the people who had them. With few exceptions the girls he'd grown up with had set out to dabble in careers that were "fun" while they worked at making a brilliant match with a wealthy man.

But by her own admission Page Linstrom wanted nothing more than to make a success of a business she'd created herself, and Ian admired her. She was independent, motivated... And she apparently wasn't worldly in the accepted sense. He turned warm and shifted slightly in his seat. She had a wonderful mouth, very soft. Out of practice with men, she'd said. He'd like to kiss her, teach her to kiss him. It would suit him fine if she never got "in practice" with any other man ever again.

ABOUT THE AUTHOR

Before turning to writing full-time six years ago, Stella Cameron edited medical texts. Her dream then, and even as a child, was to become a writer. Stella and her family live in Washington State.

Books by Stella Cameron

HARLEQUIN AMERICAN ROMANCE
153–SHADOWS
195–NO STRANGER
226–SECOND TO NONE
243–A PARTY OF TWO

HARLEQUIN SUPERROMANCE
185–MOONTIDE

HARLEQUIN INTRIGUE
50–ALL THAT SPARKLES
83–SOME DIE TELLING

The Message
Stella Cameron

Harlequin Books

TORONTO • NEW YORK • LONDON
AMSTERDAM • PARIS • SYDNEY • HAMBURG
STOCKHOLM • ATHENS • TOKYO • MILAN

For Charlotte Cameron
who welcomed me as a daughter
and became a dear friend

Published October 1988

First printing August 1988

ISBN 0-373-16268-5

Chapter One

"Hey, hard body! How's business?"

"Busy, Peeler, busy," Page said. She dodged the off-duty guy from another bike courier service and rode on.

Getting mad wasted valuable energy and time, but the next smart aleck with a wisecrack was likely to get the full benefit of her inventive tongue.

To give her tailbone a rest, she stood up on the pedals of her bike and coasted, gathering speed, down Kearny. San Francisco could be a bike jockey's nightmare. It could also be a dream. Despite too many hours on duty, tonight Page thought the city was terrific. An autumn fog was rolling off the bay, and the cold, pungent air bore scents of exotic food to mix with the wreathing damp that turned the lights ahead of her into converging neon wires of red, blue and green.

The radio, hooked to the neck of her purple satin racing shirt, crackled. She pressed a button and lowered her head. "Yeah, Waldo?" At this time of night, Waldo Sands was her only customer. She made the 10 p.m. to 2 a.m. deliveries for his twenty-four hour delicatessen, Touch Tone Gourmet.

"You on your way, kid?" Waldo always called her that. Page smiled. At twenty-seven, a woman had to be grateful to be called kid by anyone.

"On my way." A cable car clanked alongside and a cab cut in front of her. "Laguna and Green, right?"

"Right. They just called back. Been waiting twenty minutes for their truffle pâté and champagne, they said. Need it pronto."

Need it. Who *needed* truffle anything at midnight? Maybe the customer was pregnant. "They'll get it when they get it. Soon. Talk to you, Waldo." She cut him off, jumped the curb and shot far enough forward to overtake the cab and bump back to the street.

She mouthed, "So long," over her shoulder at the cabbie and made it through a light just tickling red.

This job for Waldo was a blessing and a curse. A blessing because starting your own bicycle courier service in San Francisco was a hit-and-miss undertaking and any extra money she could make took her that much closer to success. The curse in working for Waldo lay in spending a good portion of every night, when she should be sleeping to get ready for the next grueling day, delivering goodies to people who didn't have a thing to do in the morning.

Still, she'd always be grateful to her roommate, Tanya, for finding Pedal Pushers the extra work. One day maybe she'd parlay the unusual aspect of a nighttime delivery service into a real money-maker. At the moment she didn't want to ask any of the four riders she employed to take on more than the relentless ten-hour shifts they already shouldered. In time there would be more riders. Page pedaled harder. In time there would be mopeds—and real quarters for the dispatcher and repair shop, rather than the garage behind the house where she and Tanya rented an apartment.

The cab caught up, passed, and the driver called to Page through the open window. "Hiyah, toots. Don't you ever take a night off?"

She aimed a foot toward a dented rear fender, grinned at the man's raised fist and made a sliding left turn onto Green. Uphill again. This was where the legs took it. Unlike any of the people she employed, Page preferred her single-geared, balloon-tired Schwinn to a racing bike, but the machine didn't make it on the steep grades of San Francisco without a lot of muscle help.

At Laguna, Page took a right and started looking for house numbers. The Pacific Heights area had always appealed to her, with its big Victorians, each one unique—and each one worth more than her fledgling delivery service was likely to net in more years than she wanted to consider right now.

This was it. White, big columns, fretwork around the windows and too big to miss.

Page considered going to a side entrance just visible through a trellis archway, but opted instead for the front door. She hauled her bike up wide redbrick steps and across the portico.

No bell. The hollow thunk of the brass knocker made her flinch and step back. An insistent beat of music played too loudly came from inside. Page lifted the distinctive black-and-gold Touch Tone Gourmet box from the basket attached to her handlebars.

The radio blipped again. "Yeah, Waldo? Making delivery now."

Waldo had his own radio at the store and enjoyed using it more than Page would have liked. "Do it fast and get back. We've got another rush job." He chuckled. "You sure are quicker than me taking the van out half a dozen times a night."

"I'll be there." She switched off and knocked again. Waldo looked like a sleek, well-fed cat when he laughed like that—a big, handsome, sandy cat. Page wondered, not for the first time, just how close Tanya and Waldo were. Tanya had evaded the question when Page asked, and just said they were friends. But Waldo Sands wasn't a man who spent time with a beautiful woman like Tanya just for friendship.

Despite the music, no light showed through the leaded-glass panels in the door. Maybe she had the wrong address.

Page leaned her bike against the wall and jogged back down the steps to look up. Ah, a steady glow shone against pale draperies at three of the upstairs windows.

She knocked once more, waited a couple more precious, money-making minutes, then turned the handle cautiously. The door wasn't locked. Either the owner was overly trusting or careless. From the delivery slip in her hand, the truffle pâté and champagne lover-in-residence was an Ian Faber. From the volume of the music, she decided he probably couldn't hear her knock, any more than he'd hear any other intruder.

As she opened the door, a pale wedge cut across the darkened hall, crept over walls covered in watered silk, glistening curved banisters, and up wide stairs.

Music blared down.

"Delivery!" Page called.

Nothing but unintelligible melodic yells from the entertainment, and high-pitched laughter. Damn. She couldn't afford this kind of time waste. Muttering, she hauled her bike inside onto Italian marble and shut the door. If the choice was between leaving a little dirt on the floor and losing her wheels ... there wasn't one.

By the size and weight of the box she carried upstairs, she'd been turning a magnum of champagne into a bubbly shake all the way from Sutter Street on the other side of Chinatown. Page made a wry face. Better warn the customer. Then, if he cared as little as she had a hunch he would, she'd get clear of the blast area before the cork went into orbit.

At the top of the stairs Page shouted, "Delivery, Mr. Faber." The noise came from the left where a wall sconce at the entrance to a corridor spread blush glow on thick red carpet.

She advanced, the box held in both hands, until she came to closed double doors.

For an instant she considered knocking, setting down the box and sneaking away. But she needed payment and a signature on the delivery bill. She knocked, waited, knocked again. Waldo wasn't going to be pleased with her efforts this evening.

There was nothing else to do but open another door she'd rather not touch.

An eardrum-puncturing blast met her, and the gyrating vision of a stocky man with curly brown hair, his pleated evening shirt open almost to his black satin cummerbund, dancing with two stockinged-footed women. Another man lay, one hand over his eyes, along the length of a beige leather couch.

"Excuse me." Page cleared her throat.

One of the women, a generously endowed blonde, wiggled past, her upper torso moving independently of a strapless white dress. Her eyes were tightly closed.

Page took in a litter of highball glasses and scrumpled napkins on a coffee table in front of the couch and decided this crew didn't need any champagne. Not that what they needed was her business. What she needed was a signature, immediately.

"Ma'am." She walked all the way into the room. "Hey, excuse me."

Finally she was sighted. The second woman, a diminutive siren with waist-length black hair that slipped around white shoulders to form a cape over a green chiffon creation, opened her eyes and stopped undulating.

"I don't believe it!" Her voice came to Page as a scream with words. A long red fingernail stabbed in her direction. "Kiddies, will you *look* at this?"

Amid choking guffaws, three pairs of eyes studied Page. She noted dimly that the man on the couch, his head propped on one arm, his feet on the other, seemed to be asleep.

The woman in green turned the music down a fraction. "Who *are* you?"

"Delivery for—" Page glanced at the sheet beneath her fingers "—Mr. Ian Faber." Her face felt as luminous as her skintight purple shirt and matching cycling shorts. Her daytime customers were used to the way she looked, and until tonight she'd never had to go farther than the front door on any of her deliveries for Waldo. In this setting she must seem clownish.

"Mr. Faber appears to be no longer with us. I'm Mr. Martin Grantham the third. Will I do?" he offered, while indicating the supine, dark-haired figure.

"Is that Mr. Faber?" Page asked, trying not to picture the way her long brown hair puffed up between the reinforced bands of her white racing helmet. "I need his signature and payment. All after-hours deliveries are paid for on receipt."

The woman in green inspected Page more closely. "Is it Halloween do you think, darlings? Let me see—" she consulted her watch "—no-o-o, another two weeks to go yet. So no treats for you, my pet. A pity. Such a good costume. What are you supposed to be, anyway?"

"Would you like to pay for this so I can get to my next delivery?" Page spoke to Martin III who rocked from heel to toe and back again with a fatuous smile on his flushed face. He didn't appear to hear her.

"I'm Deirdre," the black-haired woman said and giggled. "Who are you?"

"Page Linstrom for Touch Tone Gourmet." Irritation and weariness tightened the muscles in Page's jaw. "We Always Deliver" was Waldo's unoriginal slogan, and keeping this job with him depended on an ability to find any location fast and not leave until the transaction was completed.

"You really are quite pretty," Deirdre told her. "Isn't she, Liz? Not everyone could carry off that outfit, but she does. Do the elbow and knee pads come in other colors? I can't wear black."

The laughter that followed, the tears that squeezed from Grantham's eyes while the women leaned on him, held hysteria. Contempt dissolved Page's embarrassment. People like these, empty with empty lives, were to be pitied. Busy and focused every waking minute of her life, she didn't understand them and didn't want to try.

"I think that's about enough," the man on the couch spoke and his voice was the antithesis of hysteria. Cool, deep, tinged with disgust, it startled Page and stopped every other sound and movement in the room. "What the hell do you think you're doing?"

Ian Faber—at least she presumed that's who he was— stood up, fists on hips beneath his rumpled dinner jacket.

Page wasn't interested in the reactions of the three comics. "Are you Mr. Faber?"

"Mm, what?" He shifted dark, dark eyes from a furious stare at his companions to Page. "Yes, yes I am."

"If you'll just take delivery of your order I'll be on my way."

He glanced at the box. "Of course, my *friends'* midnight snack. Martin's very good at ordering things in my name." The comment elicited no response from Martin, and Faber added, "I apologize for my guests' behavior. Let me take that from you."

The package was heavy. She handed it over gratefully and waited while he went to a teak desk between two of the windows and took out a checkbook. "My boss insists on cash," Page told him while the others, snickering explosively from time to time, drifted to sit in various chairs.

Page concentrated on Faber. His curly hair was as dark as his eyes and he was tall, slender, elegant even in the suit he'd slept in. He was reaching inside his jacket for a wallet.

Page didn't like or understand Waldo's cash only rule. It embarrassed her when she had to tell customers about it, and carrying sums of money around at night couldn't be totally safe.

A muted noise from her radio made Page shift anxiously from foot to foot. Waldo wasn't going to like being kept waiting, not at all. She'd once seen him lose his temper with an inept store clerk. He'd fired the man on the spot. This episode could bring her the same fate if she didn't make up a lot of time on the way back for pickup.

"Here you are." Ian Faber tucked some bills into the envelope provided and signed where she'd marked an X on the outside. "Let me show you out."

Without a backward glance, Page left the room, Faber close behind. She trotted downstairs, shoving the envelope into the pouch belted to her waist.

"I don't think I caught everything that was said to you." Faber reached the hall neck and neck with Page.

"You didn't miss anything worth hearing," she told him.

"Forgive me, please," he insisted. "I don't put up with people being insulted in my house."

"*You* didn't insult me." She adjusted the Velcro bands at the wrists of her gloves and pulled the bike to rest against her waist. "And in this business you get used to smart comments."

"I don't suppose that means you have to like them."

"No. But you develop a thick skin. You have to. Don't give it another thought."

"That may be easier said than done." He opened the door while she tightened her chin strap. "Isn't this unusual?"

She paused to look at him. An angular, handsome face and a nice smile, pleasant mouth. He was very tall, tall enough to make her five feet ten inches seem less than usual, and he was solid in a graceful way. "What do you mean by unusual? San Francisco's full of female messengers."

"Not at night. It seems dangerous."

"Not if you know what you're doing," Page told him. He was attractive, almost too attractive. She felt him beside her, big, commanding. "Well, enjoy your pâté."

There wasn't room to push her bike past him in the doorway.

"Do you just do this at night?"

His interest puzzled her. Her work wasn't something that she talked about to anyone but her employees and other people in the business. This obviously privileged man came from another world, and she hardly knew what to say to him.

"Do you?" he repeated.

"No. We're a new service. Started eighteen months ago. I've got four riders, a dispatcher and a part-time mechanic, and most of our trips are during the day—all of them except these deliveries I make for the deli."

"And do you work every night?" He stepped outside and turned to face her. There still wasn't room for Page to pass.

"Most nights. When you're building clientele you can't turn down an account."

His features sharpened in the muted light from the hall. Long, arched brows showed clearly above slightly up-slanted eyes, and shadows heightened his cheekbones and settled at the tilted corners of his mouth.

A prolonged silence became awkward. "If you'll excuse me," Page said. As if surprised when she spoke, he drew in a breath and moved aside.

When she jerked her bike over the step he stretched out a hand to help, met her eyes and smiled. "You know my name. What's yours?"

She shrugged. "Page Linstrom." Why he wanted to know escaped her but she didn't mind telling him. With a last glance at his eyes, she bumped the bike down to the sidewalk and mounted.

His goodnight came to her distinctly as she rode away...so did the memory of his face.

"Goodnight, Mr. Faber."

IAN LEANED AGAINST a column and crossed his arms while he watched the woman speed off. In a few minutes, when he'd decided what to say before he kicked Martin and his two buddies out, he'd go back.

Tires squeaked and he straightened to see more clearly. Mist verging on fine rain drifted in swathes before a street-light. Crashing on a bike would be easy in these conditions. She moved fast. Even at a distance he saw the glitter of whirling wheel spokes. Then she turned a corner and was gone.

Page Linstrom might be interesting to know. He hadn't met a really interesting woman in a long time, and he'd sensed something deeper than the lovely exterior she presented. Slowly he sank to sit on the steps, lifting his face to the mist and liking its soft touch. She was certainly lovely; tall, statuesque but graceful. And the effect of blue eyes and brown hair had always intrigued him.

A roaring, grinding sound came from the sidewalk and a gang of teenagers on skateboards shot by. Shiftless kids hungry for kicks. San Francisco seethed with potential danger at night, people on the hunt for petty, malicious diversion . . . or a chance for hard-boiled crime.

It took a gutsy woman to tackle these streets alone in the dark. The danger of accident on slick streets aside, any female would run the risk of attack.

Ian stood, an unfamiliar mixed-up feeling in his stomach. He had no reason to feel concern for a woman he didn't even know. But it might be worth trying to see her again. How could he pull that off, he wondered, if for no other reason than to find out if she was as intriguing as she seemed?

He glanced back at the street, silent again now. Throughout the advertising industry he was considered innovative, inventive—Faber the whiz. His family's lucrative business didn't flourish under his leadership because he was short on ideas. The idea pressing in on him now was fuzzy around the edges but sharp at its center. Meeting Page Linstrom again definitely appealed, so did learning more about her. Exactly how was the hazy element.

Chapter Two

Four hours' sleep didn't cut it. Six o'clock came around just as Page was really getting comfortable, but there was no choice but to get to work. Her hair still damp from the shower, she wandered into the kitchen easing blue Spandex shorts into place.

"Good morning, sunshine."

Tanya. She sat at the scrubbed white wood table in the middle of the room. Page halted just inside the doorway, squinting. She had the start of a headache, something very rare for her. "What are you doing here?"

"I live here, remember?" Tanya tossed curly, shoulder-length red hair and hooked an elbow over the back of her chair. "You look awful. What time did you get to bed?"

Good old Tanya. Always on cue with the comment that made you feel worse than you already did. "I made my last delivery at two. Your friend Waldo makes sure I keep at it till the bitter end of the shift."

"You can always quit." Tanya slid to sit on the edge of her ladder-backed chair and stretched elegant, black silk-clad legs. Her black leather miniskirt rode high on her thighs.

Page considered reminding Tanya that without a steady infusion of money Pedal Pushers would all too quickly be a memory, but decided the effort would be wasted. The child of wealthy, indulgent parents, even at twenty-three Tanya had no concept of what it was like to be responsible for one's own fate.

"I need the job with Waldo. I'm grateful for it—and to you for giving me the lead. It's hard work but it pays well, and I get to keep the whole tag price instead of splitting it with another rider. That's a real plus."

Tanya yawned. "I don't understand all that tag price stuff. There has to be an easier way for a girl to make a living. But right now I'm more interested in your social life."

Getting annoyed with Tanya was a futile exercise. Page tossed her gloves and pads on the table and pushed aside a newspaper strewn with bicycle brake parts. The air was chilly. Winter was here, and expensive or not, they'd have to turn the furnace on.

"Did you hear what I said?" Tanya persisted. "It's time you did something besides work. And I wish you'd keep this bike stuff out of the kitchen—and the hall, and the bathroom..."

"I don't put it in the bathroom. Usually the parts are in my bedroom, but I needed the table."

Tanya rolled her eyes. "I'd love to hear how you'd explain all those oily lumps piled up in your room to a man. It isn't *sexy*, Page. In fact it's downright eccentric."

"Leave my bedroom out of this," Page said, but she laughed. "No one but me is likely to see it—except you when you decide to invade my space. Stay out, and your delicate sensibilities won't be offended."

"More's the pity that no one else sees it," Tanya said, frowning at a fingernail.

Page picked up a brake block and inspected it. "You know how I feel about that. I'm not suggesting men don't interest me." Men were Tanya's favorite topic and she refused to believe Page didn't share the fascination. "One day I may decide I have time for a relationship with someone—

if I can find a man who's prepared to understand that what I've started here is too important for me to give up.''

Taking a chair, Page sat down next to Tanya. "It's been a long haul. At the beginning I thought getting enough money together to leave Anchorage and just exist somewhere else would make me feel fulfilled. But that was barely the beginning. Making this operation fly is going to take years, and I have to do it alone. Men have a way of doing two things. First they can make a woman forget she has a right to be her own person with her own dreams. Second, if the romance fades she can be left with nothing but the habit of living as an appendage to someone else. Neither appeals to me.''

Tanya clasped her hands behind her neck and looked at the ceiling. Like the walls, it was painted a shiny yellow. "Just because your mother and sisters are doormats to the men in their lives, you don't have to expect all relationships to be that way.'' She sounded almost truculent and Page glanced at her sharply.

"*You* can love 'em or leave 'em, right?'' Page said. "No man will ever own you.'' She thought of Waldo Sands.

"You've got it. But that doesn't mean I think men aren't important. And the romance doesn't have to go out the window once the vows are said, the way you seem to think. Anyway, regardless of your theories I think you spend too much time working or thinking about work. That's all you do. It's not that I don't admire what you've done. Starting a business on a shoestring has to take guts. But you know what they say all work and no play does to a girl.''

"In other words I'm dull. I guess I can handle that.'' The brake block left oil on Page's hands. "James W. will have to take a look at this.'' James W. Amwell, jr. was a sixteen-year-old who lived with his grandmother in the apartment above Tanya and Page, and on weekends and after school he worked as the Pedal Pushers' mechanic. The boy was a studious recluse who loved repairing the bikes, although when asked he insisted his job was "mindless therapy for one of superior intelligence."

Tanya moved her coffee mug listlessly back and forth on the table and gazed into space as if she'd forgotten Page. Bluish shadows underscored her downcast eyes. Her full mouth was drawn into a tight line.

"What time did *you* get home?" Page asked.

"Oh—" one beautifully manicured hand fluttered "—a while ago."

"Figures. In other words you haven't been to bed yet."

"How do you know I didn't decide to get up and go for an early run?"

"In a miniskirt and spikes? Tanya, when's the last time you and I were in the kitchen together before I went to work?"

"You're being judgmental."

"When?" Page smiled and Tanya's wonderful green eyes slowly took on the lazy sparkle that was part of her beauty.

"Okay, okay. Never. Some of us have more sense than to brave the streets in the dullest hours of the day. I'm a night animal, friend."

Page noticed the red light on the coffee maker. "Oh, Tanya, you're wonderful. You made the coffee."

"Yes. I could have gone to bed, but I knew you'd be crawling out here in one of your elegant getups, too exhausted from putting on your makeup and doing your hair to take time for the simpler things of life. So I decided to take care of you."

"Sure, mother. And I bet you made oatmeal and put out my vitamins." Another of Tanya's pet complaints was Page's lack of concern about leisure clothes and her preference for little makeup and a simple hairstyle. She decided this morning was a good time not to take the bait on that subject. She poured coffee and returned to her chair beside her roommate. Up close she didn't look so radiant. "Is everything okay with you? You don't feel ill or anything?"

Usually Tanya fell into bed the minute she got home and left
for classes at a local art college a few hours later while Page
was at work.

"I feel terrific. I always feel terrific. Don't I look it?"

"Sure. I guess you do—if you can look terrific and exhausted at the same time."

"I'm not exhausted," Tanya said too quickly. "Why
should I be?"

"No reason, I guess." Page caught sight of an open
Touch Tone Gourmet box on the counter. Remnants of a
sweet roll littered a paper towel beside the box. A parting
gift from Waldo this morning? Previous subtle comments
by Tanya had revealed that she waited in Waldo's apartment over the shop until one of his employees took over orders and dispatches at two in the morning. Then they spent
hours together there. That worried Page. They seemed so
different. Tanya always put on a worldly front, but Page had
a hunch she wasn't as tough as she'd like everyone to believe. Waldo, on the other hand, *was* tough. He was the kind
of man some women found magnetic simply because he was
the take-charge type. Page prayed Tanya would be strong
enough not to let Waldo hurt her.

Tanya met Page's eyes and smiled, but not before Page
saw a shadow of anxiety. "Maybe I am a bit tired. Having
a good time gets exhausting sometimes, that's all. I'm
probably worn out from enjoying myself."

"You going to school today?" Page asked.

"Later maybe. I've got some errands to run after I sleep
for a few hours."

Page closed her mouth firmly. Her friend's attendance at
classes had become more and more erratic. Something else
that worried Page. When they'd first met after Tanya had
answered Page's advertisement for a roommate, Tanya had
been determined to show her influential Texas family that
she could go to school, become a dress designer and pursue
a career successfully. At that time, almost two years ago,

Tanya had worked as a waitress, insisting that she didn't want financial help from her parents. That resolve hadn't lasted, but Page understood Tanya's accepting money from her parents to go to school—as long as she went to school. What she didn't understand or approve of was what she knew her friend did most of the time: stay out all night, sleep most of the day, skip all but very few classes and use her family's generosity to support an addiction to expensive clothes. She looked at Tanya now and sighed. Not liking her was impossible. A funny, spirited charmer who was the best friend Page had ever had, she was all too easy to love. And at the back of her mind, Page didn't believe Tanya was happy.

A furious hammering on the front door almost made Page spill her coffee. "What now? If Lilian's upset the Zipper again I'll croak. I'm not in the mood for one of their spats." She pushed back her chair and went into the hall. Lilian Sweeny, a divorcée with a three-year-old daughter, was Pedal Pushers' intrepid slick-tongued dispatcher. Willy Kowalski, an ex-jockey who was better known as the Zipper, had been the first messenger Page hired. The two warred constantly, when they weren't trying to look after each other. The rest of the staff, Page included, shared a secret hope that the two would get together permanently.

The instant Page unlocked the door it swung sharply inward. If she hadn't jumped back her nose would have joined the never-ending list of injuries, minor and not so minor, that were an accepted blight in the life of a bicycle courier.

Rather than the Zipper or Lilian, Buzz Collins, nineteen and Page's youngest rider, stalked into the apartment, her bleached white hair gelled into four-inch spikes. "I gotta see you, Page."

"Sure." Resigned, Page led her into the kitchen. Tanya had left the room. "Sit down and tell me what's on your mind," Page said. "Want some coffee?" Buzz, officially Beatrice Collins, wasn't a complainer. The closed expression on her pale face spelled trouble, and that concerned Page.

"No coffee," Buzz said. She hooked her thumbs into the waistband of leopard-skin tights. "We gonna do something about what's going on?"

Page cleared her throat. "Aren't you people getting along?"

Buzz stared. Her mouth was an iridescent mauve slash, and indigo bands outlined her eyes. Page often longed to tell the girl how pretty she'd be without all the paint, the rows of earrings dangling from each ear, the bizarre clothes and studded leather wrist straps. But Buzz's mission in life was to be different.

"I asked what's wrong, Buzz."

"Zipper didn't say anything to you yesterday? Or Perkins or Ken?"

"No. What are you talking about?"

"Lilian didn't clue you in?"

Page's stomach made a slow revolution. "I just told you I don't have any idea what you're talking about. So spill it. I need to get to the garage."

"They said they were going to have a meeting with you."

Impatience jerked the nerves in Page's face. She took a slow breath. "Okay, let's take this a step at a time. There's something wrong between you people, right?"

"Wrong."

Page frowned. "There *isn't* anything wrong between you?"

"Right."

"Damn it, Buzz. Enough of the guessing games. If you've got something to say, say it. Otherwise get to work so I can, too."

Buzz crossed one foot over the other and bells jingled on the laces of her high-topped sneakers. "I knew you'd get mad. That's why I couldn't figure why you didn't say anything yet. Those chickens promised they'd talk to you so I wouldn't have to. They know I hate arguments."

"I'm trying to be patient...."

"Yeah, yeah. Well, we've got problems."

"So I gathered."

"It's this messenger outfit we don't recognize. We've all tried to track them down, but they take the kind of risks you'd kill us for taking, and we've given up trailing them every time. But so help me, the next time one of those turkeys trashes me I'm gonna ride like there's no tomorrow."

"That's it. Enough double talk." Page pulled out a chair and pointed to it. "Sit. And tell me what's going on. All of it."

Buzz perched her small shapely body on the edge of the chair and hugged her knees. "Some guys from another bike courier service are on our case."

"You mean you're getting hassled on the road? What's new about that? Banter between riders from competing companies goes with the territory and usually it's harmless."

A tinge of pink showed through the powdered white on Buzz's cheeks. "This isn't the usual. They know each other, we can tell that, but we've never seen any of them before. Or we don't remember if we have. And they're mean. Look—" she worked one tight pantleg above her knee to show a series of deep scratches "—and I wasn't going anywhere when it happened."

Page shook her head. "I don't understand."

"I was headed for a drop at about five yesterday. Traffic was max. This guy was beside me while we waited for a cable car to cross Pacific at the bottom of Grant. He kept looking at me."

"It isn't a crime to look, Buzz."

"It oughta be a crime to *accidentally* ram a foot into someone's spokes just when they're taking off."

The little hairs on Page's spine rose. "It had to be an accident."

"Like hell. He used his shoe right between a spoke and the forkblade. I fell on my face, and that's when I got the gravel rash. The Zipper's had a couple of run-ins and so's Perkins and Ken, and I've had it. I just want you to know I'm fighting back from now on."

"Whoa," Page said. "Hold it right there, lady. You know my policy. We're a clean outfit. Spills are part of the game, but safety, particularly for other riders and pedestrians, comes first. No exceptions. Got it?"

"You mean we're supposed to lie down for these turkeys? They're after us, I tell you, Page. There's a war on and we don't even know who the enemy is."

Page tried to think clearly. Stories about this kind of thing abounded in San Francisco, but she'd never put much stock in them until today. "Okay. Down to the shop. We'd better have that summit meeting before one of you does something we'll all regret."

She swept up her gloves and pads, gathered the brake parts and led the way out of the apartment and into another gray October day.

From the garage, Lilian Sweeny's voice rose above the standard morning hum of chatter and the familiar clanging of tools and equipment. "If you ate properly, maybe you'd grow. How's a man supposed to live on hot dogs and fries and pop?"

Page grinned at Buzz, whose face relaxed into a smile. "Some things never change, huh?" she said.

"You said it. Another day, another round of baiting between our resident lovebirds. Poor Lilian, she thinks if she could feed the Zipper up he might get to be taller than five two."

Inside the garage Page was confronted by typical workday chaos—with the addition of Jemima, Lilian's little girl.

The three-year-old sat on a tattered car seat amid piles of spare bike wheels, tires and heaps of nuts and bolts.

Lilian spied Page immediately. Standing, the woman was close to six feet. She was standing now, leaning over the radio to glower down at the Zipper.

"Morning, Page," Lilian bellowed. Her dark eyes, as dark as her wildly curly hair, narrowed on the Zipper. "Will you help me with this guy? Cold hot dogs for breakfast, and he wonders why he's a runt."

Most days Page would have entered into the debate. She enjoyed her colorful employees. They were loyal to her and to one another, the closest thing to a family she had here. But she wasn't in the mood to be flip.

She ducked a hanging bike frame that had just undergone the ugly painting and taping necessary to protect it from theft. All over the city, Peugots, Raleighs, Bridgestones and dozens of other expensive machines masqueraded as wrecks to save them from sticky fingers. Locking before making a drop took more time than most riders could afford.

"What's Jemima doing here?" Page asked, smiling to take any sting out of the question.

"She's got a cold." Lilian shrugged. "What else could I do? The day-care center wouldn't take her."

Jemima sniffled on cue, stuck a thumb in her mouth and clutched an old pink blanket to her face. Page went to ruffle the child's black curls. This happened regularly. Page had decided that whenever the dispatcher was short of money she brought Jemima to work to save day-care fees. Lilian had a hard time making ends meet, and although a smelly garage wasn't an ideal place for a tot, Page didn't have the heart to complain.

"You can put her upstairs in my bed when it's time for her nap. I'll leave you a key," she said. Sometimes the responsibility she felt for all these people weighed her down.

"Okay you lot, let's talk about these incidents you've been keeping from me."

A chorus of dissent went up. Then Ken Moore, a muscular, sandy-haired man with green eyes who had dropped out of law school when he decided the only boss he ever wanted to work for was himself, took the center of the floor and shushed the others. He was a confident, natural orator whom Page considered wasted in his present occupation. She could only hope he'd make more of his talents one day, although at twenty-eight he seemed happy in his present lifestyle and intent only on perpetuating his reputation as a lady-killer.

For the next half hour Page listened to stories of unprovoked mischief by an unknown group of riders. Inquiries among messengers from other services had suggested Pedal Pushers was the only group being singled out for the unwanted attention. Even the Zipper, naturally stoic, seemed concerned. He repeatedly passed a callused hand over his head, which he shaved "to cut down wind resistance," and fiddled with the many pockets on his leather vest. Perkins, the fourth and quietest member of the troupe, added his list of incidents, and Page was forced to believe they had a serious problem.

"All right. I get the picture. All I can think is that it's a completely new outfit and they've decided to try cutting down the opposition one firm at a time."

"So what do we do?" the Zipper asked.

"Nothing, except watch out for ourselves. You know the police are never on the cyclist's side. Not that I blame them in many instances. But we don't have any official place to go. Ride defensively. If you see one of these clowns, get clear. Don't get drawn into any arguments. Don't react. Just get out of their way. Sooner or later they'll move their attention elsewhere. Meanwhile, we've got drops to make, so let's get on with it."

To Page the day seemed endless. Business had picked up steadily in the past few months. Two more law firms, a prestigious architect and a busy printing outfit had been added to her list of customers. She should be ecstatic. She was ecstatic. She was also deeply upset at the possibility of being under siege from whomever was picking on her riders. Why hadn't she encountered personal attack? Maybe the answer was obvious. She'd been marked as the owner of Pedal Pushers, and the word was that she'd be best undermined through her employees.

In between worrying about her business she thought of Tanya. Buzz's morning interruption had been ill timed. Page became convinced that Tanya had stayed up to talk because she'd been upset and was trying to find the courage to confide. Page hoped the opportunity hadn't been lost for good.

AT ONE-THIRTY the next morning, Page wheeled her bike into the white-tiled entrance of the Touch Tone Gourmet deli for the fourth time that night. She pushed open a second set of swinging double doors and entered the store. Ropes of onions, dozens of huge sausages and string-cradled wine bottles hung in swags from the ceiling. Glass-fronted cases displayed an overwhelming array of delicacies. The aroma was of cheeses and grains and dried bunches of herbs. "If you want it, we've got it," was yet another of Waldo's rash boasts for his customers' benefit. Page wondered, not for the first time, just how cost-effective the ten or so deliveries she made a night were. Waldo insisted they paid very well, but that the main function of round-the-clock service was to promote goodwill. He believed so strongly in the concept that he'd invested in his beloved radio especially for the purpose. She guessed he knew his business.

Several minutes after she'd rung the bell on the counter, Waldo came down the stairs from his apartment. To Page's sharp eye he looked slightly mussed, and involuntarily she

glanced upward. He probably had a woman in his bedroom. When she met Waldo's pale blue eyes an instant later,
a flicker of understanding seemed to pass between them.
Page immediately busied herself removing delivery envelopes from her waist pouch. Tanya was likely to be the
woman with him. Why was the thought so upsetting?

"Big order," Waldo said in his heartiest voice. "And
there's a little one you can drop on the way, too. Then you're
through for the night." He pushed a large box along the top
of a display case and put a small one on top. "I think this
part of the service is getting more popular. I might ask you
for a second rider before too long."

"Wonderful." Why couldn't she feel triumphant? One of
the others would probably be delighted to make some extra
money. If not, she could hire a new part-time person.

"How're things going?" Waldo asked pleasantly. His
straight, sandy hair fell over his forehead. He was a big,
good-looking man, and he was always charming to Page. So
why didn't she like him?

"Pretty good," she told him. "I figure I'll need more
staff before long. Space in the garage is becoming a problem too, but it'll be a while before I can do anything about
a new place."

"I suppose you'll want to go to computerized dispatching one of these days."

He was an informed man who seemed to know a lot about
any subject that came up. "I wish," Page responded. "But
I'll have to get a lot bigger first."

"Let me know if there's anything I can ever do to help,"
Waldo said, his tone earnest. "You're a go-getter and I like
that. I want to see you succeed."

Page couldn't think of a response. She smiled and nodded. His interest in her business puzzled her. Sure, he was
committed to his night deliveries and needed her services,
but she didn't do anything a dozen other outfits couldn't be
persuaded to do if approached with a good offer.

She took the boxes and left the store with the sensation that Waldo was watching her. Not looking back took control.

Once on the road she checked the first delivery docket, then the second, planning her route. Easy shot.

Easy... Good grief, she knew the second address. How could she forget? After a long hard day, a two-hour nap and another foray into a drizzly evening, she was to be rewarded with a repeat trip to Laguna and Green.

The small delivery was to an elegant house near Lafayette Park. Afterward, with the payment envelope safely in her pouch, Page pedaled toward Ian Faber's house. Did the man throw a party every night? She prayed someone would answer the front door this time. If they didn't, she wasn't sure she could handle another scene like the one she'd experienced the night before.

When she arrived at her destination her spirits lifted a little. Lights shone through the colored windows in the door, and lamps flanking the entrance had been turned on.

She hauled her bike up the front steps and knocked on the door firmly. A breath caught in her throat and she pursed her lips. So Ian Faber was an attractive, interesting man. He was also out of her league. He'd probably laugh if he knew that, at this instant, the woman who delivered his late-night snacks and who must look to him like a refugee from a modern vaudeville show was standing outside his house trembling at the prospect of seeing him again. She *was* trembling—and breathless. This had to be the result of what Tanya had talked about. Too much work and not enough play. Why else would a realistic, intelligent woman go hot all over at the thought of a man she knew nothing about?

Footsteps sounded inside the house, hurrying footsteps. Page prayed, *Don't let it be Martin Grantham III.* She couldn't take any teasing at this hour. Almost frantically she tore her chin strap undone and pulled off her helmet.

The door opened. "Hi, Page," Ian Faber said. His smile crinkled the corners of his eyes. "Come in, please."

Speechless, Page lifted the box from her bike basket and gave it to him.

"Thanks. If you'll come up I'll write a check."

She hesitated, took a step inside the door and thrust out the envelope. "I'll just wait here." An uncomfortable jumpiness filled her chest. "And it's cash, remember?"

"Right, cash." He closed the door behind her and hunched one shoulder. "Might as well keep the cold out. Had a busy night?"

Page swallowed. Was she imagining things, or was he nervous? "Pretty hectic," she told him.

He shifted the box from one arm to the other. "How late do you work?"

She shouldn't feel uncomfortable because a man tried to be polite. "Until two," she said and attempted a smile. "Time to go home now."

"That's what I thought. Please come up."

Without waiting for her response he walked upstairs.

Page watched until he reached the top and looked down at her. If she stayed where she was he'd take her for an insecure ninny. She set her helmet on the floor inside the door and followed him.

Ian led the way into the room she'd seen the previous night. Once she was inside he set the box on the coffee table and began to unpack and examine the contents.

A bottle of wine, a wheel of Brie, several boxes of crackers and an assortment of other containers were arranged on the table. Page sighed loudly and snapped the elastic on an elbow pad. He gave no sign of noticing.

"Is everything there, Mr. Faber?"

"Ian." He didn't look at her.

Page opened her mouth but couldn't think of a thing to say. Tonight he wore black pants and a black crewneck. His dark, curly hair looked even darker than she remembered;

so did his brows, and his eyes when he finally looked at her. She also hadn't noticed the deep cleft in his chin before, or the olive tone to his skin that suggested a tan, or the frown line between his brows that seemed at odds with a constant hint of a smile. Was stunning a suitable description for a man? Ian Faber was stunning, compelling... an overwhelming presence that made the air around Page very still.

"Are you tired?" he asked abruptly, returning her stare.

She took a breath. "No... Well, yes, I guess I am."

He went to a bar in one corner and returned with two glasses. "Would you like some wine?"

"No thank you." He was a stranger and his behavior ought to frighten her. "If everything's all right I'll leave you to your... Ah, I'll leave you." She was more excited than frightened, which probably made her a fool. For all she knew, the man could be dangerous, and he was too big to escape from if he decided he didn't want her to go.

"They told me at the deli that delivery shifts changed at two." He'd opened the bottle, poured the wine and now he offered her a glass. "I tried to work it so I'd be your last customer, and I pulled it off."

Page's heart made a slow revolution. "Why would you want to do that?" The question sounded like a fishing expedition. "I mean why...?"

His laugh was anything but confident, and Page glanced behind to locate the door. Maybe if she ran without warning she'd catch him off guard.

"You're wondering why I pulled a stunt like this, right?"

She looked at her feet.

"Right. Well, last night you hit a chord I'd forgotten all about. You interested me. You still do. Is that okay?"

If this was a come-on it was definitely a new one to Page.

When she didn't answer he set down the glasses and started to pace. "Anyway, I just wanted a chance to talk to you again and tell you I don't think it's such a hot idea for a beautiful woman to be riding around San Francisco at night all alone and on a bicycle." He paused and Page met his eyes. He was serious, truly serious—at least, he looked it. "Ever since I watched you ride away I've been thinking about it."

She heard what he said, absorbed the words and felt a brief rush of warmth...before common sense returned. This was the best line she'd ever heard. Ian Faber wasn't the type of man who worried about grunts hired to tend his whims. She scanned the room, half expecting to see his friend Martin contouring his stocky frame behind the trunk of a ficus tree near the bar, or pressed beneath the keyboard of a baby grand piano at the far end of the room. She could almost imagine him betting Ian that he couldn't pull off this practical joke.

"I've caught you off guard," Ian said. "I'm sorry. I just didn't know any other way to get in touch with you. Asking the guy at the deli where I could reach you didn't seem like such a good idea."

"Why?" Page found her voice, but it sounded strange.

Ian looked as if he was surprised that she'd spoken at all. He stopped pacing and passed a hand over his thick, well-cut hair. "Isn't it obvious?"

"Not to me." Nothing about this encounter was obvious to Page.

"I was afraid he'd think you were, uh, well, you know."

She was beginning to be dimly afraid she did know. "Perhaps we should stop this conversation right now. I may be getting the wrong impression, and neither of us would want that."

"Oh, no, no, Page. Listen, I only meant I didn't want to risk giving your customer the impression you were using your deliveries as a chance to make friends..." He threw up his hands. "Oh, hell, I don't know what I mean. None of this is coming out right. It's straightforward, really. I wanted to see you again. You intrigue me..." His color heightened. "This sounds dumb. Put simply, I'd like to get to know you better. Last night I didn't think to ask you the name of your company, so I had to resort to this, okay?''

Not okay, Page thought, stepping backward. He might be the first man she'd looked at—really looked at in a long time—and he hadn't actually made a physical move on her yet, but she didn't intend to wait around and find out if he would. Being lured to a house where no one would think to look for her, by a stranger who was unlikely ever to be connected with her disappearance if it occurred, was reason to panic. At any second she was about to do just that.

He came toward her.

"Don't come any closer." Page took another step backward and stumbled on the edge of the rug. Her arms flailed and she recovered her balance. Crouched, she held out both hands. "Let me leave or I'll scream."

Ian stopped, his hands at his sides. Page saw his eyes widen and the color leave his face. "I frightened you. Good Lord, I've never frightened a woman in my life."

Her thighs and calves cramped. He looked . . . shocked.

"Please listen to me," he said. "I thought this would be an amusing way to get to know you. It even seemed clever at the outset. I really am sorry if I've scared you. Good Lord." He picked up a glass and swallowed some wine, watching her as if he expected her to start screaming.

Slowly Page straightened. Dull heat throbbed in her face and neck. "You really are trying to be nice, aren't you?"

He nodded, frowning deeply.

"Oh boy. I feel like a fool. I guess I'm tired and out of practice."

"Out of practice?"

The heat in her cheeks throbbed more. "With men," she said, feeling miserable.

"I see."

She doubted if he did see at all, and she still didn't fully believe he could be interested in her. There was never any doubt in her mind that she was attractive—enough men had told her so—but Ian Faber obviously moved in circles where beautiful women were plentiful.

Nothing like this had ever happened to Ian. He watched her warily, half expecting her to leap from the room and dash away. If she did he'd have no alternative but to let her go. Her reaction had made him feel like an ass, an adolescent playing silly games. And he had genuinely scared her. He hated that.

"Could we call a truce, do you think?"

She lifted the long, windblown mass of dark hair off her shoulders. Her eyes were bluer than any he remembered seeing. Damn, why didn't she speak? He looked at her mouth, wide, soft, parted a little over very white teeth.

"Here. Have some of the wine. You look as if you need it."

She laughed, and relief rushed into his tense body. Still laughing, she took the other glass and sipped, smiling tentatively at him over the rim. Ian took another swallow and quelled what could only be a self-destructive urge to hug her. She'd probably slap him.

"You must think I'm a nut," she said at last.

"Because you thought I was related to Jack the Ripper?" He wrinkled his nose. "Nah. All the women I lure here think that. I'm used to it."

She laughed again and his stomach tightened. Relaxed, she was even more appealing. Her skin shone slightly. She appeared to wear no makeup and didn't need any. Every feature was clearly defined and the light in her eyes held honest warmth.

He realized his mouth was open. "Um, sit down, sit down, please. If you've got time?" he added hastily.

"I really should go...."

"Please?"

With a faint shrug she did as he asked, choosing one end of the couch. "You have a beautiful home," she said. Her voice broke slightly. He liked the effect.

"Thank you. It's too big for me. That's why I live on the second floor—unless I have a lot of people to entertain. I'm always thinking I'll fill the whole place up with a family one day." Brilliant. She could certainly make something of that comment if she thought about it for a while.

Page only nodded and rotated the stem of her glass. She was tall, with long, shapely, muscular legs. Her body, inside a pale blue leotard and knee-length shorts, made Ian think things he probably shouldn't think, at least for now. Page Linstrom had the kind of body any man would react to.

She met his eyes and glanced away quickly. He made her uncomfortable. "Where do you live?" he asked. Getting personal could be hazardous, but if he didn't say or do something fast he'd probably never see her again.

"Russian Hill."

"Is that where your business is?"

She held her bottom lip in her teeth for an instant. "Yes. I rent the garage behind the house where my apartment is."

"And you call yourself...?"

"Pedal Pushers."

"Cute. How long have you been there?"

The teeth dug into the lip again. "Two years."

"You come from San Francisco?"

"Anchorage."

"Alaska. You're a long way from home." How many more questions before she told him to mind his own business? "I was born here. My family's in advertising. Faber and Faber. Maybe you've heard of us."

She shook her head.

Ian took a long, slow breath to calm his leaping nerves. He didn't know why for sure, but the tougher this got the more determined he was to break down her defenses.

"Do you live alone?"

Her eyes darkened slightly. She didn't reply.

He grimaced. "Dumb question, right? Jack the Ripper question. I only meant, I wondered if you... Scratch the question."

"I share an apartment with another woman." She looked into her glass, but he saw her amusement. "And I like my job. I've got big ambitions for expansion. San Francisco's the most exciting city I've ever seen, and I intend to spend the rest of my life here. What else do you want to know? Oh, I'm twenty-seven, single, never been married—and don't intend to be. Parents living, one brother, two sisters, no pets, except for my dispatcher's three-year-old daughter, and I'd steal her if I didn't know her mother would put up a fuss." She paused, grinning broadly now. "There, total disclosure, though I don't have a clue why you care about me one way or the other."

Ian scratched his head. She was gorgeous, bright, appealing, and she didn't know it. He was going to have to step right up and see if he couldn't do something about that. It might take a lot of effort but of the most pleasurable kind.

"My turn. Then I'll ask you another question."

She gave a mock groan and leaned back. He watched the play of muscle and soft flesh and stiffened his jaw. "I'm a marital holdout, too. Thirty-six and an only child. My folks are still in the area, and Dad sits on the board while I do the dog work around the firm."

Page watched him from beneath lowered lashes and after a short pause said, "And?"

"And nothing. That's all of it that's worth reporting. How about some of this Brie? I bought all this stuff to share with you."

"No thanks, Ian." She checked her watch. "Oh, no, three o'clock."

He frowned. "What happens at three? Do you turn into a pumpkin or something?"

"It's not what happens at three that counts. But at six I have to get up and start another day's work, so if you'll excuse me—"

"I won't." He put a hand on her arm. "Not until I say what I set out to say tonight."

She stood up, moving away from his grasp. "Haven't you said it?"

"Not quite." Quickly. He had to think of something this instant or he'd miss what could be his only chance to ask to see her again. "I wondered if you take necessary precautions on the streets at night." Boy, that sounded weak.

"Thanks for the concern," she said, "but I do know what I'm doing."

She probably did. Now he had to go for it and get to the point. "Yes, well, actually there was another thing I wanted to ask you."

She was edging toward the door. A few more seconds and he'd blown it.

"Goodnight then, Ian."

He closed his eyes and swallowed. Not one of his friends would believe this. "Page—" he rubbed his hands together "—how would you like to spend Saturday night in Sausalito with me?"

Chapter Three

From the corner window of Faber and Faber's boardroom in the Embarcadero Center, Ian could glimpse San Francisco Bay. A shifting web of fog separated an ominous late-morning sky from the flat gunmetal water. It wasn't the picture-postcard image thousands of tourists sent home, but he liked it well enough. Dismal fitted his mood.

"Did you hear what I said, Ian?"

Samson LeBeck was holding forth on something or other. "Why don't you recap for me, Samson," Ian said, focusing his eyes if not his whole attention on the corpulent little man. Samson was a pedantic pain, and if he didn't own a big block of Faber stock Ian would consider telling him as much.

"I was addressing the question of expansion," Samson said, puffing up his chest inside his navy pinstripe suit.

Ian concentrated on a straining jacket button. The man should address the matter of his own expansion, he thought, his mind slipping away again, away from the vast rosewood table and away from the men who surrounded it.

He could hardly bear to remember last night, what he'd said, the way Page had recoiled and bolted. She'd thought he was asking her to go to Sausalito with him for the night— literally for the night. By the time he'd recovered she'd been vaulting downstairs like a hurdler and there hadn't been time to explain that he meant he'd like to take her to see his parents' home. Damn it.

The drone of voices persisted. Faber had long ago become a major force in the advertising industry, his father was pointing out. Their west coast headquarters hadn't proved a handicap, but they should think of leaning more heavily toward the New York scene. Grant Maxwell, their vice president of operations for the east coast, was doing a fantastic job, but the time had come to show him a vote of confidence and cut him loose a bit more. Grant needed a freer hand. Ian smiled at Robert Faber. His old man still had it. He never stopped thinking, moving.

Ian pushed the blank notebook in front of him back and forth, grabbed a pencil and wrote furiously: "I was a fool last night." He scratched out the words and tried again. "Forgive me for last night. I know how it sounded, but I honestly wasn't asking you to sleep with me."

"Are you with us at all, Ian?" His father sounded uncharacteristically irritated. "We need your vote on this."

"Yeah, right—you've got it."

He raised a hand, and as he did so, Clemmie, his secretary, gathered his notebook onto the pile she'd collected.

"Just a minute..."

The notebooks were handed to his father who cleared his throat and adjusted his glasses on his thin, high-bridged nose. "Okay, we've got one, two, three, four, five...yes votes. And..." His smooth, still taut skin turned an interesting shade of puce. He looked up at Ian. At seventy, Bob Faber remained a very handsome man who, with a look from eyes as dark as his son's, could wither even the most intrepid. His son was the recipient of one of those looks now. "This isn't very clear, Ian. This is your pad, the one with the, ah, explanation?"

Ian crossed his arms and nodded.

"And I take it your vote is to give Grant more leeway?"

So much for secret ballots. "Yup." He'd better get hold of himself and prepare for an onslaught from his mother. She was the only person his father would mention the note to, and then the subtle interrogation would begin. Any hint of an eligible female on the horizon sent Rose Faber's grandmotherly antennae skyward. She and his father made no bones about their impatience for Ian to marry and have children. Usually he made sure they knew nothing about his love life.

"Next on the agenda is the question of fees for television campaigns...."

Several sentences later Ian stopped listening again. What would Page look like in a soft dress, a swimsuit... in nothing at all? He swallowed and spread his hands on his thighs. He'd be lying to himself if he didn't admit the lure of a different kind of woman from the type who buzzed through his life with nothing in mind but a brilliant match.

By her own admission, Page Linstrom wanted nothing more than to make a success of a business she'd created herself, and Ian admired that. She was independent, motivated... He turned warm and shifted slightly in his seat. She had a wonderful mouth, very soft...

"Now, Ian. Is there something you'd like to—"

"Not a thing." He pushed his chair back so hard he had to stop it from falling. Addressing his father he said, "Forgive me, Dad. I seem to be having difficulty concentrating."

Bob Faber grunted, but the beginning of a smile was obvious.

"Anyway," Ian rushed on, "I've got a lot on my mind and I think the sooner I take care of it the better. So if you'll all excuse me, and if you can all clear your calendars for an hour at, say, two—we'll reschedule the meeting for then."

Murmurs of surprise followed him to the door where his father's voice stopped him. "Good luck, Ian. I'll look forward to hearing how things come out."

Ian returned to his office. For three years he'd held the presidency of Faber and Faber, which meant that his father stayed in the wings as chairman of the board and pretended to be semiretired while he continued to watch every move his son made. And Ian took pleasure in knowing he hadn't disappointed him.

"Mr. Faber!" Clemmie followed Ian breathlessly into the big, striking room he'd decorated himself. "Mr. Faber, your father asked me to give you this. He also said for you to let him know when you're free for golf."

"I'll call him later." Ian took the folded sheet of paper Clemmie proffered, knowing roughly what it was. He waited until she retreated, closing the door smoothly and softly over dove-gray carpet.

He unfolded the lined yellow paper and read what his father had written underneath his own scribbled efforts: "When you want something and it's worth the effort—go after it." Smart man, his father. He and Ian shared a special closeness, and Bob Faber was bound to have recognized that his son's behavior this morning had been out of character.

Yeah. If a man wanted something badly enough he should go after it. With purposeful strides he crossed to the simple mahogany desk that sat between two floor-to-ceiling windows.

From his pocket he took a card on which he'd written a telephone number. There was one instant when he hesitated, but only an instant. Then he picked up the phone and dialed.

"PEDAL PUSHERS. You got something to peddle? We got the push. Name your game."

Aghast, Page listened to Lilian answer the phone. Something must change around here in the telephone answering department. Success and a professional approach went hand in hand.

"Oh yes, sir," Lilian said, standing up and saluting. "Yes, *sir*."

Page whispered, "Cool it." Surely Lilian didn't ham it up every time a customer called. Usually Page was on the road and didn't hear much of this end of the business. Half an hour earlier she'd jumped the curb to avoid an opening cab door, wrapped a wheel around a fire hydrant and been forced to come back for a repair, otherwise she wouldn't have witnessed this exchange.

She'd deal with Lilian later. Deftly, she slid on a fork tip and reached for a wrench.

"Perfectly possible, sir," Lilian was saying. "Ms. Linstrom is in her office. She may be in conference, but I'll buzz her and see if she can talk to you."

At that Page stood up, hands on hips, grinning and shaking her head.

Lilian tilted up her nose. She covered the receiver. "Sounds like *big* business. He won't speak to anyone but the owner." Lilian leaned heavily on the word owner.

Wiping her hands on an oily rag, Page stepped over the bike and went to the cluttered radio table where a pile of dockets partially buried the telephone.

"Sir," Lilian said into the phone, "Ms. Linstrom for you."

Page took the phone, frowning at Lilian who chortled silently into a fist.

"Page Linstrom here."

"Don't hang up."

Ian Faber. She opened her mouth, but the air went out of her lungs instead of in. All her blood drained downward. Glancing at Lilian, she said, "I believe we spoke before, Mr. Faber, and as I told you then, we are definitely unsuited to what you have in mind."

Lilian had sat on the tattered car seat and picked up a magazine.

"Page, listen to me. You may not believe this, but I could find a hell of a lot of people who would vouch for my reputation."

"I'll bet."

He expelled a gusty sigh. "Geez, lady. I feel like I'm jinxed with you. All I have to do is open my mouth and my foot automatically finds it."

Page rubbed her eyes and smiled a little. He sounded desperate.

"Are you still there?" he asked.

"Yes, I'm still here. You ordered me not to hang up, remember?"

"Will you please forgive me for saying such an asinine thing last night?"

"Ian, I—"

"No, don't say it. Don't cut me off."

"You do have a way of wanting to tell me what to do, don't you?"

She heard him tap the phone at his end. "I want to start this conversation again. Last night was a mess. What I was trying to do was to find a way to ask you out without you thinking I was ... was ... you know."

He had such spectacular eyes when he was being serious. In her mind she saw those eyes now. Penetrating, sexy. And she was nuts. She had no time for this. "Thanks for the call, Ian. Don't give last night another thought."

"Please," he moaned, "don't do this to me. Say you'll go out with me. Just once if that's all you'll give it. Or just once to see if you can stand me. I'll go anywhere, a museum, grocery shopping, you name it. I just want to find out if what I feel about you is worth pursuing."

He immediately groaned and Page laughed. "Oh yes, you do have a way with words. But I understand and I thank you. If I had time I'd say yes, but—"

"But you'll make time. And by the way, all I meant last night was that I thought it might be nice to take you over to

Sausalito for the evening. My parents live there. I thought if I invited you to their home you wouldn't feel threatened."

Page sat heavily on the edge of the table. She loved the sound of his voice. He was special. If she cut him off completely would she regret it later? And would it hurt just to go out for once?

"Page, are you thinking?"

"Yes."

"What are you thinking?"

"I'm thinking that it couldn't be such a sin to take a few hours off—"

"Wonderful! Terrific! When?"

"Just a few hours and just once. I'm not the right kind of woman for you, Ian, but I'd enjoy going out anyway." She liked the sensible ring of her voice.

"Can you go tonight?"

"Impossible. The only night I don't work, or have to get ready for work, is Saturday."

"Today's Thursday." He sounded disappointed.

"Right."

He sighed again. "Okay, Saturday it'll have to be then. Name the place."

"Wherever you want to take me."

"Okay. Dress very casually. I'll pick you up at . . . three? I've got the address."

He would have the address by now, Page thought wryly. "Three's fine." If they went early, she could get back early. "Goodbye."

"'I'm getting married in the morning. Ding dong the bells are going to chime . . .'"

Page had forgotten Lilian, who reclined in the seat, her hands clasped behind her head, smiling beatifically as she sang.

"That's enough," Page said and climbed back to her spot beside the bike she'd been repairing. "Don't make something out of nothing and don't mention what you heard to any of the others.''

'''You do have a way with words,''' Lilian said in a high voice. "And what did happen last night, boss?" She jumped up and stood beside Page. "Tell Auntie Lilian all."

Page looked up and realized, not for the first time, that Lilian was a beautiful woman in a strong, unconventional way. She sat on the dirty floor and clasped her knees. "Last night, Lilian, I met a magnetic, rich, handsome, incredibly sexy guy who asked me to spend the night with him next Saturday. And I just told him I would."

With that, she got up, tested the wheel and left the garage.

Chapter Four

Spray whipped over the bow of the ferry. Page licked her lips and tasted salt. Even in her fur-lined, army-surplus parka and jeans and with thick socks inside her tennis shoes she was cold. She suppressed a shiver but pulled up her hood and tucked her hair inside. The wind was cool but not so bad that she should be shivering. Tension must be closing down her circulation.

She shouldn't have come. She didn't belong here with Ian Faber of the charming smile and easy manner. At least, his manner had been easy when he picked her up. An hour in her uncommunicative company had made him as silent as she was.

After he'd ushered her into a glistening black Mercedes coupe and seated himself behind the wheel, he'd announced that he'd decided to follow his first instinct and take her to Sausalito. His parents might or might not be at home, he'd said. Page instantly decided they wouldn't be there. A man didn't take a woman home to meet Mom and Dad on a first date, particularly when he was simply "deciding if she was worth pursuing." Why had she agreed to come?

They'd parked at Fisherman's Wharf, boarded the ferry and were now among a handful of passengers brave enough to venture from cover onto the foredeck. Ian sat beside her on a slatted wooden bench, his arms spread along the back, one ankle propped on the opposite knee. Page peered at him from inside her hood…and he looked back and smiled. He was dressed much as she was, but his parka was navy instead of the drab olive Page knew didn't suit her, and his jeans fashionably faded rather than just old. His polo-necked sweater, also navy, of heavy oiled wool was obviously expensive, and Page hoped she could get through the outing without having to take off her coat. Her own high-necked sweater was dark gray and did suit her, but the elbows were baggy and many washings had stretched the bottom edge. For once she wished she'd heeded at least one of Tanya's attempts to make her buy some new clothes.

She turned her head away and scanned the scenery. They sat facing the boat's starboard side. Over her right shoulder San Francisco's skyline was a hilly gray jumble against dense white cloud. Abreast of the vessel lay the barren rock pile that was Alcatraz Island.

Page got up and went to lean on the rail. Sausalito grew steadily clearer through a film of mist, its colorful buildings stacked from the waterfront to the top of steep, lush slopes.

Ian joined her, resting his chin on crossed arms. "Not much of a day, huh?" he asked. The wind flattened his hair, then tossed it forward.

Page sensed tension under his nonchalance. "I like it," she said and pressed her lips together. If she thought before she spoke she might at least manage to say something less argumentative.

He stood up and faced her, hooking his elbows over the railing. "What *don't* you like? Apart from me."

Heat rushed to her face. "I don't even know you."

"And you don't want to?"

She wasn't equipped for this.

"Why did you agree to come, Page? You're obviously hating every second you're with me."

"I . . ." She pressed her hands to her cheeks. "I'm sorry. Really I am. But you're wrong. . .and right in a way." She'd never felt more foolish or more trapped.

Ian tilted his head. "Could you expand on that?"

He had a right to be terse. "The other evening I told you a bit about myself," Page said. "I explained that I was out of practice with men. I should have said I was out of practice with anything but work. Not that I'm apologizing for that. But I am sorry I accepted your invitation."

"Thanks." He walked around her and stared at the faint outline of the Golden Gate Bridge.

Page took a deep breath. This was awful, absolutely the pits.

She wasn't a kid. Life in an Anchorage suburb hadn't exposed her to a lot of smooth repartee, but surely she was mature enough to spend a few hours with a perfectly nice man without insulting him.

Page rubbed her temple, praying for a graceful exit line. Then she noticed two women watching them from a bench. Watching Ian would have been more accurate. A "perfectly nice man" was a lousy description of him. He was one of those rare males who would capture attention wherever he went, probably until he was at least a hundred, yet he appeared unaware of the effect he had on women.

"Ian." She touched his back, half expecting him to shrug away.

He didn't. Nor did he say anything.

"Could I try again, do you think?" she asked.

"I pushed you for this date." He faced her. "If it's a flop it sure isn't your fault. You gave enough signals you didn't want to go out with me. We can stay aboard when the boat docks and go right back to the city. And I'm sorry, okay?"

"Not okay. Please, Ian. Let me say something."

Before he could respond the boat caught the wake from a passing tanker and nosed into a trough. Page stumbled and Ian steadied her as he was thrown against the side. He held her while the bow came up again. His body was solid, his braced legs hard where they touched hers.

He held her only until the deck leveled. When he dropped his arms they stood almost toe to toe for several seconds. His eyes, so serious and questioning, mesmerized Page. She stared into them. When she'd said she didn't know him it had been the truth. But she'd like to know him—well.

She breathed in and became aware of her fingers clutching his parka. Flustered, she let go. "Thanks," she said.

"For what?"

"Stopping me from falling flat on my face," she said and laughed. "Now let me see if I can crawl out of the hole I dug myself into."

He smiled and the effect electrified Page. She had to smile back. The somber set of his face was transformed into captivating expectancy.

"You know how it is sometimes," she told him. "Each time you open your mouth you just keep putting your foot in it."

He laughed aloud. "I think you just stole my line. Must be a catching condition. You'd better watch it."

"I'll try. But I do want to go to Sausalito with you. I need the break and I need to learn to let go a bit. What I was trying to say when I made such a mess of it was that, although I don't know you very well, I do like you. The reason I said I wished I hadn't come was because I feel so awkward." She paused, watching for his reaction. He nodded and she gained courage. "I'm comfortable in my own arena, Ian, but I guess I feel out of my depth with you."

"You're very honest." He put an arm around her shoulders and pulled her beside him at the rail. "Can I let you in on a secret?"

"I—"

"Good. I knew I could. I'm a bit nervous around you, too. Whoever perpetuated the myth that men are always sure of themselves did his fellow males a disservice."

His arm was warm. Page leaned a little closer. He felt nice, very nice. "Maybe it was a woman who did it to all of you. Some women want men to be in control."

He turned toward her and she met his gaze. "You wouldn't want that at all, would you?" he asked.

"It's not something I need to think about one way or the other."

"If you say so." He pointed at the nearing headland. "When was the last time you were in Sausalito?" he asked. He took his arm from her shoulders. Page wished he hadn't, then wished she didn't care.

"I've never been there," she told him.

"Never?" He leaned to see her face. The ferry was nudging into the dock. "It's just a hop, skip and a jump from Fisherman's Wharf. If you stood on the roof of your house you could probably see it. Everyone goes to Sausalito. Some of the best art galleries in the area are there."

The gap between them was yawning again. Page had a quick vision of her bedroom with its bent-bicycle-parts motif. She tried not to compare it to Ian's sumptuous home, but failed. "I doubt if *everyone* goes to Sausalito," she said. "Some of us spend more money on bicycle equipment and tools than we do on art."

He pursed his lips as if deep in thought. "Bicycle equipment. Are you really hooked on this courier stuff? Or do you think you'll grow out of it?"

Page poked his chest with a long finger. "You know how seriously I take my business, and if I didn't know better I'd think you were trying to pick another fight with me."

He raised his right hand. "No. Honest. But can I just say that someone as elegant as you would look a damn sight better in a gallery than shuttling around San Francisco on a filthy old bike?"

"Aha." Page grinned. "You are trying to bait me. Listen, my friend. My filthy old bike isn't a filthy old bike. It's a very expensive bike deliberately made to look like a heap of junk to discourage anyone who happens along with sticky fingers and no wheels of their own. Every machine used by my riders looks that way."

"Fascinating," Ian said. "You'll have to tell me more, but if we don't get off this ferry we'll be going back to San Francisco whether we want to or not."

They joined the line of disembarking passengers. Page noted how many cyclists were aboard and checked to see if any appeared to be messengers. "This might be an interesting place to expand to," she said, thinking aloud. "I don't think I know of an outfit that comes over here. It wouldn't be cheap for the customer. You'd have to allow for the ferry fare and the lost time, but if you consolidated—"

"Page."

She glanced up, reluctantly shifting her mind from her new idea to the slightly exasperated expression on Ian's face. "Yes?"

"We're on a date. For a while we aren't going to talk about bicycles. Okay?"

"What are we going to talk about?"

He threw up his hands. "I give up. Let's grab a cab."

"Mr. Faber, sir!"

A man's voice. Page swung around, searching for its owner. She heard Ian mutter something that sounded hostile before he gripped her elbow and guided her from the ferry landing to the sidewalk.

"Good afternoon, Mr. Faber and Ms....ah?" A portly man in a chauffeur's uniform, his cap under his arm, held open the door of an immaculate black limousine.

"This is Ms. Linstrom," Ian supplied in a tone Page interpreted as surly. "How did you know I was coming, Banks?"

The chauffeur's surprise looked genuine. "Why, your folks told me, sir. They always send me when you're coming." He squinted at Ian as if considering his mental state.

"My folks?" His hand tightened on her arm. "My folks said they'd be..." Page thought she heard his teeth snap together before he arranged his face into a bland mask and stood aside to let her get into the car.

She slid across the softest leather seats she'd ever sat on, buried herself in a far corner and hid a smile by shading her face to look through the tinted window. *My parents may or may not be at home.* He'd been pretty certain they wouldn't be, but his little plan for an exclusive get-together had been scuttled. She did wonder how the Fabers had known Ian intended to come here.

He joined her. His smile went no farther than his mouth. Page saw the way he wiped his palms on his jeans, and her amusement at the failure of his little deception fled. She felt her own small welling of apprehension. These parents of his must be formidable if they intimidated their own son. Then another thought hit. She didn't want to meet his parents. She hadn't thought about the possibility becoming reality. And she also wasn't dressed for an audience with people who must be used to the best. That was Ian's fault. He'd been the one to tell her she should dress casually. She'd been grateful, since she had a limited wardrobe, but she wasn't grateful now. Who was she kidding? She wouldn't have come at all if there'd been any question of meeting his family.

Banks started the engine and turned into traffic along the busy, tourist-clogged waterfront. Ian chewed on the inside of his cheek. Clemmie would hear about this. She'd found out the ferry schedule for him. The pieces were already dropping neatly into place in his brain. He might have known his father—or more likely his mother, after his father reported on the note—would grill Clemmie for any information on a new woman in his life. Rose Faber could wheedle information out of anyone. Ten minutes of logical reasons that Clemmie, for Ian's own good of course, should spill anything she knew would be all Rose needed. Not that

Clemmie knew more than that he'd intended to go to Sausalito while his parents were in San Francisco. But his mother could easily make a nice little package of possibilities out of his reasons for going without telling her of his intention. At this moment he felt less than a loving and respectful son.

He hadn't meant to lie to Page, but he did think his parents' home would be a good place to take her. He'd considered and quickly discarded inviting her to his own place. Too threatening after their last encounter. And his father had said he and Ian's mother planned to spend the weekend at their city apartment, damn it.

Ian felt an unfamiliar fury welling. He glanced at Page, but she stared out the window. Her throat moved sharply. He must be giving off tangible waves of annoyance, he thought. "You'll like my parents," he said, deliberately pulling his shoulders down and settling into the seat. "They'll want you to call them Rose and Bob. They're informal, easy to get along with. Everyone gets along with them." He was talking too much.

"Yes," Page said. Her voice, a pitch higher than usual, caught him off guard. She was nervous. Holy hell, just when she was starting to overcome her distrust of him, they were back to square one.

"I didn't expect them to be here," he said, resigned to revealing all. He'd never been good at deceit.

"I know."

Ian turned to her sharply. "You did?"

"Mmm. Taking a woman you just met home to Mom and Dad doesn't sound too likely, does it?"

His face burned for the first time in as long as he could remember. "I guess it doesn't." Trying to protest that he was more than casually interested in her wouldn't help at all. Maybe he should analyze his reasons for wanting to be with Page. She wasn't like any other woman he'd ever known or dated. His parents wouldn't miss that fact.

He pictured how she would look to them. To him she was lovely, fresh, with a sparkle that came as much from the inside as the outside. And he liked her dedication to independence, her unconscious femininity that wasn't diminished by her less-than-glamorous job. He found her incredibly sexy. How would his parents see her? As odd, too quiet, lacking sophistication? Would they be horrified if they found out what she did for a living . . . or even that she did anything at all for a living? His mother had never worked and made no secret of her hope that one day he'd end up with a woman who would mold her life around him and their children.

Ian closed his eyes. He didn't intend to marry the woman, for God's sake, only to cultivate what might become a relationship that would ease the boring routine he'd fallen into outside the office. He did find his job exhilarating, but he wasn't fool enough not to know that living for Faber and Faber alone wasn't enough.

Banks had cruised along Front Street as far as Napa and turned up into the hills. Ian crossed his arms and tapped his feet. His parents lived about as high up as you could go in Sausalito, which was pretty high. He loved the house, Spanish outside, all glass and dark wood inside and with a view over the water that didn't quit.

"How far is it?"

Page's voice had the effect of making him want to sink inside himself. With effort he said, "Not far. About ten minutes more at the most."

"You look uptight," she said softly.

He turned toward her. "I'm not uptight." *Liar.* "Just thinking. I feel guilty that I wasn't honest with you from the outset. I wanted us to go somewhere quiet so we'd have a chance to get to know each other. But you don't believe that, do you? You think I planned to take you to an empty house and seduce you."

She colored, and he rammed a hand into his hair. Ian Faber, silver-tongued devil, had struck again.

Page's hand closed on his wrist, and she pulled his hand down. "I didn't think that. Not consciously." She gave a short laugh. "Although it may have crossed my subconscious. Truly, I know I've blown way out of proportion what should have been very straightforward and simple. And I feel like a fool about it. You're great to be with and I'm a pain."

"No—"

"Yes, yes I am. At least let me wallow in my humility for a while."

Now Ian laughed. She was wonderful when she showed herself as she really was. "Okay," he said. "Wallow if you like."

"Thanks. I've finished now. Everything's fine. I can tell you aren't thrilled that we're getting a reception committee. Frankly neither am I, particularly when I'm not dressed for one, but we'll make it through."

Damn it all, he was pouting and she was coaxing him along, trying to convince him they were having a great time. "You bet we will," he said. She still held his wrist and he covered her hand, holding it between both of his. "I'm beginning to think I'm a good judge of character. I could tell there was something more interesting about you than the fetching purple outfit and those delectable knee pads you were wearing the night we met."

She wrinkled her nose, but before she could respond the limousine made a sharp right turn and started down a steep driveway.

Below her, behind a vine-covered, white stone wall, she saw a red-tiled roof. Huge skylights dotted its surface. Banks parked on a gravel swathe by the wall and leaped out to open Page's door. She took the hand he offered and emerged into air scented by orange trees.

"Thank you, Banks," Ian said. He had followed her out. He put a hand on the back of her neck and walked her down some steps into a shady courtyard, where jade plants grew higher than their heads. The house was of white stucco. No windows faced the area. They passed through black, wrought-iron gates into an atrium, where a small fountain bubbled amid random clusters of flowering shrubs in containers.

Page's heart sped. She was definitely out of her element.

The hand on her neck began a massaging motion. "Loosen up, will you?" Ian said in a low voice. "I could play these muscles in your back like a guitar."

She breathed through her nose, pulling her mouth tight. "I'll be fine," she told him, not at all sure she would be. "I'm always nervous when I meet someone for the first time."

With his hand still firmly on Page, Ian opened a brass-studded oak door and walked into the house. She was relieved to notice that he, at least, seemed more relaxed. He even smiled when he called, "Hello. Anyone home?" The smile turned to a narrow-eyed grin when a small, dark-haired woman rushed across terra-cotta tiles to throw her arms around him.

"Ian, darling. What a lovely surprise!"

He held her off. "Hi, Mother. Surprise, huh? Do you send Banks down to meet every ferry just in case I decide to surprise you?"

She made a little, slightly coquettish moue and lowered thick lashes over a pair of bright blue eyes. "You know I don't. I meant it was a lovely surprise to find out you were coming."

"Mmm." Ian bent to kiss her cheek. "We'll talk more about that later. Mother, this is my friend Page Linstrom. Page, this is my mother, Rose."

Page cleared her throat, extended a hand and finally found her voice. "How do you do, Mrs. Faber." Ian's petite mother made her feel like an Amazon, and the sensation didn't help her composure.

"Hello, Page. Please call me Rose. Everybody does."

Reluctantly Page relinquished her parka to Ian who made an apologetic face as his mother dismissed him, insisting that he search out his father while she showed Page the house.

"So," Rose began, her high heels clacking as she led the way down a corridor lined with illuminated curio cabinets. "Your name is Page. Very nice. Simple. I've always liked simple names."

Page murmured what she hoped was a polite response and followed Rose into a vast, airy kitchen, tiled floor to ceiling in dramatic, umber Indian patterns.

"Sit down." Rose pulled out a stool from a butcher-block counter flanking three sides of a central cooking island. "Ian and Bob will be talking business for a while. They won't miss us, and we need to get to know each other."

Not asking why they needed to get to know each other took restraint. Page slid onto the stool and watched Rose pour coffee into two mugs.

"Cream and sugar?"

"Black, thank you." Any minute now this woman would find a way to tell her how unsuited she was as a companion for Ian. And Page would gladly agree and go home.

Rose sat on a stool where she could face her guest. "When did you and Ian meet?"

It was coming. "Um, quite recently...about a week ago, I guess." The next question would be how they met and then even the composed Rose Faber was likely to have difficulty thinking of an appropriate response.

"Have you always lived in San Francisco?"

For an instant Page's mind blanked. "I'm sorry?"

"I wondered if you were a native San Franciscan."

"I'm from Anchorage, Alaska," Page said, relaxing slightly.

"How long have you been in California?"

"Two years." A few more minutes, and Rose would probably know how much Page had in her bank account. She sipped her coffee to hide a smile.

Rose drank, too, her small, perfect hands laced around the mug while she fell into a moment of thoughtful silence. Planning attack, Page thought, without rancor. Ian's mother gave off vibes that felt friendly.

"How about your family?" Rose asked at last. "Are they still in Alaska?"

"Yes."

"They must miss you."

"We aren't particularly close. We talk on the phone regularly and I went up for a visit a year ago. I like to know they're fine, but I don't get homesick."

Rose frowned. "That's sad. Don't you get lonely?"

This was an area Page avoided. "I'm usually too busy to be lonely." She made sure of that. "But there are times when I envy close families. My folks were always too engrossed in working hard enough to pay the bills. They barely kept ahead most of the time. There wasn't much time for getting to know one another the way most families do. But that kind of childhood teaches you independence, and I'll always thank them for it."

She cleared her throat and closed her mouth firmly. There was something about Ian's mother that invited confidence. Page couldn't remember the last time she'd given conscious thought to her not-too-cozy childhood.

"You know how to make the best of things," Rose said, dropping her voice as a woman in a white overall bustled in with a basket of vegetables. "We'll get out of your way in a minute, Cass," Rose said, and turned back to Page. "It doesn't do any good to mope about things gone by, does it? You can't change them, so you might as well learn from them. When you have your own family you'll be able to give them the attention you didn't get. I expect you want a family?"

"I . . ." Page couldn't think of a reply.

Rose smiled and her eyes held genuine warmth. "Oh dear. I always dive in with the personal questions. Bob—my husband—says I'm intimidating, but I don't think I am, do you?"

"No," Page responded promptly and realized, with surprise, that she meant it.

"Thank you, dear." Rose checked her watch. "I'd better give you the grand tour and take you back to Ian."

For the next half hour Page trailed through spectacular rooms, each one eligible for its own page in *Architectural Digest*. And finally, feeling slightly disoriented, she followed her hostess to a library overlooking all of Sausalito and the bay beyond.

Ian sat in a dark leather chair that matched one occupied by a man who could only be his father.

"Page." Ian sprang to his feet. "We thought Mother had kidnapped you permanently."

"This is a beautiful house," Page murmured, resisting an urge to press the bottom of her sweater closer or cross her arms to cover her elbows.

"Page is from Anchorage, Bob." At full pitch, Rose's voice was big and resonant for so small a woman—like that of a diminutive contralto.

"I know." Robert Faber rose, smiling, and shook Page's hand. In comparison to his wife, he seemed reserved. "Ian's been telling me all about you, Page."

Wonderful, Page thought.

For the next hour she did more listening than talking. Although polite and interesting, Bob, as he insisted she call him, concentrated on discussing business with his son while Page became a spectator, mentally retreating to a place where she observed the two men as if from outside a thick glass window. Rose had left to "do something about dinner."

Page's gaze followed the path of heavy beams to the apex of the vaulted ceiling. Then she rested her chin on a fist, lowered her eyes and let the soft blues and greens of the huge rug lull her.

From time to time Ian or Bob spoke to her, but the father immediately steered the conversation back to business, and she couldn't go there with them.

The sweeping green arches on the rug cradled endless blue circles, one after another. Page was getting drowsy. On Saturdays she usually tried to get some extra sleep. Sighing, she glanced up directly into Ian's eyes.

While his father thumbed through a sheaf of papers, Ian looked at her. She thought he had probably been looking at her for some time. The corners of his mouth twitched up, but not in a real smile, only in a signal that came more from his eyes. He was telling her silently that, despite what she might have thought, his mind was more on her than whatever he was discussing with his father.

Then Rose called them to dinner and the moment passed.

At the vast shimmering table in the dining room, Ian tried and failed to concentrate on what was said around him. Page was a trouper. He'd seen her occasional tugs at the old sweater she wore and longed to tell her she was a woman who could wear a flour sack and still command the rapt attention of any man in the vicinity. But she held up under his mother's not very subtle interrogation and his father's pleasant but irritatingly disinterested comments.

At last a maid removed the dessert dishes and began to pour coffee.

Ian looked at his watch. "Good Lord. Eight-thirty. I had no idea it was that late. We'd better get going." He pushed back his chair and Page did the same.

"Nonsense," Rose said. "You men have done all the talking and now you want to go home, Ian? We want our liqueur, our coffee and your undivided attention for a while, don't we, Page?"

With a sensation close to horror, Ian avoided looking at Page.

"We certainly do," he heard her say in a firm voice, and he blessed her courage. This had to have been one tough experience for her. He'd have hated it if he'd been in her position.

"Right," Rose said, clearly satisfied. "Bob, tell Madeleine we'll take our coffee into the library."

With that Ian's mother led the way and fussed over seating them all in the leather furniture he'd always found uncomfortable.

"Now," Rose said when she was settled with her coffee and a generous measure of Cointreau. "Back to you, Page. I'm sure Ian told Bob all about you, but he hasn't told me. How did you come to settle in San Francisco? You have decided to settle here permanently, haven't you?"

Now would come the questions Page had hoped Rose wouldn't ask. "I intend to stay in San Francisco," she said. "It excites me. That's why I chose it."

Rose was silent for several seconds as if digesting the idea that someone might choose where to live on the basis of excitement. "There must be more to your decision than that. I've always thought it was a wonderful city to raise a family in. Don't you?"

"Mmm. I suppose it would be," Page said. This was definitely a woman obsessed with one subject. Since her own life probably revolved around her husband and son, she must expect everyone else's interests to be similar.

"Mother, I do think Page and I should—"

Rose interrupted. "You don't have to rush off. The ferries leave all the time and Page and I are only just getting to know each other."

This would probably be their first and only meeting, Page thought. She could cope with anything once. The sooner she told Rose Faber everything she wanted to know, the sooner she could get out of there. "I don't know if Ian told Bob *all* about me. Not that I'm very interesting. I run a bicycle courier service out of a garage behind my apartment." She caught Ian's eye, and the amusement she saw there warmed her. He really was attracted to her, and she had the feeling he admired her just as she was. She gathered confidence and turned back to Rose. "I have six employees. Four of them are riders. I ride myself. I guess you'd call Pedal Pushers a seat-of-the-pants operation." She realized she was digging her nails into the arms of her chair and carefully relaxed her fingers.

There was a short silence, then Rose clapped her hands. The effect was like hearing a child holler in a library reference room. Page took in a breath and held it.

"Do you hear that, Bob?" Rose said, her eyes round. "Page has her own business. My, I do admire your courage, dear. And you ride those bicycles around the city yourself? In and out of all that traffic and up and down the hills?"

"Yes." An almost childish defiance fueled Page. "I enjoy it. Particularly at night."

"At night?" Rose whispered now. "Oh, Page. You *don't* go around the city at night, dear. Not on your own."

Page glanced at Ian. He shook his head slowly, a rueful grimace on his face.

"I'm very careful," Page said, tempering what she would have preferred to say. "And I'm always in radio contact with my client. Ian will tell you how careful I am." Let him try to help her out if he felt she wasn't doing so well in this exchange.

"Page is very sensible," he said, but he didn't return her smile. "She always weighs what she does."

And that, Page thought, *can be taken any way you want it.*

"Well," Rose continued after a sip of Cointreau, "I think it's very good for a young woman to have some experience in the world before she gets married and settles down."

Ian felt himself shrink in his chair. He'd assumed his parents would disapprove of Page. The kind of remark his mother had just made suggested the opposite. He checked Page's expression. It showed nothing.

"Have some more Drambuie, dear," Rose offered. Page shook her head, smiling. "As I was saying," Rose went on. "I've always thought it's easier for a woman to be satisfied to spend her life backing up her husband and children if she's already had a good look at the world."

News to me, Ian thought, looking at his father this time. His eyes were lowered, and his face betrayed nothing of what he was thinking.

Rose gathered momentum as she talked. "So many of my friends have married children with families of their own. And they tell me over and over how these young wives feel they've missed out if they were never on their own for a while. I think I understand why. Once you've been on your own, you not only gain maturity but you get ready to really appreciate a good husband who can take you away from all that nastiness out there."

Ian cringed. His mother sounded like someone in a matrimonial agency. He couldn't believe it. For some reason, occupation and background aside, she'd decided Page was a prime candidate to become Mrs. Ian Faber. And even if he'd ever considered such a thing, which he hadn't and didn't intend to, she was doing an embarrassingly thorough job of making sure Page would never want to see him again, much less consider any kind of deeper relationship.

When Page suddenly stood up, Ian started. "Ian," she said, "I'm having a wonderful time, but six o'clock in the morning comes around early and I'd better go home."

Ian stood also, as did his father and mother. "Six?" Rose squealed the word. "You get up at six?"

"I have to be at work shortly after that on weekdays and on Sundays I still get up at the same time because I have to catch up on my chores and paperwork." Page smiled with a genuine warmth, which Ian appreciated, and submitted to his mother's hug. Oh, but she was lovely, and graceful, and so sexy....

"Well, if you have to go you have to go," Rose said and Ian could tell she wasn't feigning disappointment. "But promise me you'll make Ian bring you back."

Page cast him a pleading look. "Thank you for the invitation," she said. "I'll remember it."

"Thank you for coming." Ian's father spoke with less enthusiasm, and he and his son exchanged sympathetic glances. They were both used to Rose's attempts to push Ian into marriage, but this had been one of her more flamboyant efforts.

Throughout the ride back to the ferry and the crossing itself, Page said little, and Ian allowed her the peace he knew she must need. Again and again he looked at her, watched the play of emotion over her elegant features. The wind had turned her hair into a riotous mass that caught shining slivers from the boat's spotlights.

Minutes from Fisherman's Wharf, the ache of expected disappointment hit him. If things went as he expected, he'd drive her home, she'd thank him politely and he wouldn't have the gall to press for another date. Then he'd go back to fantasizing about her when he should be doing other things, and probably make a fool of himself by calling and being turned down.

"May I kiss you?"

They were alone on the deck in the gathering darkness. Had he really said that? He couldn't have asked her to let **him kiss her, out of the blue, not when they'd had a rotten** few hours together in the company of his parents and no chance to even approach closeness.

"Yes."

Page's voice came to him as a muffled whisper. She stood in front of him at the railing where they could see San Francisco emerging from the gloom.

He didn't move immediately. He'd asked and she'd said yes.

Page faced him, her arms at her sides. Her eyes shimmered, and he was afraid she was close to tears. This was all beyond him—the emotion he felt, the answering emotion he felt in her.

The pressure of her hands on his chest was light. She pressed her palms flat on his sweater beneath the parka. Then she wound her arms around his neck and pushed her fingers into his hair. Her face replaced her hands on his chest.

"Pretty awful afternoon," he said. "I'm sorry."

"Don't be. Your folks are nice." She rubbed his neck, and Ian's stomach tightened.

He touched her hair, stroked it, kissed it. He had to see her again. He had to.

In the gloom she raised her face, and he brought his lips slowly to hers. Soft. She felt so very soft and warm. Her mouth moved beneath his, brushed with exquisite care, then opened a little. She wasn't leading or following, simply doing what seemed so right to him and, he knew, also to her. He let the seconds slowly unreel while they touched fingertips to one another's face and brought their mouths together again and again. Then he stilled her head and made the contact harder. With his tongue, he parted her lips, tested the soft places just inside and reached. And Page held him close again, forced her body against his until he was certain she felt his arousal and equally certain that the wanting wasn't all on his side.

She pulled away a little, rested her forehead on his jaw and he felt her tremble. Why didn't he feel euphoric? Why did he feel so incredibly sad? Was it too late for his shot at enjoying someone like Page Linstrom, for as long as they wanted to enjoy each other?

"We'd better get off this thing."

Her voice startled him and he turned his head. The boat had docked and the last few passengers were moving down to the landing.

With his arm around her shoulders, Ian walked Page back to the Mercedes, settled her inside, then got in himself. The sinking sensation wouldn't go away, the conviction that even though she'd kissed him with passion she might not want to see him again.

The drive to her apartment took too little time, and when they got there she opened the car door and was on the sidewalk before he could turn off the engine.

He joined her and tried to take her in his arms.

Page bent her head and held his wrists. "Thank you for taking me. I hope I haven't embarrassed you with your parents."

The desperation he felt was like nothing he'd ever experienced before. "They liked you. Couldn't you tell?" It had surprised him how much they had liked her.

"They're too polite not to try to make someone feel at home. I'm sure they're wondering where on earth you found me." Her laugh was unconvincing. "I'd better go in. I'd invite you for coffee, but I really do need to sleep."

"Yes," he said. There was nothing else to say. "May I see you again?" He was sure he didn't have a pulse at all.

Her indrawn breath was soft but still audible. "I wish I could say no. I ought to say no. But I can't. Not right away though, Ian. Let's both do some thinking and decide if we should even try to go on with this. I'm not sure we should."

"I am." He could barely stop himself from grabbing and kissing her.

"You may not be tomorrow when your parents start pointing out how unsuitable I am for you even as a casual acquaintance."

"I'm the one who wants to be with you, not my parents. Can I pick you up tomorrow when you finish work?"

She chuckled. "At two in the morning?"

"If you like. Call me from wherever you make your last delivery and I'll come and get you."

"You didn't hear what I said." She stepped back. "We have to think our way through this. I don't have any idea how soon we'll see each other again, only that I'd like us to. Think about my work schedule, okay? And think about how hard it will be for us to do more than grab a cup of coffee and a sandwich while I'm on my lunch break or before I start my evening shift. It could be something you don't want to bother with."

He opened his mouth to protest, to say that he didn't give a damn about anything *but* bothering with her right now, then managed to stop himself. "Go on in," he said with what he hoped was restraint.

She leaned close, kissed his mouth so quickly he barely had time to feel her lips, and turned to run up the steps.

"I'll call you tomorrow," he said as she opened the door.

"What?" She was silhouetted against light from the hall.

"I said lock the door."

"Right," she said and disappeared inside.

Ian did a soft shoe jig on the sidewalk. "I'll call you tomorrow, Page," he said aloud. "And the next day. I'll eat sandwiches for lunch, and dinner every day if necessary— until I can persuade you that there's more to life than work."

He drove home, noting with satisfaction how short a distance he lived from Russian Hill.

Chapter Five

The phone rang as Page replaced a last handful of books on the cinder block and plywood shelves in her bedroom.

"Hello." She expected to hear Tanya, who hadn't come home again last night.

Ian said, "Hello yourself. You aren't still sleeping, are you?"

Page's hold on the phone tightened. So did every muscle in her body. "Yes. I'm still sleeping. I'm snoring. Can't you hear?" She made several snorting noises.

He laughed. "Okay. Dumb question. I meant I hope I'm not waking you."

If he only knew how little sleep she had managed since they'd parted the night before.

"Did I wake you, Page?"

"No, of course not. How are you?"

"Lonely."

She closed her eyes. "I'm sorry."

"Are you lonely?"

Yes, yes, but I can't get in too deep with you. "I'm too busy to be lonely. Today's cleaning day. This afternoon I'll get a nap if I'm lucky, then tonight I'm back on duty for the deli."

"Can't you make enough money by working normal hours?"

He wasn't getting the message. "No, I can't, Ian. I've already explained that."

"Why?"

"Because my business can still go either way, and I need all the money I can get my hands on. The daytime stuff isn't enough yet. If that sounds crass I'm sorry. But it's also life—my life. Now please, have a nice day and let me get on with mine. Sunday's catch-up time, and there really are a million things to do around here."

"Don't hang up."

She sighed. "You like saying that, don't you?"

"No, I don't. But I don't like feeling you're going to smack the phone down in my ear, either. How about going for a drive this afternoon? We could—"

"I can't, Ian. I already said I'm knee-high in work."

"You couldn't leave it just for an hour or so?"

She wanted to. How she wanted to. "No, I can't. But thanks anyway."

Silence followed. Page could almost hear Ian formulating his next offensive. "What time are you off for lunch tomorrow?" he asked.

She didn't believe this. She must have become some sort of challenge to him. He was determined to beat her down. "I'm not sure what time I'll get a break."

"I'll call your dispatcher and she'll let me know. Is that all right?"

Page remembered Lilian's last poetic telephone effort with Ian and rolled her eyes. "Don't do that. I'll call you when I'm free."

"Sure." Sarcasm didn't suit his voice. "Then you'll give me a location I can't get to before you have to go back to work again. I don't think you want to see me."

"That's not true." Damn, she shouldn't have said that. "I mean I would like to have lunch with you, but you could be right, it could be very tough to pull off."

He was silent for a moment. "Got it. Pick a location where we can meet. How about Golden Gate Park?"

"Well—"

"Yeah, Golden Gate Park. Right by the Baker Street entrance to the Panhandle. First bench you come to. I can take a long lunch tomorrow. I'll get there at eleven-thirty. You wouldn't be there before then, would you?"

Page tugged at a piece of hair. "No, but—"

"Great." He spoke rapidly. "I'll be there at eleven-thirty then, with lunch. And I'll just wait until you arrive."

He was cutting off any escape route. "What if I can't get away before one? That happens sometimes."

"You may not get much lunch." His laugh made her laugh, too. "Get back to work and be careful tonight. See you tomorrow."

He hung up without giving her a chance to say anything else. She considered looking him up in the phone book and backing out, but didn't. If she didn't want to go, she wouldn't. It would be his fault if he sat in Golden Gate Park for two hours. Not that she believed he would. After all, she hadn't agreed to go.

Page pushed at her hair with the back of her hand. She'd already flipped a duster through the apartment and cleaned the kitchen. Her own bathroom, tiled in shocking pink, was immaculate. Ugly, but clean, right down to the cracked pumpkin-colored linoleum. Finishing her bedroom was all that remained of her weekly domestic chores.

As she pulled the magenta down comforter over her futon, another jolting ring of the phone startled her.

Maybe it was Tanya. "Yes," Page said into the receiver, more shortly than she intended. She was worried about her roommate's increasing moodiness and repeated absences.

The telephone line crackled before a woman's voice shouted, "Page? Is that you?" Page's mother had never accepted that she didn't need to shout on the phone just because she was thousands of miles away.

Page sank to the floor and crossed her legs. "Yes, Mom. How are you?" The old guilt came. She should remember to call home more often.

"Fine, fine," Molly Linstrom yelled. "Got to keep this short. Costs, these long-distance calls, I can tell you."

"I know, Mom." Page rested her forehead on the heel of one hand. "Why don't you hang up and I'll call you right back?"

"Just wanted to let you know your brother has a new baby boy," her mother went on as if Page hadn't spoken. "Nine pounds and doing great. He looks just like Tony."

Her brother had a boy. Not her brother and sister-in-law had a boy. Not that Sally was or wasn't doing well. Linstrom women were supposed to be no more than conveniences for men. "That's good news," Page said. "How's Sally?"

"Good," her mother said. "Anyway, that's all I wanted to tell you, so—"

"Mom," Page interrupted. "How are you and Dad and everyone?"

"Oh, we're the same as usual. I've got to go."

"Yeah." *And how are you, Page? We think about you sometimes.* She was a dreamer and should know better by now than to care about being a nonperson to her parents. "I'll send something for the baby. Tell Tony and Sally... Tell them I love them."

Her mother had already hung up.

She sat still for a moment, her head in her hands, before the chime of the old clock in the sitting room reminded her she couldn't afford moping time.

One of her Sunday tasks that she hadn't mentioned to Ian was her consultation with James W. Amwell, jr., upstairs neighbor and part-time mechanic for Pedal Pushers.

When she'd done everything possible for her bedroom, Page made a giant tuna-fish sandwich and put it in a brown sack with a large bag of potato chips, an apple, a banana, a

pint carton of milk, and two cans of cola. James was one of
Page's favorite people. When she allowed herself to analyze the reason, the answer made her sad. James reminded
her of the Page she used to know—optimistic, single-
minded, invincible. He hadn't yet learned, nor admitted that
anything could make his goals more difficult to reach than
his lack of money and family support already did.

Whistling breathily, she made her way out of the house
and down the alley leading to the garage. Classical music,
played at James's favorite high volume, met her. Wagner's
Valkyries were doing their thing, as James would put it.

With a finger jammed in each ear, Page entered the garage through the small side door. "James!" She couldn't see
him. "James, where are you?" Scrambling, she climbed
onto a pile of boxes to snap off the button on his cassette
deck.

"Where . . . ? What on earth are you doing?"

James sat on the floor in the lotus position, his eyes
closed, hands turned up atop his knees. Each forefinger and
thumb touched in a circle. He didn't answer.

Immobile, his thinness was more pronounced. Usually he
was in perpetual jerky motion, and although the sticklike
wrists that protruded from too short sleeves were something no one would miss, his animation overcame what
might have been an impression of frailty. Sitting still, he
looked pale and poor, and Page's heart contracted.

She approached on tiptoe and whispered, "James, it's
me. I made too much lunch, so I brought you some." She
said the same thing every Sunday, and every Sunday he accepted her offering solemnly but never ate until she'd left.

Page worried about him. He wanted one thing in life—to
become a structural engineer. For that he needed a college
education, and the only way he'd get it was by his own efforts. From the day she'd met him, a scraggly fourteen-year-
old who needed braces he still didn't have, he'd talked of his
savings for college. Page had long ago figured out that one

of the ways he saved was by not eating very often or spending money on clothes. He lived with his youthful grandmother, a self-centered woman who tolerated James as long as he kept out of her way.

He opened his eyes slowly and blinked several times. "Yoga," he said. "It helps you focus your inner self and avoid distraction."

"So I've heard," Page said. "How does everything look?" He would have been working since early morning, oiling, greasing, checking the machinery and the radio.

James pushed long, tow-colored hair away from his face, leaving oily stripes on his forehead. "Not so good."

"Good . . . what?" She paused in the act of setting the paper sack on the radio table. As far as James was concerned, "terrific" was the prime word around here. Everything was always terrific.

"Ken was in yesterday while I was working," he said. "He wanted to talk to you, but you were out."

"He came in on Saturday? Why? He never puts in an extra minute if he can help it."

James unbent and got to his feet. "He said he wanted to talk to you and only you. When he got in Friday night you'd already left to do deliveries for Waldo Sands, so he came back yesterday."

"Did he tell you what his problem is?" Page asked. Ken was often surly, but he did his job and he did it fast without undue complaining.

"Look at this." James ambled to a bike leaning against one wall. Page recognized the machine as Ken's Peugeot. "He didn't say anything about it. Or I guess he did. He said to leave the damn thing alone." The boy colored slightly. "Sorry. Just quoting. Anyway, I didn't touch it, but I did look."

Page dropped to her knees and examined the bike. "What about it, James? Looks the same as usual to me."

"Drive chain," he said shortly.

She put her finger on top of the chain and moved it. "Oh, hell. I see it. Geez, I don't believe it. Someone took a hacksaw to the thing. It's almost cut through. Ken should have contacted me somehow." Not that she had any idea of what she was going to do about it.

"He was so mad he punched me out of his way," James said. "Went on about someone trying to kill him and how you didn't pay him enough to take the kind of risks he was taking."

Page got up and went to sit in the old car seat. She was still such a simpleminded idiot. She'd assumed that, in this business, hard work and determination would get her where she wanted to be. That she'd have to deal with threatening competition had never occurred to her. "Did Ken say anything else?"

"Not much. Just that he wasn't wasting any more of his weekend, but he'd see you on Monday."

"I guess I'll have to wait till tomorrow morning, then," Page said, more to herself than James.

"Afternoon," he said. "He was also going on about all the extra hours he'd wasted coming in here looking for you. He's taking the morning off. Look for him around two, he said."

"Two!" Page buried her face in her hands. "Just what I need. One less worker for a whole morning. Then I suppose he'll get everyone else riled up."

"It'll be okay."

She lifted her head. James stood beside her, his big hands knotted together. Anxiety pinched his face.

"Sure it will." Smiling, she held out a hand and he hauled her up. He was a tall boy, taller than she was. One day, when he put some meat on his bones, he'd be a big man. "I'm not used to this kind of thing, James, that's all. Will you do something for me?"

"Anything."

"Replace the chain on Ken's bike and give the broken one to me. I don't want him giving some sort of performance and getting the others uptight. I'll talk to Lilian in the morning and have her make arrangements for a meeting after lunch."

James shifted uncomfortably. "I heard about the guy who kicked Buzz."

"Her bike. He kicked her bike, not her."

"Yeah." His grimy fingers made their way through his hair again. "But some outfit is picking on our guys."

She wanted to snap at him that she didn't know what she could do about it and that all she wanted was to be left alone. "Don't worry," she said, and patted his shoulder. "Like I told Buzz, this kind of thing happens. The best way to defend ourselves is to stay calm and not get dragged into a petty war."

"Is cutting a drive chain petty?" He turned the power of sincere blue eyes on her. "If that thing had broken while Ken was flying, it could have been all over for him."

Everything he said was true, but she didn't have the answers he hoped for. "Just fix the chain, okay?" she said. "I'll figure it all out and calm everyone down. Now I've got to check out my own wheels. Sunday night's busy for Waldo." She had a hunch she was going to get more and more grateful for Waldo's business. It might be good strategy to look for more night clients and another rider or two willing to take on the work. Then there was her Sausalito idea. The realization that being down one courier could throw her completely off schedule made her all too aware of the need to grow and grow fast.

"WHAT MADE YOU CHANGE your mind about playing today?"

Ian watched his father's ball soar off the tee and track a straight course down the fairway. "Guilt probably, Dad," he said with only a twinge of remorse at the deception.

When Page had refused to spend the afternoon with him he'd immediately called his father, then headed for Sausalito and the golf course.

Bob Faber stood back. "Guilt, son?"

"I haven't been spending enough time with you lately." He met the older man's eyes and smiled. "I've missed our times together." And that was completely true.

"Me, too, Ian. Let's take time to catch up again."

Ian's own shot angled high and veered to the left, disappearing behind a stand of trees. "Hell, I'm rusty." He crammed his club back into the bag and they trundled off. They'd long ago decided to spurn jitneys in favor of getting some exercise.

"You seem different lately," Ian's father remarked, squinting at the gray sky. "Quieter somehow. Do you still see Martin and the others?"

"Martin occasionally." Though he no longer enjoyed his company as he once had. "We play the odd game of racquetball. The others have kind of slipped away. Guess I'm getting old, slowing down too much for them."

"Or growing up too much for them?" Bob Faber arched a brow. "I liked that young woman you brought over yesterday." Now he stared straight ahead.

Ian suppressed a chuckle. Neither of his parents could contain curiosity about their only child's love life for long. "I like her, too," he said evenly.

"Pretty spunky, doing a job like that. Can't say I'd fancy it."

"Page has guts." Maybe more than were good for her.

They'd reached Bob's ball, and Bob fussed, drawing and replacing several clubs, then leaning on the one he finally chose. "You like her a lot, don't you, son?" He didn't wait for a response. "I can see you do, and your mother said the same thing."

"You didn't think she was a little offbeat for the Fabers?"

"Not at all." Bob took a practice swing and lined up on the ball. "Can't tell an orange by its skin, I always say. Not that she doesn't have great skin...." He paused, shook his head and bent over the club once more. "Could be elegant in the right clothes. And she speaks well. Sounds bright. Sturdy girl, too. Make a good wife and mother, I'd think. At least, that's what your mother was saying. Some man's going to be very lucky."

Ian blew into a fist and remained silent. His parents were unbelievable. Wonderful but unbelievable. He really couldn't accept yet that they wouldn't prefer to see him attached to some socially prominent woman; yet, faced with the possibility that he might be an indefinite marital holdout, they would push him into the arms of the first candidate for whom he showed more than a casual interest.

"What do you think our chances are on the Daniel Max account?" he asked, determined to change the subject. "Samson's talking as if we've got it in the bag, but I think it's too soon to relax a muscle."

His father's ball sailed in another straight line but landed in a sand trap. "Damn." He stuffed the club back in his bag and shoved his hands into his pockets. "I'm with you on Max. We're the best and we've got the best concept, but like they say, it isn't over till the fat lady sings. Somebody else could still get the account."

"Yup. But we're up front, I know it. Max wants to change its image from middle-priced merchandise for middle-income customers to upscale products at prices the average folks can afford. By forming a link with a British manufacturer who's prepared to keep costs down for the size of the account, and leaning heavily on the prestige of wearing British-made stuff without spending a fortune, it can work beautifully. With the right advertising, that is. And we're the right advertising."

His father laughed and slapped Ian's back. "Right, son, right. And with you spearheading we could probably refuse the account and then have Daniel Max crawling to our door begging us to change our minds.''

Ian had to smile. ''I do get carried away, I guess. But only around you. The rest of the world thinks I'm made of ice.''

''The rest of the world, son?''

''All of it.''

''Including Page Linstrom?''

Ian stared at his father, who pursed his lips in a soundless whistle. ''Dad,'' Ian said, ''sometimes you aren't too subtle.''

IF HE WASN'T THERE—right now—she wouldn't wait. She shouldn't be taking time out to stop for lunch at all.

Page rode through the entrance to the park. All morning she'd rushed from job to job with a sense of barely contained panic at the prospect of the interview with Ken and the rest of the riders that lay ahead. At eleven she'd made up her mind she wouldn't attempt to meet Ian. By eleven-twenty she wasn't sure she'd get through the day at all if she didn't see him, talk to him . . . ask his advice maybe.

Benches lined the walkway in the center of the narrow strip of Golden Gate Park dubbed the Panhandle. They all seemed occupied, but there was no sign of Ian. People strolling alone and in twos, joggers, children, dogs—the place was crowded for eleven forty-five on a Monday morning. He must have come with the same thought as she had, that he wouldn't be kept waiting, and left almost immediately when she didn't show on time.

Page dismounted and slowly took off her helmet. She felt close to tears. He'd said he would be there, until one if necessary, and he hadn't even lasted fifteen minutes. If he'd come at all. She knew she was being unreasonable, that she'd considered not coming herself, but that didn't matter. She needed someone. She needed Ian.

A jogger passed and whistled. Page dropped her helmet into the bike basket and braced herself against the seat. The silver satin racing outfit she wore had been a frivolous waste of money bought because for once she'd given in to temptation. She knew she looked good in it, good enough to make sure she got the kind of attention the runner had just given her. And she'd worn it for Ian. Even while she'd pulled it on early this morning, denying all the time that she intended to meet him today, she'd been visualizing his reaction.

So much for that. She guessed he wasn't lonely anymore. She reached for the helmet.

Pressure on her back brought the start of a shriek to her lips. "Don't put that on." A broad hand climbed to rest beneath her hair. Ian kissed her before she could speak, drew her against him with both arms wrapped tightly around her body. "Wait here," he whispered. "I'm going to catch up with that jogger and kill him. But I'll be right back."

Page gasped and kept her hands tightly locked behind his neck. "You'll do no such thing."

"For what he was thinking he deserves to be punished."

She laughed. "How do you know what he was thinking?"

"Mmm." He rubbed his cheek on her hair. "I know because I've been watching you for five minutes and thinking the same things."

Warmth suffused her and she laughed. "Where were you?"

"On the first bench, like I said I would be."

Turning her head, Page saw that she'd ridden into the park without noticing a bench immediately inside the gates. "I thought you hadn't come."

Satisfaction loaded his smile. "You were afraid I wouldn't, huh? You've been missing me since yesterday?"

For an instant she felt off balance. Then she returned his smile as coolly as possible. "I came, Ian, because I'm too polite to leave a busy man sitting in a park on his own for two hours."

"Afraid someone else might get me?"

"You're impossible."

"I'll take this." Pushing the bike, he returned to the bench with Page beside him. A willow spread its almost naked branches over the area and he leaned her Schwinn against its trunk.

"Don't do that around anyone but me," Ian remarked, taking her hand and guiding her to sit down.

"Do what?" Page asked. She glanced at her watch. Much as she wanted to be here she mustn't take long.

"Wiggle when you walk. And while we're on the subject, I don't think you should wear that outfit at all."

She bowed her head and looked up at him. "You've got a lot of instructions to pass out today."

"Yup. Got to take a little control around you. Show you how strong I am—and possessive. Lady, in that suit I can see just about all of you and my imagination fills in the rest. I don't think I like the idea that other men are doing the same thing."

She'd wanted this, so why did she feel irritated? "The suit's no different than any other piece of functional equipment. It serves the same purpose for me that your clothes serve for you. Fits the image and feels good. And by the way—" it was her turn to do some careful eye work "—no man should look the way you look in a business suit. You, Ian Faber, are a first-class knockout. Navy blue is your color, and the way that shirt fits has to have every woman in your office wanting to take it off. And your legs—did I tell you I'm a leg woman? Ian, the way those pants fit your fantastic legs makes me want to see you in shorts."

First he turned pink. Then he laughed, tipped back his head and howled until his lashes were wet.

Page crossed her arms and, with a struggle, kept her face perfectly serious. "Didn't Rose teach you how to accept compliments?"

He sobered a little but continued to chuckle and wipe his eyes. "You are something. No woman ever said those things to me."

"You didn't like it?"

"Well." He coughed and straightened his tie. "I didn't say I didn't like it. In fact, when would you like to see me in shorts? How about after work tonight?"

She wasn't getting dragged into another when and where battle. "How about the lunch you said you'd bring? I'm starving."

"Chickening out on the sexy come-on?" He grinned, and the effect was definitely wicked.

"Lunch, Ian?"

"Right, right. Lunch. I was afraid I'd be late, so I ran into a deli and bought sandwiches, coffee and fruit. Is that okay?" He looked suddenly anxious. "If it's not we can hop in the car and go to a restaurant."

"What kind of sandwiches?" He made her feel good, lighthearted in a way she'd almost forgotten.

She hadn't noticed a big box under the seat. Ian pulled it out and opened the top. "Pastrami on rye, or ham and swiss, or roast beef or vegetarian. There's egg salad and tuna salad and liverwurst and shrimp croissants. I got some bagels and cream cheese and—"

"Stop. You bought out the whole store. I don't know about you, but I only eat one sandwich at a time." Amazed, she peered into the crammed box.

Ian shrugged. "I didn't know what you liked so I brought one of everything."

"That's a waste."

"We'll give the rest away."

"Sure." Page looked around, wondering if he intended them to go from person to person offering food. "I'd like the shrimp, please."

They ate without speaking and drank coffee from Styrofoam cups. Being silent with Ian beside her felt all right, comfortable. Page began to wish they could stay here indefinitely and that she didn't have to face the afternoon.

"Something's wrong, isn't it?" Ian said suddenly.

Page almost spilled her coffee. "No. Everything's fine."

"There's something else you should know about me," he said, taking the cup from her and setting it on the ground so he could hold her hand. "I'm psychic. I can see inside your head."

"Of course you can. Just the way you can see inside my clothes." She winced. That was the kind of thing she never said. "I didn't mean to say that."

"It's perfectly okay. I bring out the worst in you. I understand. But I still want to know what's on your mind."

It would feel so good to let it out. She had no one to talk to about the decisions she had to make, and earlier she'd considered telling him. But she was supposed to go this alone. That was what she'd set out to do from the day she'd left Anchorage.

"Page," Ian said, keeping his voice low, "tell me, please."

She sighed. "A long time ago I promised myself I was never going to need anyone's help to make my way."

"Everyone needs help sometimes," Ian said and raised her hand so that he could kiss her knuckles. "I sure need help from time to time."

"You're something, Ian. Do you know that?"

He hitched an ankle onto the opposite knee and shifted to look at her. "What's up?" One slightly rough fingertip traced the tendon from beneath her ear to her neckline and back.

Concentration was tough when he touched her like that, but she began, haltingly, to explain what had been happening to her riders. When she'd finished he didn't say anything, and she began to feel foolish. Maybe she was overreacting, making a lot out of very little.

"I'd better get back," she said when several minutes had passed. "I have my little summit meeting to attend and a lot more deliveries before tonight rolls around."

Ian opened his mouth. What he was feeling was totally foreign. Fear. Possessiveness. Anger. "You're not going anywhere," he heard himself say and immediately cursed the patterning that made him forget he couldn't order this woman around. He clamped a hand on her arm to stop her from getting up. "I mean, I don't want you to go, Page. Not yet, please."

"I've got to. I'm going to be late if I don't."

"Too bad," he said between clenched teeth. Then he took a deep breath and tried to relax. "I don't have one damn right in the world to tell you what to do, but I can say what I think."

She was trying to look calm. He could see and feel her effort to shrug off the importance of what she'd just told him. If he had to guess, he'd say she was already wishing she'd refused to confide in him.

"What's the name of this outfit that's causing the trouble?" He still sounded like a schoolteacher, or a father. The breath he took through his nose did nothing to take the knots out of his jaw. "A name, Page. Give me a name so I have something to go on."

What he saw in her eyes next was a mixture of annoyance and panic. "I didn't tell you this because I expect you to take care of me. And I don't know who they are. My people haven't seen any of them before."

She'd be next. Ian swallowed acid. One day soon he'd call Pedal Pushers and find out Page had been injured . . . or worse. "We're going to the police." He started shoving sandwich wrappers into the box.

"We are not going to the police." Page grabbed his sleeve and waited until he looked at her. "I shouldn't have told you. I didn't have any idea you'd react like this. All I wanted was ... was ..."

Tears welled in her eyes, and horror. She attempted to turn away, but he held her shoulders. "All you wanted was what?"

"I don't know. Someone I trust to talk to, I guess."

As if she'd turned on a heater somewhere, some of the fear dissipated, and he warmed, glowed. She trusted him. "And I blew up like a faulty grenade. Sorry, sweetheart." He saw her lashes flicker at the term he'd used, and he smiled. "Tell me what you intend to do and how I can help you."

Her breasts rose as she took a deep breath. "I'm going to line up all the incidents that have happened. Then I'm going to make an all-out effort to find out who these people are. We've talked to other courier services and none of them say they're being hassled. That may or may not be true. This is a closemouthed, competitive business. I am going to file a police complaint. Not that it'll do any good."

"How come?"

"The police don't like us. Or they don't like bicycle couriers, I should say. There are a lot of accidents every year caused by careless riders. My riders aren't careless, but the cops have no way of sorting out who's who most of the time."

He felt sick and out of his depth. "I wish you didn't have to go through this." And he wished he knew how to help.

"So do I, but I don't have a choice." She stroked his cheek, and the blood in his veins felt like water. "I need the money. Period."

There had to be a way. An idea came to him, and so did her likely reaction. "Why not get a business loan to carry you until things really take off? That way you could stop riding and concentrate on the administrative angle.'' He didn't like to think of her out there, and so vulnerable.

"I'm already paying off two loans." She crossed her arms and stared at two small children chasing a ball. "I don't intend to owe any more money."

Careful. "I could help you—"

"No!" She was on her feet, marching around to get her bike. "Thank you. I appreciate your concern, but I don't borrow from friends."

He met her as she wheeled from behind the bench. Standing astride the front wheel, he placed his hands on hers. "I respect your feelings. And I admire you one hell of a lot." At least he was a friend now, and he was trusted. Whatever happened he had that to get started with.

"Thanks. The feeling's mutual."

The effect she had on him was a heady thing. "Will you at least help me out by saying you'll be very careful?"

"Yes. I'll be very careful. And I will get to the bottom of this. I've got a hunch it'll all blow over if we keep cool."

"You really think so?" She could be right. He hoped to God she was.

"I do. I've got an idea where I can go to get some information on new people coming into the business."

"Where?"

"Just a bar at the Hotel Utah where bikers hang out after work." She looked at his hands, but he didn't move them.

"Let me come with you."

Her burst of laughter stung him. "No. Thanks for the offer anyway."

"What's so funny about my wanting to come to a bar with you? You shouldn't go alone."

Page nodded, still smiling. "I won't go alone. I probably won't go at all. I'll get the Zipper to go for me, and maybe Perkins."

Something close to jealousy turned him clammy. "Who are the Zipper and Perkins? Friends?"

"They work for me." Pressure against his locked arms conveyed her anxiety to be gone.

"How did last night go? Lots of deliveries?"

"Ian, I've got to get back to the garage."

He sucked in his lower lip. She wouldn't agree to meet him again like this if he made it tough. "Go then." He stood aside and gave her a mock salute. "May I call you when you get off duty tonight?"

"I don't—"

"I won't talk for long."

"I may not be back before two-thirty or so." She was already moving away.

This was hopeless, exactly the kind of thing that had never happened to him. He was handling her all wrong. She said she trusted and liked him. The next move should be hers. "Two-thirty is kind of late. I forgot for a minute. Listen, give me a call some time if you feel like it and maybe we'll go out again. Okay?"

The spokes stopped turning. His stomach didn't.

"Good idea," she said. "What are you going to do with all those sandwiches?"

He glanced from her to the box. He'd forgotten the silly sandwiches. "Uh..."

"If you don't want them I'll take them. I've got a hungry young friend who doesn't have much money. I can give him a couple for dinner each night."

"Fine." He handed her the box and she put it in her carrier. "I hope your friend enjoys them."

"He will. Thanks."

She rode away, turning back to give a nonchalant wave before she left the park.

Jingling keys in his pocket, Ian started toward the exit and his car. Maybe his little table-turning effort hadn't been such a hot idea.

Damn. Was it his hormones or his ego that kept him chasing one woman in a city full of delectable females?

Chapter Six

Braced for combat, Page pushed her bike into the garage. She was met by total silence.

The radio blipped, and Lilian, who sat beside the Zipper on the table, reached back to answer. "Yeah, yeah," she said in a subdued voice. Then, while she wrote on a dispatch pad she said, "Yeah," again and then, "Out."

"Hi, everybody." Page scooted her Schwinn against a wall and faced her staff. Buzz was sprawled in the car seat with Jemima on her lap. Ken Moore, his back to the room, was looking out of a grimy window. Perkins was the only one who answered Page with a soft, "Hi," from a spot in a gloomy corner.

This was worse than she'd expected. Page took off her helmet and gloves and dropped them on a pile of old sacks. "All right, folks. Let's talk and talk fast. Time's money around here."

The Zipper's fist, coming down on the table like a sledgehammer, made her flinch. "We aren't giving up, Page. We aren't creeping away like a bunch of rabbits. I don't give a...

I don't care what he says." He glared at Ken Moore's back.

"Ken?" She walked over and stood beside him. "Ken, what was said when I wasn't here?"

He gave her a sidelong glance, his dark green eyes spoiled by hardness. "I told that kid to leave my machine alone. Where's the chain that was on it Friday?"

She'd been right. Grandstanding was in Ken's nature. And rabble-rousing. He'd come in ready to whip the others into a rage, and she'd stolen some of his thunder. Page looked around. Only Lilian and the Zipper met her eyes. Ken had done a pretty good job without Exhibit A.

"Forget the chain. Fill me in. You've obviously had a head start on our discussion period. Who wants to tell me what's been said?"

"Plenty," Ken said, flexing broad shoulders displayed to full advantage in a skintight, black tank top.

Page flipped her fingers. "Gimme, Ken. Can the hints and give it to me straight." Two years with these people had taught her to put on their lingo like an extra coat.

"He says we gotta get tough," Buzz said, in a bored voice that didn't ring true. "He says we gotta fight back."

"Stupid sonov—"

"Not in front of Jemima." Page cut the Zipper off. "I called this meeting and I'll run it. In case any of you've forgotten, this is my business and I make the decisions."

Ken toed a brake block across the floor like a hockey puck. "From where I stand, boss lady, you aren't looking so good. Every one of us here has had more than one run-in with these jerks—except Lilian and you. Maybe if some sucker had taken a hacksaw to your drive chain you wouldn't be so cool."

"I'm not cool now," Page retorted. "I'm...I'm mad. But going down to their level won't solve anything."

"It'll make us feel a hell of a lot better," Buzz said, the attempt at disinterest gone. "I already know what I'm gonna do."

"Yeah," Ken said. "Me, too."

"Fools—"

"Stop it!" Again Page interrupted the Zipper, but she gave him a tight little smile of gratitude. He had always been the best and most likable of the bunch. She turned to Buzz. "What do you intend to do?"

Buzz shrugged and smoothed Jemima's curls. "Nothing much, do I, baby?" She brought her eyes to the level of the toddler's and they giggled.

"Cut it out," Page said, breathing harder. "Just answer the question."

"And for this I left law school." Ken dropped into a rickety wooden chair and looked at the ceiling. "You've missed your calling, Page, baby. You should have been a prosecuting attorney."

"Don't you ever call me baby again," Page said. "If you don't want to talk about this calmly, you know what to do."

He locked his hands behind his neck and crossed his ankles, but his face became wary. "What would that be?"

"Take a walk. And don't come back." She almost wished he would. He might be a good worker, fast and with a hound dog's nose for direction, but his attitude was bad news and she already had enough trouble.

"I say we do whatever Page says we should do."

Everyone stared at Perkins. His voice was rarely heard for more than a word at a time.

"Yeah, Perk," Lilian said. "I'll go for that."

Ken shifted and recrossed his feet. "So would I if I was safe behind a radio all day."

From the corner of her eye Page saw the Zipper move. "Speak to her like that and I'll see you don't do much talking for the rest of your life." He'd grabbed Ken's hair and jerked his head down before Page could react.

"Stop it!" She wasn't ready for this. She never would be.

"Enough, you two," Lilian echoed. She crossed the small space from the radio table and pulled the Zipper back. Page noticed she looked at the wiry little man with something close to adoration. "Zip, honey," Lilian continued, "Ken just likes to get you all riled up. We've got to do like Page says and be calm. The whole lot of you be calm." She glowered around.

"Give me some paper and a pen," Page said before anyone else could speak again. "I want a list of every incident."

"I'm carrying a coat hanger from here on," Buzz muttered.

When Page looked at the girl she kept her eyes down. "You're going to do what, Buzz?"

"You heard."

"A coat hanger?" Page nodded slowly. "Brilliant. I don't suppose you want to explain what you intend to do with it?"

"You already know."

"I hope I don't, but if it's what I think, you won't ride for me anymore."

Ken snorted. "Riders are going to get pretty thin on the ground around here if you fire us all. No riders, no business, boss lady."

"You can cut the 'boss lady' bit, too, Ken," Page told him. "Buzz, a coat hanger or anything else rigid enough to ram between spokes could kill someone. I want your word you won't pull a stunt like that."

"A foot in the spokes didn't feel so good," Buzz said under her breath.

"Your word, Buzz," Page persisted.

Buzz passed stubby fingers through her white crew cut and sighed long and low. "Are we just gonna wait till they kill one of us?"

"No, we are not," Page said. "Every one of you has had some sort of trouble, right?"

There was a chorus of agreement.

"So you must be getting some sort of descriptions you can compare. The riders, their bikes and so on."

"I've never seen the same one twice," the Zipper said.

"They can't be ghosts." Page tossed the pad Lilian had given her back on the table. "It's too bad some of the competition hasn't reported any incidents. A united front would help. But we can track this down alone, and we will."

"If I've got to do it with a smile on my lips I'll need more money to keep me sweet," Ken said, not looking at her.

Page's heart gave a big thud. She'd been expecting this, but she wasn't ready with an answer.

"Knock it off, Ken," the Zipper said while she was still thinking. "Page is working round the clock herself. We all know things are tight."

"That's not my problem."

Too bad Ken Moore was such a good rider, Page thought. She longed to tell him to leave. "Ken," she said, "jobs aren't that easy to come by, but if you want to go look for one, be my guest. I'll be sorry to see you go, because you're good at what you do. But I flat can't afford to pay you more than I do. Half the tag price is standard. You won't get more anywhere else."

"That's what you say."

"That's the way it is," Perkins said. "And I'm getting behind on my drops, so let's move."

Again Page was surprised at the quiet man's vehemence. "There is something I'd like a couple of you to do for me," she said.

"Name it," the Zipper said immediately.

"How many of you get together at the Hotel Utah with people from other outfits? You know what I mean, the after-work, horror-story session?"

Within two minutes she had four volunteers—Buzz, Lilian, the Zipper and Perkins—to go to the city's bicycle messenger hangout and ask questions. Ken made no comment one way or the other, but he did pick up his job numbers and get on the road as soon as Page said the meeting was over.

When all the riders had left, she turned to Lilian who continued fielding radio messages. "How do you think it went?" Page asked.

Moving the mouthpiece of her headset aside, Lilian gave Page her whole attention. "I think you're one gutsy lady. But I don't get any of this. It doesn't make sense for someone to pick on an outfit as small as ours. Page, for the first time in my life I'm scared to death."

"ANYBODY THERE? Tanya?"

Page opened the door to the apartment slowly. Light shone from the kitchen. She never left lights on. Too many years of patterning by a parsimonious father had made her careful about waste.

"Tanya?" Her voice cracked, and she swallowed a flash of nausea.

She was tired from the night's work, mentally as well as physically. There was nobody waiting to jump on her. She must have forgotten the lights this time. The sooner she got to bed and slept, the sooner she'd be her old calm self.

To reach the bedroom she had to pass through the kitchen. She leaned on the table to unlace her shoes and slip them off, then rose to her toes to stretch cramped insteps. A rancid odor made her wrinkle her nose and glance around. A glass stood on the counter by the sink. Page walked over and picked it up. She smelled the gin even before she raised it to her nose. Tanya occasionally drank gin—when she was depressed.

Instinctively, Page looked over her shoulder, mentally ticking off the days since she and her friend had crossed paths. Close to a week.

Page entered the narrow corridor that divided the two bedrooms from the kitchen and sitting room. Tanya's was the room opposite the kitchen. Light showed under the door.

Was this a good time to try to talk, or would Tanya resent the intrusion? Like Page, she was trying to carve a life for herself away from her family. The big difference between the two of them was that Tanya received financial help from her parents, enough to keep her in college and a spectacular wardrobe. It had always puzzled Page that Tanya had chosen to live in a less-than-luxurious apartment, but she'd never questioned her friend on the subject.

Pursing her lips in a soundless whistle, Page tapped on Tanya's door. She heard the rustle of bedclothes and wished she hadn't knocked.

The strip of light under the door disappeared and Page's reticence was replaced by irritation. Damn it. They shared this apartment and had tacitly agreed to look out for each other. Page didn't need a watchdog, and Tanya probably didn't, either, but Tanya's long absences were odd, and as a friend Page felt she was owed an explanation.

She stood, hands on hips, jiggling a socked foot for several seconds, then knocked again—loudly.

No response.

Page opened the door and walked firmly inside. "Tanya. Sorry to barge in, but—"

"I'm sleeping."

Page took a step backward and half turned away. No. Something was wrong here. The voice was blurred but not by sleepiness. Tanya had been drinking—plenty.

"Um, Tanya, can we talk for a few minutes?"

"Sleepy," Tanya responded.

And I'm sleepy, too, Page wanted to retort. Instead she approached the bed and switched on a bedside lamp. Only a fan of red curls showed above hauled-up covers. This was ridiculous.

"Do you have an early class?" she asked.

Tanya didn't reply.

"Darn you, Tanya. Speak to me, will you? Let me in to whatever's going on in your life. I've got troubles of my own. Sharing them with you wouldn't be so bad, either. Will you give me a break and talk to me?"

Long fingernails curled over the covers and Tanya's face emerged, fully made-up, flaming red lipstick smudged, mascara caked into the paths of dried tears. "What d'you want, Page? I don't want to talk right now." A gold ribbon, bow askew, sagged over her forehead.

In a swift motion, before Tanya could react, Page pulled the covers farther down. "You're still dressed," she said, nonplussed. "What is it with you?"

"Leave me alone." Tanya rolled away, hiding her face. She wore a rumpled, red satin dress with a peplum and short shirt. A high-heeled red sandal with rhinestone-encrusted straps still clung to the toes of one exposed foot.

"Are you sick?" Page asked, real fear coiling in her. "Where have you been all week?" *And when did you manage to get in and out of here to change clothes, and have you been to school?* She mustn't pile on all the questions that screamed for answers.

"With a friend," Tanya said, a fuzzy, sullen coating on her voice. "So what?"

"So nothing, as long as you're all right."

"Don't worry about me."

"I do. I can't help it. We're friends, remember?"

Tanya rolled onto her back, one hand over her eyes. "If we're friends, don't push, okay? I'm not having such a hot time right now. Happens to everyone."

The arm Tanya had raised was thin, thinner than it should be. And the dress, which Page had never seen before, fitted so tightly that it showed prominent hip bones and ribs. Something near panic rose in her throat. "How is school going, anyway?" She tried to sound casual, cheerful. "I'm living for the day when I see fashions by Tanya at the end of some TV show, or in a magazine layout."

"Don't hold your breath."

Page sat on the edge of the bed and took a thin hand in hers. The skin was unnaturally warm. "Is it a man?" She didn't want to say Waldo specifically. If she did, Tanya would have immediately protested that he wasn't the only male on her horizon.

"I think I kind of love someone." The statement amazed Page. She couldn't think of an answer. "He loves me, too, only he's fighting it. That's a tough scene, Page. If it ever happens to you, you'll know how it feels."

Page Linstrom, the workaholic without a heart. She looked at their joined hands. "I guess you're right." Some of the feelings she was having about Ian came close to pain. There were a lot of potential stumbling blocks to a relationship, and while they might vary from couple to couple, they didn't hurt or confuse any less because a woman seemed directed in other areas of her life. In many ways, having a goal you couldn't give up made caring for someone even harder.

Tanya had closed her eyes. Page looked at the ceiling. She'd turned to Ian when she was desperate for support. Did that mean she wasn't as comfortable with her lone existence as she liked to think?

"Do you want to tell me who he is?" she asked, keeping her voice soft. "It might help to talk about what's happening." Even as she asked she tried to remember the last time someone had come to the apartment to pick Tanya up. Months ago. Tanya always left alone in a cab.

"I can't tell you. He doesn't want anyone to know."

"How could it hurt for you to tell me?" She gently pushed the ribbon to the top of Tanya's head.

"That's the way he wants it."

Page sighed. "Okay. You love him and he loves you. Why is it tearing you apart?"

"It's not." But Tanya's voice rose a pitch and she pulled her hand free.

"Of course not." Pushing wasn't Page's style, but she sensed Tanya's need and her vulnerability. "You've got it all together. That's why you've been drinking, and that's why you're in bed with your clothes on and makeup smeared all over your face. Why—"

"Leave me alone!"

Tanya swung her feet to the floor. When she stood an ankle gave out, and she caught herself clumsily against the wall.

Page knew roughly what the answer would be but had to ask. "Please let me help you. This man, whoever he is, isn't doing you any good."

"Don't say that." Tanya sat down again and buried her head in her hands. "We'll work things out."

"Maybe you need a break. You could go home to your family for a while and—"

"No! No. You don't understand." She straightened, smoothing the wisp of red satin over her thighs. "Anyway, Mommy and Daddy are in Europe at the moment. And I'm fine," she added, casting Page a defiant stare.

"Sure you are." She was weary now, too weary to go on fighting, and a fight was what this felt like. "I'd better get to bed and let you do the same."

Tanya didn't answer, and Page left the room to go to her own. On the way home she'd planned to take a relaxing bath, but it no longer sounded like a panacea for her over-crowded brain. The growing problems with Pedal Pushers and her constant dread that she wouldn't get ahead fast enough to make the business a success were now crammed together with her concern for Tanya. At least where the business was concerned she could keep doing something. About Tanya she was helpless, unless Tanya allowed her into whatever the trouble was.

Preoccupied with the stream of questions that passed through her head, Page stripped off the silver racing suit and stretched out nude on the futon. Even in winter, San Francisco seemed warm to her, and she enjoyed the freedom of not wearing clothes to bed, a luxury Anchorage had never afforded.

She'd scrap the bath altogether and make do with a quick shower, although even that seemed too much trouble.

Ian had told her to give him a call when she felt like it. She felt like it.

But he'd also let her know that he didn't want to be disturbed very late. She looked at the clock on the bedside table. Only two. Tonight the deliveries had been light and Waldo sent her home early. Ian had thought she wouldn't be back before two-thirty.

Page curled on her side. She was splitting hairs. Two was almost as late as two-thirty. He hadn't been as persistent about seeing or talking to her again as she'd expected. Not that it mattered. Better that way. If they did have a chance to be friends, even very casual friends, that would be nice. But it could never be more.

The phone was on the same table as the clock. But maybe he wasn't listed in the phone book. No, probably not. She ought to take that shower.

She kept the phone book under the phone. There wasn't another convenient place for it. Propping herself on an elbow, she eased out the book and scuffed aside pages. A listing for Ian Faber stood out as if in darker print, which it wasn't.

Calling was out of the question. What if this wasn't the same Ian Faber? She rested her head down again. A little nap before the shower sounded good.

There weren't two Ian Fabers, not living on Laguna.

Damn. She wanted, more than she remembered wanting anything before, to talk to Ian. Without sitting up, she pulled the phone onto the floor beside the futon and punched in the numbers.

"Hello."

He'd answered immediately and he didn't sound sleepy. For a moment Page listened, half expecting to hear music and laughter. All she heard was Ian breathing on the other end of the line.

"Page, is that you?"

Annoyance flickered. Was he so sure of himself that he'd assumed she'd call him after work? "Yes." She was being childish. Who else was likely to call him at this hour?

"I thought you were going to be too tired to talk to me."

She was a fool. Dozens of women might call him in the early hours of the morning. "Does that mean you're too tired, Ian?" On the other hand, hers had been the name to come automatically to his lips.

"I've been sitting here trying not to call you. It's not two-thirty yet. I'm not sure I was going to hold out once it was."

She smiled, then smiled more broadly at her own transparent pleasure. "I just wanted to thank you for the picnic. It was fun."

Seconds ticked by before he replied. "That's all you wanted to say? Now you want to say goodbye?"

He wasn't attempting to hide how much he wanted to talk to her. She ignored his questions. "How was your afternoon?"

"Busy. Things are hopping at the office. Ask me how my evening was."

"How was your evening?"

"Dull. I played racquetball with Martin—you remember Martin Grantham? He was drunk the one time you met him, but he's really not such a bad guy. Only he beat me tonight, which doesn't usually happen. I guess I wasn't concentrating."

"That's too bad." Talking to Ian was taking away the tiredness.

"It was all your fault. You and that silver suit you had on today. I kept seeing it when I should have been seeing the ball."

She turned hot. She rested a hand on her breast and then remembered she was naked. Her fingers groped for something to cover her body, before she registered that no one could see her.

"Page?"

"I'm here. My afternoon was awful." She hadn't intended to, but she went on to tell him about her problems when she got back to the garage.

"Sounds as if you coped well."

His response surprised her. Some remark about how unsuitable her job was would have been more in character. "Thank you." More seconds passed. "I guess I'd better let you get some sleep."

"Don't hang up."

They laughed.

"I know, I know," Ian said. "I'm always saying that. Page, can I tell you something—honestly tell you something without your getting offended?"

She sat up and pulled the comforter over her knees. "That'll depend on what you tell me."

"I'd better not say it."

He was manipulating her, making her insist that he say his piece. "Don't keep me in suspense." She'd play his game.

"I'm in bed. Where are you?"

She swallowed. "Sitting on my bed."

"I wish we were in the same bed."

Page breathed in but felt suffocated. She had no slick answer for him.

"Does that offend you?"

If she wasn't careful she'd be admitting she wished the same thing. "No. I'm not a kid."

"You sure aren't, thank God."

She pressed a palm to her flaming cheek.

"Are you still there, Page?"

"I'm here. And for some reason I'm suddenly overheated."

"Maybe you wear too much to bed." She heard him pull in a breath. "Sorry. I'm not saying the right things tonight."

She *must* be suffocating. She imagined his big, well-formed body stretched out on a bed. She made a mind picture of him lying on his back, a sheet around slender hips, one hand behind his head while he talked to her. His broad chest would be covered with dark hair, his biceps flexed. The ridges of muscle on his stomach would be hard and lean....

Ian listened to their shared silence. He lay a few miles, only minutes from her. One day that distance would be put aside. The conviction hit him with exhilarating force.

Tonight, after Martin had left, he'd sat sorting through emotions that were virgin for him. For the first time in his life he wondered if he could be moving toward feeling something more than physical attraction for a woman. Oh, Page wouldn't be the only woman he'd ever liked, as well as wanted for a lover, but there had never really been anything deeper than that.

He sat up and hugged his knees with one arm. "Page, forget anything I've said that you found offensive, okay?" Staying rational was the answer. The different element here was that she wasn't falling into his arms and his bed. That made her more desirable.

She sighed into the phone. "You didn't say anything offensive. And Ian, the heat had nothing to do with what I've got on. I don't wear anything to bed."

Chapter Seven

When had Faber and Faber become big enough to employ five people in the mail room? Ian clasped his hands behind his back and walked slowly between long, Formica-topped counters lined with wire baskets.

Two women who appeared little more than teenagers continued to work, feeding envelopes through a postage meter. Each had flashed him an acknowledging smile before returning to their tasks. Probably didn't know who he was, which was just as well.

The other woman in the room, and the two men, gave him their full attention.

"Is there a problem, Mr. Faber?"

He looked at his shoes, then returned his attention to the woman's face with a brief detour to her name tag. Mrs. Pellett.

Smiling, he pulled a high stool from beneath a counter and sat down. "Not a thing, Mrs. Pellett. I decided it's been far too long since I checked in with some of Faber and Faber's most important departments." Too much. Too effusive. He coughed. "I wanted to make sure you people know that although you don't see some of us very often we don't forget you, or the essential work you do down here." That sounded okay.

"Thank you, sir," Mrs. Pellett said. But she looked uncertain and Ian noticed from the corner of his eye that the other two women had paused to listen.

"It's good to see you, sir." One of the men—Ian noted his name was J. Grimes—held out a hand. "Feel free to look around. Not very exciting, I'm afraid." While Ian shook his hand, Grimes blushed and added, "Not that excitement is what we expect... I mean, efficiency's the thing, isn't it, sir?"

Ian squared his shoulders, broadening his smile. "Absolutely. How long have you been with us, Mr. Grimes?" Most other departments were on a first-name basis. The formality felt strange.

"Fourteen years, sir." A faint suggestion of pride entered the dry voice.

"Fourteen years?" Ian nodded and wondered how he himself would survive for fourteen years in this narrow room filled with transient things. "A long time, Mr. Grimes, and we're grateful for your loyalty."

"Thank you, sir."

It occurred to Ian that he might sound as if he were working up to a gentle firing. If there was such a thing. "We thank you, Grimes." His sincere smile took in the entire mail-room staff. "We thank all of you."

He got up quickly and started reading cards on the fronts of baskets. Eventually he found one marked local, then another beside the first.

"Was there something in particular...?" Mrs. Pellett's voice trailed away, as Ian pretended to be deeply engrossed in the contents of the two baskets.

Twenty-six packages and envelopes addressed to businesses in San Francisco. Ian riffled through them again, checking his count. Twenty-six extra deliveries in one day, or even half that number, should bring in as much money as any one bicycle messenger could make on several nights.

"I have been wondering about our local deliveries," he said, not raising his eyes. "How do we deal with these?"

"Courier," Mr. Grimes said promptly.

Ian picked up a cardboard tube addressed to a seafood firm with offices on Bay Street. "Any particular service?"

"We use several. A lot of these outfits come and go, so we keep our options open and spread the business around. Keeps them all on their toes that way."

Ian admired Grimes's directness. "True," he told the man. "But with all these outfits do you find the reliability factor constant?"

"They do vary, sir." Mrs. Pellett crossed her arms. "In fact they can be a bit of a nuisance. Here one day and out of business the next."

"I see," Ian said. "In that case I think I'll look into this and see if I can come up with one or two firms that'll really give us the service we demand."

His last impression of the room as he left was one of stillness. There would be lively discussion over coffee this morning.

Rather than use the elevator, he charged up flight after flight of stairs, his shoes clanging on concrete. He needed exercise—and a chance to get over the awkwardness he'd felt in the mail room. But it had been worth it. Now he could proceed with the plan he'd devised while he'd lain awake in the night after talking to Page.

He reached his floor and paused for breath before opening the door to the plushly carpeted hall. While he walked swiftly toward his suite, he smoothed his hair and settled his jacket more comfortably on his shoulders. He felt hot. But he felt hot every time he thought of Page.

"There you are, Mr. Faber." Clemmie rose from her desk the instant he entered the anteroom. "Your father wants to know if you'll have lunch with him."

Ian waved her back into her seat. "Clemmie, be a dear and call Dad back for me. Tell him I'm caught up in something and can't make lunch. Ask him if we could get together around three. We'll have coffee in his office if he likes and catch up a bit." All this was said while he walked into his office. Before Clemmie could answer he closed his door.

He checked his appointments for the day then called Pedal Pushers.

"You got something to peddle—"

"Yes." He smiled, wondering if Page knew about her dispatcher's answering technique.

Minutes later he hung up and settled smugly into his chair. He'd never thought of himself as devious, but he was learning. "*Big business. Guaranteed volume. Chance to increase that volume.* He'd baited his hook carefully, grateful Page was "unavailable." And he'd made sure the dispatcher told him when Ms. Linstrom *would* be available before suggesting she come to the offices of Faber and Faber at eleven-thirty for an interview.

He buzzed Clemmie. "I'm expecting an eleven-thirty appointment," he told her. "Until then I'm out. To anyone."

There. Page wouldn't be able to reach him to question or cancel the date. If she chose not to turn up, there was nothing he could do about it. But he didn't believe she wouldn't show. If there was one thing certain about the lady, it was that she would be unlikely to turn down business.

For an hour he tried to work up a treatment for a toothpaste television commercial. He'd long ago passed the point where he had much time for hands-on work in the creative end of the business, but he still enjoyed involving himself as a copy writer on the ground floor of occasional projects.

By eleven-fifteen he gave up. Photos of smiling mouths, puckered mouths, mouths kissing mouths, littered his desk—the pad where he'd scribbled theme line and jingle ideas was a crosshatched disaster.

He felt disheveled. In the compact bathroom off the office he splashed cold water on his face, scrubbed it vigorously with a towel and made an ineffectual attempt at taming his hair.

Eleven twenty-five.

Damn, he'd splashed water on his pink silk tie. It would dry in puckered circles. Usually he kept a spare in a drawer but he'd used it and forgotten to bring another.

Eleven thirty-five.

She was a hardheaded, cantankerous tease. So what if she didn't show? There were plenty of other women waiting in the wings. All he had to do was pick up the phone and he'd have dates every night for as long as he wanted them.

A sharp pain at the end of his right index finger startled him. He'd chewed a fingernail to the quick. That was it. The end. No woman would reduce him to this. He stopped pacing and sat behind his desk once more. A buzz from the intercom jolted him like a blow. He flipped the switch.

"Your, ah, eleven-thirty appointment is here, Mr. Faber."

A beatific calm slipped over Ian. He wasn't sure why he felt that way, and he wasn't going to analyze the reason. "Show her in, please." How could he have doubted, even for a second, that she'd come?

Page came through the door Clemmie opened for her. Ian avoided looking at his secretary before she left. He didn't have to see her face to know what her expression would be.

"Come in, come in." He stood and waved Page to a chair on the other side of the desk then sat down again. "I'm glad you could make it. Coffee?"

She shook her head. "What's this about, Ian?" Her blue eyes glittered with skepticism.

Ian rocked back, lacing his fingers behind his neck. "Business," he said. She'd obviously been working. Her hair was windblown and she wore the purple outfit she'd worn the night of their first meeting.

"Business, Ian? What kind of business?"

Her waist was so small. Did she wear leotards and shorts all winter? he wondered. He'd feel better if she wore oilskins, or even jeans and a baggy sweatshirt. There were so many kooks out there—watching.

"You make me uncomfortable when you stare," she said.

He started. "I wasn't staring. I was thinking."

"And staring."

"Yeah, I guess I was." He puffed up his cheeks and slowly expelled the air. "I was wondering…" All he needed to do to ensure failure with her was deliver a lecture on how she should dress. "Did your people find out anything at the Hotel Utah?" he asked, suddenly inspired.

"You didn't ask me here to talk about that."

This was one woman he'd never be able to snow. "Not entirely." Swinging forward, he rested his elbows on the desk. "But I think of you as a friend, Page. You don't need me to say that I'd like to think of you as more than a friend." His concentration slipped quickly from her eyes, her mouth, to the toes of purple, high-topped sneakers.

Page shifted and he glanced back at her face. She was blushing and it suited her. "I don't think this is the time or the place to get into personal stuff," she said, and lifted her hair from her neck.

Her turn to feel hot, Ian thought with satisfaction. "Possibly not. But can we at least agree on the fact that we are friends? I'll settle for that for a while." As if he had a choice until she changed the rules.

"I think of you as a friend, Ian."

"Good. What about the Hotel Utah?"

In an unconscious gesture, Page gathered her hair together and piled it at the back of her head. The action, the way it lifted her breasts, arched her ribs, mesmerized him.

"I don't know what to think about it all," she said. "Not only didn't they get a good look at any of the guys who've been giving us trouble, but no one else seemed to see them, either. Not a single description. It doesn't figure. How can a whole group of riders be invisible to everyone?"

"Pedal pushers—I mean the pants—are fashionable again now, aren't they?" As soon as he asked he felt ridiculous.

Page looked blank. "I don't follow trends. Why?"

He made an airy gesture. "Oh, I don't know. It just popped into my head that it would be kind of cute if you wore pedal pushers and sweatshirts for work. Kind of a trademark, you know?" *Hell.*

When she laughed he wasn't sure how to react. "You haven't met my people," she said. "There's only one other woman apart from me, and if it doesn't have spots or glitter, or if it isn't made of leather with studs, she won't wear it. And the guys might not think pedal pushers were too cute."

He didn't feel like smiling, but he managed to turn up the corners of his mouth. "I bet they wouldn't. Forget it. Just the old advertising instinct rearing its head. So, no leads on these people, huh?"

"No leads. But so far today we haven't had trouble, so I'm keeping my fingers and toes crossed and praying they've lost interest."

Ian's prayer was the same, but dread still lay in the pit of his stomach. "Let's hope so."

"I don't want to hurry you—" she looked at her watch "—but we'd better keep this really short. In fact I have to get on the road just about now."

"Sure, sure." Even as he searched for more ways to detain her he knew it was a mistake. "It meant so much to me to hear your voice last night. When we were in the park yesterday it took everything I had not to push you for another date." He'd always been honest, but this was making him feel too vulnerable for comfort.

Page leaned across the desk and put a hand on top of his. "Maybe we're more alike than we think. Part of me was glad you didn't push. But I think a bigger part was disappointed.''

He lifted her fingers toward his mouth, studied her palm, then kissed it. ''True-confession time, huh?'' He was too old to be a cockeyed optimist, but he was enjoying these few minutes of forgetting the rest of the world.

Page couldn't help closing her eyes. Ian's mouth on her palm was soft yet firm, as erotic as if he'd kissed her lips. ''I'd...'' She swallowed. Her mouth was so dry. ''I'd better get going. But I'm glad we got to talk for a few minutes. Maybe we'll get a chance to see each other again soon.'' She wasn't used to making the moves, but if he could lay himself open, so could she.

He held her hand a while longer, then took in a gusty breath and released it. ''Yes, yes. But I almost forgot what made me get you here in the first place.''

She slid to the edge of her chair. Lilian had talked about Ian saying he had work for them. She hadn't really believed that.

Ian had difficulty concentrating on what he would say next. ''Um, I've been doing a study on our mailing department. Reliability, cost-effectiveness, you know the routine.'' This had better not sound as thin to her as it did to him.

Page crossed her arms under her breasts, and Ian quickly averted his gaze. At least for now he was going to have to separate his mind from his libido.

''Anyway, we've decided at Faber that we'd like to deal with one or two really reliable courier services rather than go through the hit-and-miss routine of calling half a dozen in the space of every week.''

He saw interest in the serious set of her features. ''You mean you don't already deal with just one firm? That's fairly unusual.''

Ian suppressed a satisfied grunt. More ammunition when he informed the mail room that he'd decided to eliminate most of the outfits doing local work for Faber. "I agree," he said. "Now, I realize you aren't fooled by my offer. Obviously I would never have thought of you...it's because we know each other and..." He was never this bumbling. "You know why I'm doing this."

Her smile was uncertain. "Are you sure that's such a good idea? I mean, I want the business of course, but—"

"But could conflict of interest become a problem? Why should it? You and your people will come and go from the dispatching area and you probably won't ever see me. Whether or not you and I continue to...ah... Whatever happens between us need never affect the other."

She stood up, beautiful, lithe, unself-consciously graceful. "Then I'd be happy to take on the work. Thank you. Do I talk to your dispatch people?"

"I'll do that," he said in a rush.

"We won't expect any preferential treatment, Ian. If there's a problem, I want to hear about it."

"Oh, you will." And he meant it.

Page inclined her head. "Then we have a deal. I'll tell my dispatcher to expect calls."

"You got something to peddle?" Ian grinned and was rewarded by a grimace from Page. "I've spoken to her about that," she said. "I guess I'll have to speak some more. What kind of volume are we talking about, by the way?"

She was more in control than he was at the moment. "Ah, minimum of twelve to fifteen packages a day, I'd say. Could be much more on occasions."

He noted triumphantly that she was surprised. "That much? Great. Thank you very, very much. We'll perform well for you, I promise."

Much as he longed to address the question of her giving up riding and spending all her time on management, he gauged that the timing was wrong. "I'm sure you'll do just fine. By the way, this isn't very professional, but since getting in touch with you isn't the easiest thing, what are you doing on Saturday?"

That old uncertainty entered her eyes. "I've got a lot of catching up to do around the apartment," she said. "And shopping. Tanya says it's time I stopped—"

The abrupt snapping shut of her mouth intrigued him. So did her heightened color. "Tanya's the woman you live with?"

"Yes, anyway, I really do have loads to do on Saturday."

"I wasn't thinking of the daytime." Actually he'd been thinking, or fantasizing, of all day and all night. "How about dinner?"

"Well . . ."

"Come on." Cajoling was foreign to him but he could learn. "Be a sport and keep a lonely man company for an evening. We'll go somewhere spectacular. Do you like to dance?"

"Yes, but I don't have anything—"

"Wonderful. It's a date, then. I'll be by around seven. We'll go somewhere for a drink first and eat late. How does that sound?" A mistake, he realized instantly. Never go for the close on a question.

"It sounds very nice." Her smile was fixed and he felt her rallying for a turndown.

"Good. Saturday at seven, then. And now, you'd better get back to work and so had I."

Swiftly he went to put an arm around her shoulders and usher her to the door. It opened the instant before he reached for the handle and his father put his head inside. "Busy, Ian?"

He thought fast. "Come in, Dad. You're exactly the man I wanted to see. Page was just leaving. You remember Page?"

"I remember Page very well." Robert Faber came all the way into the room and shook her hand. The flicker of his eyes was subtle, but not so subtle that Ian didn't know it had taken Page in all the way to the purple sneakers. He pushed his shoulders back and hoped he didn't look as off balance as he felt.

"Good to see you again, Mr. Faber." Page was polite but not effusive. "I intend to write Mrs. Faber and thank her for a wonderful dinner. Please tell her she'll hear from me when I have a few minutes. I'm sure having too much to do and not enough time to do it is something she understands."

Ian couldn't hold back a pleased smile. To hell with the way she dressed and her oddball occupation. Any savvy man or woman would admire her. His father's appreciative expression suggested he certainly did.

When Page had left, Bob Faber faced his son with raised brows and a quizzical smile on his face. "She's quite a woman, Ian. But I guess you've noticed that."

"ARE YOU SURE, operator?"

Static crackled in Page's ear before a nasal voice repeated, "There is no listing in Dallas for a Jasper Woodside, jr."

"Wait!" She had to be absolutely sure that her hunch about Tanya's family was right. "Is there a Jasper who isn't a junior?"

"No, ma'am. But I have two J. Woodsides. Would you like those numbers?"

Page listened and scribbled, hung up and immediately tried the two J. Woodsides of Dallas, Texas. Neither John nor Jerry had ever heard of someone named Tanya.

This time Tanya had been gone three days and Page's concern approached panic. That the wealthy family that supposedly supported her friend's every whim didn't exist wasn't a surprise. The pieces were falling into place. Tanya's choice of an inexpensive place to live. Her saying she didn't receive mail from home at the apartment because she had a post-office box.

On Tuesday and Wednesday nights, after she returned home from working for Waldo, Page had considered calling the deli to see if Tanya was there. Each time she'd decided against the idea, afraid she'd run the risk of having Tanya shut her out completely. Maybe it shouldn't matter so much, but it did. In a city where Page had arrived as a stranger, Tanya had been her first friend, and she didn't make friends easily. She didn't want to lose her.

Tonight, Thursday, Page felt an unaccustomed emptiness. The work she'd started getting from Faber and Faber was a wonderful shot in the arm to her cash flow. Page had made several pickups there herself, and each time she entered the building she couldn't help hoping for a glimpse of Ian. She never saw him, and her disappointment had grown.

When she thought of Saturday, her stomach turned queasy. Somewhere spectacular, Ian had said. And dancing. Before seven o'clock on Saturday evening she'd have to break down and buy a dress. She didn't even know what was in fashion anymore. If Tanya were around she could help.

Tanya took over her thoughts again—the way she'd looked on Monday night, thin, drawn. With more difficulty than she would have liked, Page turned aside her preoccupation with Ian and went to stand in the doorway of Tanya's room. She switched on the light. Everything looked as it had on Tuesday morning.

Her mind a blank, Page wandered about the room. Tanya was so tidy. No wonder her own disorderly space was an irritation sometimes. Tanya must have a family. If only there was a clue somewhere.

Page opened the drawer of a warped writing table on one side of the bed. A jumble of papers confronted her. Odd. So tidy on the outside, so disorganized on the inside. She left the drawer open and checked the closet for a suitcase. But then the idea that if one was missing she could assume this was a planned absence immediately made no sense. Surely Tanya would have said if she was going away for a while—

if she knew she was going anywhere. The problem remained the same. These disappearing acts had no pattern, and Tanya was definitely in worse shape each time she returned.

The closet was also messy. Page closed it, feeling like a snoop. She also felt helpless. Where could she go for help? And she was more and more convinced that whatever was happening to Tanya was serious enough to necessitate help from someone.

Back at the writing table, she lifted one scrap of paper after another, hoping to find a telephone number, or an address to lead her to Tanya's parents. Bills, mostly unpaid, messages and notes that made no sense, checkbook stubs; the mishmash was endless and also useless for Page's purpose.

She sat on the bed and continued searching. There had to be a lead here somewhere. Idly flipping through sheets of paper, she came to another checkbook stub and picked it up. The first page showed a large deposit. A huge deposit even for Tanya, who always seemed to have plenty of money. Page squinted. Her eyes were tired. A rim of shiny black caught the light. Awkwardly easing her hand under the tabletop to free the object, she pulled the drawer all the way out. Crushed at the back was a familiar, shiny black box. Touch Tone Gourmet. The gold lettering was creased, but plain. Hesitantly Page opened the flaps and looked inside. Bills, wads of new bills in big denominations. There had to be thousands of dollars.

Page's skin prickled. Waldo had a preoccupation with cash. He wanted things paid for in cash, and it made sense that he would pay for what he got in cash, too. She closed the box and shoved it forcefully back, hating to touch it, to think of what it might mean...that Tanya was tied to Waldo by her own dependence.

"Find anything interesting?"

At the sound of Tanya's voice, Page jumped so hard her neck hurt. She slammed the drawer shut. "Thank God. Where have you been? Where do you keep going? I've been so worried about you."

"You don't have to be. I've already told you that. And I don't need a keeper, Page. I don't like the feeling you're watching me. I left home to get away from that."

Goosebumps shot up Page's back. She stiffened, totally at a loss for something to say.

"What are you going through my things for?" Tanya continued. "Would you like it if I waited until you were out and searched your room?"

This was a side of Tanya that Page hadn't seen before. Her roommate was sober, but there was a meanness about her. "I'm not interested in your things," Page said. "And I'm sorry if I'm trespassing on your turf. I was worried, okay? You haven't looked well for a long time." And with this she took in the rumpled man's shirt Tanya wore and loose jeans and tennis shoes. She looked as if she were dressed in a larger woman's clothes, and haggard didn't describe the condition of her face. "The only reason I opened this drawer was to see if there was a phone number or address for your parents. If I'd found either I'd have used it." This wasn't the right moment to bring up the issue of why Tanya had lied about her family. "I also checked your closet to see if you might have packed for a trip. Then I realized I wouldn't know anything more about what's going on with you if I found out you had taken a trip. That's it. All. If you want to call it quits as friends, fine. Otherwise tell me what's eating you so I can help you."

If Page didn't feel so dried up by the effort she'd just put out, she'd cry.

"I'm sorry." Tanya did cry. "Look, I'll try to give you a call or something if I'm not coming home. Would that be all right?"

Page nodded, unable to speak.

"And I shouldn't have said all that stuff. You're very important to me, Page. You're kind of... well, kind of my anchor, I guess."

"I want you to see a doctor." Page hadn't planned to say that, but as soon as she had she was glad. "You've lost too much weight."

Tanya fidgeted before she answered. "You're having your own troubles, Page. Maybe that's making you blow mine out of proportion."

The avoidance of her suggestion didn't escape Page, but she was more interested in what Tanya said. "How do you know I'm having problems? We haven't discussed that."

Tanya's back was to her. "I... I just heard some things, that's all."

"What things?" Page needed to know if there was some general talk about Pedal Pushers. Not that it made sense for Tanya to have heard any gossip.

Tanya shrugged. "Not a lot. Just about some accidents and things."

Page took a deep breath and let it out slowly. "Ken told you, didn't he? He's made comments about you from time to time. Did he find a way to talk to you, to talk about Pedal Pushers?"

"That's right, Ken told me." Tanya turned around, smiling. "He's quite a hunk, that guy."

"I might have known it," Page muttered. "He may be a hunk, but he's no prize. I wonder how many other people he's told."

Tanya turned around. "I wouldn't worry about that. I just happened to bump into him the other day when I was leaving, and he started a conversation. The bike accidents were probably the first thing that came into his head to say."

"Yeah," Page agreed, "you're probably right. I wish I didn't need him, though."

"Listen. Nothing's changed with me. Remember the man I told you about?" Tanya didn't sound as if she needed an answer. "Well, we're still working things through and it's hard on both of us. Go to bed and stop fussing over me. I promise I won't drop out of sight without a word again."

Tiredness was making Page's head fuzzy. There was a great deal more she and Tanya should talk about, but at least they'd made a start at openness. "Thanks," Page said. "I feel a bit better hearing you say that. I guess I will hit the hay."

She closed Tanya's door as she left. Maybe they should keep a pad on the kitchen table for messages in case there wasn't time to bother with a phone call.

She opened the door again to tell Tanya the idea.

Tanya stood bracing her weight on the foot of her bed, her back arched over. She'd taken off the shirt and the black lace straps of her bra were stark against her white skin.

So were clusters of purple and red bruises.

Chapter Eight

"Don't come in here!" Tanya straightened and whirled around, clutching the shirt to her chest. More bruises marred her thin arms.

"Oh, Tanya. What's happened to you?" Page put a trembling hand over her mouth.

"I fell." Tanya pulled the shirt back on and crossed it tightly about her. "Stupid accident. You know the way these things happen?"

Page was wide awake again. "I never saw that many bruises from one fall."

Tanya's eyes flashed and she spoke through gritted teeth. "Are you calling me a liar?"

Page flinched but stood her ground. "I'm not calling you a liar. I'm just asking questions."

"You ask too many questions. We already went over that."

"And you said our friendship meant something to you, and in future we were going to be open with each other." She began to feel angry.

"I know," Tanya said quietly, "and I meant it. I'm extra touchy at the moment, Page. I wish I weren't." She sat on the end of her bed. "I fell down some steps and I rolled over and over. It hurt a lot."

Page went to sit beside her, started to put an arm around her shoulders, then changed her mind. She gave an awkward laugh. "I'm afraid to touch you. You must still hurt a lot. Where were the steps?"

Tanya's mussed red hair obscured her face. "At a friend's house. The man—you know who I mean. I ran out of there after an argument and slipped. There are metal railings down each side of the steps and I think I hit some of those, too." Her voice cracked.

The little room felt stuffy and dismal to Page, and Tanya's perfume smelled cloying. "When did it happen?" she asked.

Tanya shrugged. "Yesterday, I think."

She thought? Wouldn't a person know when they'd fallen hard enough to do the damage Page had seen? "Did you hit your head as well?"

"No." Tanya turned her face, and up close she appeared even worse than Page had feared. A smile did nothing to improve her appearance. "And I'm so hardheaded it probably wouldn't have hurt me anyway," she added.

Page smiled back. "Thank goodness for that. Boy, I don't know about you, but I'm just about too tired to sleep. Would you like a hot drink? I'll make it."

"I don't think—"

"Please. I need your advice on something."

One delicate eyebrow raised, and Tanya's green eyes regained some light. "What kind of advice?"

Page feigned shyness. "Something to do with a man. You don't have the corner on that market, you know."

"Really?" Tanya got up, buttoning the shirt. "You've got my full attention. Lead the way to the kitchen."

An hour later Page crawled onto her futon and, as she always did, pulled the comforter over her head. Her plan had been to get Tanya talking and then draw her out about what was really happening in her life. It hadn't worked. Tanya had wormed out the whole story of Ian and shown

genuine delight that Page was at last interested in someone
and something other than work. No matter how hard Page
tried to turn the conversation back to Tanya, it remained on
herself, until finally she gave up and asked for some hints on
what kind of dress to buy for Saturday.

The magazines Tanya had rushed to collect were now beside the futon. Pages were marked to give guidance to shops
Tanya preferred and styles she thought would suit both Page
and the occasion.

Page wasn't sure she could afford Tanya's taste, but she'd
do her best. And it wasn't the dress that kept her awake now.

She stared unseeingly into the darkness and remembered
bruises on pale skin . . . and money stacked in a black box.
Were Waldo and Tanya just in an unhealthy relationship, or
something more?

THE HALIBUT WAS probably wonderful. Page couldn't taste
a thing, concentrate on a thing. *Eyes for no one but you.*
She didn't remember where the line came from, but it fitted
Ian's present state. Without looking at him, she knew he
watched every move she made. Her hands seemed to have
grown larger and clumsier, and she was sure the heat in her
face must show as ugly red.

"Good?" Ian asked.

She glanced at him and then at the elaborate hairstyle of
a woman seated behind him. "Very good. How's yours?"

"Good."

Page toyed with her wineglass, took a sip and picked up
her fork again. Their conversation had been this way from
the moment Ian came to the apartment for her. Desultory.
She really wasn't comfortable with him in his natural settings. That confirmed her theory that, as much as they were
attracted to each other, and they were, they didn't belong
together. Wasn't that what it proved?

"That dress looks wonderful on you."

Was he eating at all? "Thank you. Actually it's two pieces." She set down the fork and placed her hands in her lap. He didn't want to know silly details about her clothes.

"Something wrong, Page?"

She looked up at him. "No...yes. Ian, I'm lousy company. Admit it. You bring me to this wonderful place—" she indicated the mirrored walls of the restaurant, the crisp linen cloths, the flickering candles and fresh flowers on each table "—and I clam up. Frankly, after our last official date I'm surprised you asked me out again."

Coming perilously close to settling a shirt cuff in a candle flame, he reached for and caught one of her waving hands. He laughed and trapped her wrist on the table. "Why must you always analyze? Why don't you just *feel*? You know perfectly well why I asked you out again. You also knew I would and that you wanted to come."

She relaxed slightly. "Pretty sure of yourself, huh? What was your major? Humility?"

"Smiling suits you." The pressure on her wrist lightened, and he turned it to stroke the base of her thumb with his own. "So does blue. I've never seen you in a skirt before."

"Thanks. I bought this today..." She rolled her eyes heavenward. "Don't you admire a sophisticated woman, Ian? I bet all your dates let you know they buy a new dress when you're taking them out."

"Please don't get sophisticated." He trailed his fingers to the tips of hers and waited until she returned his gaze. "Keep on being yourself for as long as you can."

"You sound as if being yourself isn't easy around here. Who are you, Ian? Have I met you yet?"

"You've got me there. I don't think I put on an act most of the time. But I guess most of us have a few masks we aren't aware of."

He was showing himself now, Page thought, letting her see the way his mind worked on at least one level. "Sometimes we have to cover up," she said, "when we know we'll be taken advantage of if we don't. You should see me at work. My father should see me at work. You wouldn't believe what comes out of my mouth, or how. But Dad never did understand why a woman wouldn't want to stay home and be 'provided for.' Of course, being provided for also means—as far as he's concerned—that you're on duty and answerable for your actions twenty-four hours a day. Still, he'd see that as what I should want. He'd never work out that I find it a challenge to run a business where I deal with people, day in and day out, who can be pretty rough and tough." She withdrew her hand from his and drank more wine. She'd said too much. Too much, or too little. Why couldn't she develop better social skills?

"Your father did you a favor."

"What?" She looked at him sharply.

"He did you a favor. And me." Ian laughed. Even when he confused her, she loved the way he laughed. "He made you determined to find freedom. You chose San Francisco to do that in. Good for you and me."

She shook her head slowly. "You have a lovely way of making things sound so simple. But you're right—at least about it being good for me. Your dinner must be cold."

Ian speared a carrot and put it into his mouth, chewing thoughtfully. "My mother does that."

"Does what?" She was beginning to feel very relaxed now.

"Changes subject in mid-conversation. The dress is sexy."

Page choked and blushed at the same time. "Now who's changing subjects in mid-conversation?" She coughed and felt tears form in her eyes. "And you deliberately go for shock value, Ian Faber. Dirty pool."

"No way. I was thinking that if you wore the dress, or top or whatever it is, back to front no man in this room would eat his dinner."

"Ian! That qualifies as a lewd suggestion." The outfit, of soft, midnight-blue cashmere, was a draped, crossover-cowl style at the back, leaving her skin bare to the waist. Shopping alone, she'd been unsure it suited her, but an enthusiastic salesperson had assured her it was perfect, and Page decided it was at least flattering.

"Lewd?" Ian said when he stopped laughing. "Garbage. Wishful thinking, that's all. Not that you don't have a delectable back. In fact, you have a delectable every—"

"Thank you," she said hurriedly. "You're pretty delectable yourself."

He chuckled. "I'm crazy about the way you do that. It's sort of naughty and totally out of character."

Page gave him an arch stare. "How do you know what's out of character for me?"

"Hmm." With his elbows planted on the table, he rested his chin and started one of his disconcerting but provocative inspections of as much of her as he could see. "You'd be surprised how much I've figured out about you. And you've told me more than you think. Where did you buy the, um, dress? The skirt does nice things, too, by the way. I'm glad it's not too short. Not that I don't like looking at short skirts."

"You mean who's wearing them. But not on older women, right?" Page was enjoying herself. The banter teased something inside her, warmed her, created an intimacy that was subtly arousing.

Ian snorted. "Lady, I've seen your legs, remember? And what *wonderful* legs. The truth is I don't think a tall woman with phenomenal gams needs miniskirts. I believe long legs inside a clinging skirt are one of the biggest turn-ons there is."

A faint blush started again. "I'm glad I can give you a thrill."

"You make that sound obscene." The humor in his eyes took any sting out of his words. "But it's true. Where did you buy the outfit?"

Why would he care? Only women were supposed to care about things like that. He must be humoring her, trying to react on her level as he saw it. "Well." How did she deal with this gracefully? "I did go into Neiman-Marcus."

"Good choice." He drank some of his own wine, nodding approval. "You can always rely on Neiman-Marcus. I do a lot of shopping there . . . or, to be more precise, I shop there when I can't put it off any longer."

"You don't like shopping, either?" Page leaned forward conspiratorially. "I absolutely hate it. I know women who can't wait to spend all day making their feet swell. Not me."

"But your trip to Neiman-Marcus paid off."

"No. It was too rich for my blood. I got this at Macy's."

For an instant Ian stared, his glass halfway to his mouth. Then he set it down and laughed. "You are wonderful. Any other woman would have let it go. You just have to be honest, don't you?"

"Yes," she said tersely, and thought: too honest. He might find her simplicity intriguing, and even find her intriguing because of that simplicity. She didn't like the idea very much, or the probability that he wouldn't take long to get bored with such a simple diversion.

A waiter removed their plates. He made no comment about how little had been eaten—he didn't have to. The disapproving downturn of his mouth said it all. They ordered coffee and brandy.

She leaned back in her chair and let her eyes wander over the other diners. The ambience of the place was one of understated elegance. She was glad she'd bought the outfit. It felt good and appropriate.

"The music's nice," Ian said. He also sat back. With his hands spread on the arms of his chair, his navy suit jacket gaped to show a white shirt, probably hand tailored, that fitted him without a wrinkle. He did have a broad chest and a slim waist. Page decided some men were born to wear beautiful suits and silk ties and handmade shirts, and Ian was one of them.

"Hey, dreamer. Do you like the music?"

A pianist played a grand piano. The pieces were gentle, nonintrusive, mostly old and familiar. "I love it. This place is so peaceful, it wouldn't be hard to fall asleep."

Ian, jolting forward, startled Page. "Ruby's is supposed to be romantic. It's not supposed to put you to sleep. Or is it the company that's doing that?"

She narrowed her eyes at him while the coffee and brandy arrived. When they were alone again, she brought her face nearer to his across the table. "If you think I'm going to fall into any of your traps and tell you how irresistible you are, forget it." Up close his dark eyes appeared opaque, pupil and iris all one. She withdrew several inches. "You are pretty irresistible."

"Page—"

"Ian, darling! It *is* you. I told Martin I was sure it was, and he said I'd had one too many, didn't you Martin, darling? You're so mean sometimes."

Page looked up into the avid face of Deirdre of the long black hair and vicious tongue, and wished for divine intervention, like the fire alarm going off. Clearing out the restaurant seemed incredibly appealing at the moment.

Martin Grantham III stood at Deirdre's shoulder. He wasn't swaying this evening, and Page acknowledged, unwillingly, that in a foppish way he was quite attractive.

"Hello, Deirdre, Martin." Ian sounded as enthusiastic as Page felt, and at least one or two of her knotted muscles softened.

"Darling, we haven't seen you for simply ages. Poor Liz is pining away for you. Says you won't even talk to her on the phone." With this Deirdre pulled out a chair and sat down, motioning Martin to the other side of the table. He appeared uncomfortable. "Maybe Ian and, er... Maybe Ian doesn't want company," he said.

"Nonsense," Deirdre said. So far she'd managed to behave as if Ian were alone. She hailed the waiter. "Be a good boy and order me some more champagne, Ian. You know how I love champagne."

Ian glowered from Deirdre to Martin, who slid awkwardly to sit where Deirdre had indicated.

"We were about to leave," Ian said in a flat voice Page hadn't heard before. "Do you both remember Page?"

"You can't leave yet." Deirdre ordered the champagne herself, a bottle of Dom Perignon, then took a sip from Ian's brandy snifter. "You've got to finish this, and we just arrived."

"How are you, Page?" Martin asked. His discomfort was strong enough to make her feel sorry for him. "You are the lady we met at Ian's that night, aren't you?"

"Of course she is, silly." Deirdre made a cross moue. "I expect Ian is... Well, Ian always was one for little experiments."

Page put her napkin on the table. Cold climbed her spine and tightened her scalp. If this was so-called sophistication, she hoped she never got it. The woman was a boor. But she was also someone Ian had entertained in his home, together with a clone who must have been his date. Little experiments. Like taking out a member of the working class?

She'd bowed her head and didn't realize Ian was standing until he said her name.

"Page," he repeated. "It's time we got to that dancing I promised you." He motioned for his check.

"Aren't you going to have some of your champagne?" Deirdre asked, ignoring Martin's whispered, "Shut up, Deirdre."

"No thanks," Ian said. "And it's *your* champagne." He was making it clear that he wasn't paying for Deirdre's self-indulgence.

Martin stood and shook Page's hand. "Nice to see you again," he said. "Sorry about that other time. You know what they say: when the wine's in the wit's out? It's true."

She couldn't help liking him. "Forget it," she said. "I had until tonight, and I will again now. Enjoy your evening. You too, Deirdre." No need to take lessons from lesser beings.

As they left, Martin was reminding Ian that he owed him a rematch on the racquetball court. Ian's only response was a thin smile.

Outside the night was cool, the sky clear and silver black in the light of the moon and the city's illumination.

Sitting beside Ian in the car, Page fell silent. He'd switched on the engine but made no attempt to pull away from the curb. They both stared straight ahead.

"I'm sorry about that," Ian said.

"Why should you be?"

"Because they are friends of mine, or Martin is, anyway." He ran his hands around the steering wheel.

"Martin's quite nice, and I'm sure if Deirdre were sober she'd be okay, too." The inside of the car felt warm and Page opened her window. Night scents, dark and soothing, crept in.

"I doubt it," Ian said. "But then, I don't remember seeing her sober."

Page laughed. "Then feel sorry for her."

"You're too forgiving."

"Don't bet on it. I'm putting on a good front."

"Thank God," Ian said on a sigh. "Saints make me feel guilty. Are you up for dancing?"

She wasn't. "Um...well..."

"Neither am I. Would it make you nervous if I invited you back to my place? I'm not ready to let you go yet."

Whatever that meant. "It might make me nervous, but I'd probably say yes."

He put the car in gear.

Traffic was light and the drive from Brannan Street to Ian's place took what seemed to Page only minutes. When they eased into the narrow alley beside his house, she was still wondering if she'd appear a fool if she told him she'd changed her mind and wanted to go home.

"I hope the cupboard isn't bare," Ian said as he ushered her through the front door. "If it is, I suppose I can always call Touch Tone Gourmet." Was his laugh hollow?

Page said nothing. She was probably projecting her own tension on him.

"It's chilly in here," Ian said after showing her into the salon. "These big old houses are the dickens to heat. I'll get a fire going, then we'll raid the kitchen."

"We just had dinner," Page reminded him.

"Correction. We just paid for dinner. I seem to remember that neither of us ate too much."

She wrapped her short sheepskin coat more tightly around her. It didn't complement the blue cashmere, but was as close as she'd been able to come to something dressy.

Ian knelt on the hearth of a large, gray, marble fireplace and set light to paper beneath a pile of logs.

Page glanced around the beautiful room. "How do you keep everything so tidy?" It would take hours to clean the place.

"I have a housekeeper who comes in every other day," Ian said, still engrossed in poking the fire to life.

"Of course." How could she be so naive? It wasn't likely that the wealthy president of an advertising agency did windows.

At last, satisfied with his efforts, Ian stood. "The kitchen's downstairs. That's the one inconvenience to living upstairs. Do you want to stay by the fire while I see what I can find to eat?"

Being alone in the big room didn't appeal to her. "I'll come with you. I'd like to see the kitchen." Not strictly true.

Page didn't enjoy cooking, and kitchens had never interested her.

This kitchen was huge. Square, white tiles covered the lower halves of the walls. An incongruous paper depicting blue cupids cavorting among impossibly large pieces of blue fruit filled the space to a carved ceiling. Everything was spotless: rows of copper pans and utensils hanging from racks over a central cooking island; dishes visible through glass-fronted cabinets on two walls; a double, white enamel sink; a blue, linoleum-covered floor strewn with a hodgepodge of rag mats.

Ian watched her reaction. "Strange, isn't it? I keep saying I'm going to do something about it. I like to cook, so I had new appliances put in, but I haven't gotten around to the decor. God knows who chose this."

Page made a sympathetic noise. "I hate cooking." She applied fingertips to temples. He didn't need to know she had difficulty boiling spaghetti.

"So we balance each other," Ian said, oozing cheer. "That's exactly as it should be."

She resisted the temptation to ask if that meant he'd like to stay home and have someone like her "provide" for him.

He took off his raincoat and tossed it on a chair. "Ready to take yours off?"

She let him ease the sheepskin from her shoulders, conscious that the pattern of his breathing changed slightly and that his knuckles lingered too long on her bare back.

As soon as her hands were free, she moved. The change in atmosphere was subtle, but even without looking at Ian she knew it had happened. "May I check out the refrigerator?" she asked.

"Be my guest."

His voice was no longer falsely cheerful.

As if she spent every evening coming up with nice little snacks for company, Page took out cheese and sliced roast beef and mustard and mayonnaise and set them on a round oak table by a bay window. Then she found lettuce and a tomato, a loaf of bread and added them to the array.

While she busied herself, Ian stayed beside the chair where he'd put their coats.

"I thought you said you didn't like cooking," he said when she started setting out plates and flatware.

"I don't. Sandwiches aren't cooking, and I'm not going to make them. I just thought I'd do my bit first."

"Maybe I don't want sandwiches."

She paused in the act of opening the mayonnaise jar. He must see that she was keyed-up and not thinking straight. "What *do* you want?"

"To kiss you."

Her breathing quickened. "Are you always so blunt?"

"That wasn't blunt."

Her warmed skin turned fiery. "Can I make you a sandwich?"

"You can, but I probably won't eat it."

She made herself meet his stare. "What is it with us, Ian? Why does it feel like this whenever we're together?"

His laugh was short and jarring. "You're not that innocent."

"No. Maybe I should go home."

"Do you want to?"

Page crossed her arms and turned away. "I don't know."

She heard him move, but she still jumped when he slipped his hands under the draped back of her sweater. "If I'd been blunt just now I'd have said I wanted to make love to you."

"I know." Her voice sounded loud inside her head.

"Shall I explain exactly why we fence the way we do? Why there are all these long silences?"

He didn't need to. As he'd said, she wasn't that innocent.

"I'll tell you anyway. It's because we've got something special starting. Or already started. I felt it from the first time I saw you, and if you're honest you'll admit you did, too."

He traced bare skin at the edges of the sweater all the way to her waist. Page shuddered.

"Sexual tension can make conversation tough. That's why the silences."

His hands were inside the sweater now, circling her waist, and she felt soft wool sliding from her shoulders. She didn't try to stop it. "You sound like an expert on all this."

"Rational, that's all." He laced his fingers over her ribs and kissed the side of her neck, her nape, each shoulder blade. Only the fullness of her breasts stopped the sweater from falling completely.

Page arched her body. Rational. She didn't feel rational anymore, didn't want to.

"I'm not sorry for wanting you," Ian murmured against her ear. "But I want it to be a two-way thing. Is it?"

He rubbed his fingers back and forth beneath her breasts. Then he covered them gently, supporting their weight, touching his thumbs lightly to her nipples.

Page closed her eyes before she said, "I think it's what I want."

Ian turned her, eased her arms free of her sleeves and enfolded her, stroking, pressing his lips to a hundred small, erotic places. When he drew back they were both breathing hard.

Page loosened his tie and pulled it away, pushed his jacket from his shoulders and took off his shirt. And while she worked, Ian planted kisses designed to make her task more difficult... and more tantalizing. She smiled, evading him again and again until she finished.

She felt no awkwardness. They stood, inches apart, absorbing each other, touching. It was Page who broke first. She reached for him, pressed aching breasts against the provocative roughness of the dark hair on his chest.

Slowly, Ian moved them both backward, glancing behind him until he sat on one of the straight-backed chairs by the table with Page on his lap.

"You are something," he told her and brought his lips a whisper away from hers. "But I'm sure I'm not the first man to tell you that."

The statement-cum-question registered, nagged a little, but did nothing to stop what was happening in Page's body. "What's that supposed to mean?" she asked and ran the tip of her tongue along his lower lip.

His eyes lost some focus. Their mouths came together, and the kiss was deep and searching. Ian spread his hands behind her head and neck, and she clung to him, her nerves and skin, every part of her, open, raw, close to pain with the longing for release.

Ian bent his head to catch a nipple carefully in his teeth. And with the contact of his tongue came a deeper longing. His hand was on her leg, smoothing from knee to thigh, then gripping tight where the lace edge of her panties made a ridge through her hose.

"I'd like to be with you this way a lot, sweetheart," Ian said, moving his mouth to her other breast. Insistent pressure between her legs shocked and excited her, and she shifted, pushing her fingers beneath his belt. The rough hair continued over his belly.

"Let's go upstairs." Ian's voice was thick. He put a knuckle beneath her chin and kissed the spot between her eyes. "My bed's been too empty lately."

She turned cold.

Ian slid her to her feet and stood, wrapping an arm around her.

His bed had been too empty lately. Surely he didn't mean that the way it sounded, but he must expect her to have been sexually active. He must think... It was too soon for this.

"Ian...oh, Ian, please listen to me a minute." She ducked from his arm and struggled to pull her sweater back into place. "You and I are..." She couldn't finish, couldn't look at him.

"What, Page?" The clear note in his voice surprised her, and she turned her face up to his. The passion was still there, the evidence of arousal, but no anger. He took several long breaths. "Tell me what's wrong."

She wanted to cry and laugh at the same time, and she wanted the uncontrollable shaking in her legs to stop. "I don't want to do this now. I've let everything go too far, and I shouldn't have. I'm sorry." His bed had only been empty lately? The implication was there and she hated it.

He pulled free strands of hair that had caught beneath her neckline and picked up his own shirt. "Are you going to refuse to see me again?" The question was matter-of-fact.

"Will you want to see me again?" she said. Nothing had ever been as difficult as this.

"You just won't accept how badly I want you." He gathered his jacket and tie, but didn't bother to button his shirt. "Yes, I'll want to see you again, and again. The only difference from here out is that there's no pretense, is there? Just now you were as ready to make love as I was. I'm not sure what changed your mind, but I've always believed a man or woman's body was private property, only shared if the person was sure the time was right. All I ask is that when you are sure the time's right you let me know."

He wasn't angry. Yes, the frustration was there in the tight lines on his face, but no anger. She had no experience with men who didn't get angry when what they wanted was denied.

Page had to go home, to think. Ian made no attempt to dissuade her.

In the car they kissed before they pulled away from Ian's house, and then once more when he stopped the car in front of Page's apartment.

He saw her to her door, but gripped her elbow before she could slip quickly inside. "Don't think I'm not going to try again."

Her heart resumed its heavy beat. "I think I hope you will." She was glad the dim light hid her blush.

"Then we'll have to do something about it sooner or later, won't we?"

"I suppose so."

"I know so, sweetheart."

IAN LEANED ACROSS HIS DESK and pressed a button on his conference phone. "Faber here," he said without enthusiasm.

"Ian, it's Martin. What the hell are you doing at the office on Sunday?"

"What the hell made you think of trying to reach me here?"

"Quit answering questions with questions. I couldn't get you at home, so I decided to take a shot there."

Ian spread a series of glossy photographs in a line across the desk. "What do you want, Martin? I'm busy." And he wanted to stay that way. He was making progress as he never did during the week with phones constantly ringing.

"You're going to make this tough on me, aren't you, friend?"

"Spit it out," Ian said. "We've got a big presentation coming up and I don't have time to chat." Tomorrow Daniel Max would make their final decision on an advertising firm. Ian felt confident, but he wanted to be well prepared.

"Okay," Martin said on a sigh. "I'm sorry."

Ian waited.

"Did you hear me, Ian? I'm sorry for the way we interrupted you and Page last night."

Now it was Ian's turn to sigh. He was trying not to think too much about last night, and so far he'd been fairly successful. "Forget it. It wasn't important. Now—"

Martin laughed. "I realize it wasn't important. She's not your type, but she is a beauty."

Slowly, aware of flexing muscles in his jaw, Ian put his face closer to the speaker. "What do you mean, not important?"

Again Martin laughed, nervously this time. "I was just repeating what you said. No offense intended."

"Of course not. But for the record, friend, Page Linstrom is a hell of a lot more my type than the Deirdres of this world. Page is one special woman, and I don't ever want to hear you suggest otherwise again."

"Ian, I—"

"Goodbye, Martin. See you around." He broke the connection.

Damn Martin Grantham. Damn all the others like him. Ian reached for a mug of cooling coffee and took a deep swallow, narrowing his eyes to look over the rim at the photos. They were good. Lots of color, fine wool . . . classic style. These lines, presented his way, would be a hit all over the country.

He set down the mug and lifted a photo of a woman with long, glossy brown hair. She wore a brilliant green tartan skirt with a green cableknit sweater and a soft woolen hat pulled low over her brow. Were her eyes brown or blue? He studied the photo more closely.

Page's eyes were so blue.

This wasn't working. His attention couldn't keep being divided this way. Page's eyes were blue, her hair was wonderful, so was her body...but she wasn't ready for the kind of relationship he wanted. He didn't dare push her too hard.

The model in the photo had brown eyes.

Disgusted with himself, Ian tossed the shot on top of the others. Was something different happening to him? His reaction to Martin's comments about Page still hung in his head. Did a man lose his cool that way over a woman for whom he felt nothing more than liking and desire?

He wasn't sure he was ready to face the answer.

IN FRONT OF PAGE on the kitchen table lay her business accounts. She made it a rule to keep up the books. It would be nice to have a professional take over some of this one day, but that was a long way off. Fortunately bookkeeping was one of her strong areas, but she couldn't concentrate today. Ian, the memory of the way he looked at her last night, the way he'd touched her, repeatedly made the columns of figures senseless. She wanted to hear his voice but wouldn't allow herself to call him.

Regardless of what had happened between them, their parting message to each other had been implicit: they would continue to meet. She'd have to do some thinking about how to handle all the possible ramifications of total involvement with Ian. How would she cope if, as seemed inevitable, they became lovers but only for a while?

The sound of the doorbell was an intrusion she didn't need. But people had been known to ignore visitors.

With Ian's business and a steady increase in Waldo's, together with several other new accounts—two generated by referrals from Ian—profits looked good. The mopeds she hoped to buy were beginning to be clear pictures in her mind, and decent operation quarters, and computerized dispatching.

The doorbell rang again.

Damn. She looked awful, and she wasn't going to waste time being polite to someone selling something she didn't want.

But whoever was out there wasn't going away.

Page stood up, resting her hands on the table. Her black velour sweats had holes in the knees and she looked down at furry slippers shaped like elephant feet.

So what. She didn't have to dress up for door-to-door salespeople.

Muttering, she scuffed down the hall and threw open the door. "Ye—"

"Page! You are home. May I come in?"

Rose Faber, swathed in glossy chinchilla, gave Page a dazzling smile as she swept into the apartment.

Chapter Nine

A waft of Shalimar remained where Rose had passed. Page realized her mouth was open, closed it, and the front door.

"What an *interesting* little apartment," Rose was saying by the time Page followed her into the kitchen. "I've always thought Russian Hill was charming. When I was a little girl I had a friend who lived not far from here."

Not, Page bet, in a run-down apartment. "Really?"

"Yes." Rose slipped off black leather gloves, then her coat, to reveal a white suit Tanya would have described as a "smashing little number."

Page waited for Rose to say something more, like what she was doing here.

"I bet you wonder how I knew where you lived."

The thought hadn't come to her until now. "How did you know?" she asked.

Rose waggled a finger and tossed the chinchilla down as only someone who could afford one would. "I find out things I want to know." The words held no malice or threat, yet Page's stomach tightened. She glanced around the kitchen wishing she'd done her housekeeping stint and cleared away the papers, but most of all dressed in almost anything but what she had on. Had she even combed her hair?

"Well, Page. Come on, ask me how I found out. Intrigue isn't much fun if nobody cares about it."

Rose's cajoling tone began to grate. "How did you find out?" Page asked more tersely than she intended.

"Oh, you're cross because I didn't call first." Rose sat down. "Is it all right for me to come? I found out where you live, because Bob told me you were doing some work for Faber. I called shipping for the name of your firm and an address."

Why? was the first thought Page had. "You're welcome to come. It gives me the chance to thank you for having me to dinner. Somehow I don't seem to get to some of the things I should do. Like write thank-you notes."

"We loved having you." Rose looked around. "You must have a...shop, would you call it?"

"For the bikes and dispatching, I suppose you mean." Page propped a hip against the sink, trying not to visualize the way Rose must see her. "There's a garage at the back of the house. You know the way lots of these houses have them at the end of an alley? That's where my operations area is. That—" she indicated the table "—is my office, I'm afraid. Not very glamorous but the best I can do for now."

"Bob and I think what you've done is wonderful." Rose settled herself more comfortably. "It gives older people hope to see that there are still some youngsters with imagination and courage."

Page pushed at her hair. Rose made her sound like a child prodigy rather than one more struggling workaholic. "Thank you," she said, then remembered the importance of diplomacy. "I really appreciate the confidence Faber and Faber has shown in us. We'll prove we're worth the risk."

"Yes," Rose said. Her smile became fixed. "I'm sure you will. You know, you could be more to Ian than a business proposition."

Page blushed and bristled in unison. "I respect Ian as a businessman. I hope he's equally impressed with me."

Rose's face set in a serious mold. "Bob tells me that Ian considers you someone to be encouraged."

Someone to be encouraged. Page was sure Rose meant well, but there was still that ring of patronage: the inventive little woman should be encouraged—provided she doesn't go too far....

Page longed to be blunt and ask Rose exactly why she'd come. "Would you like some coffee or tea? Or there's some wine, I think."

Rose flapped a dismissive hand. "Tea if you have it. Preferably herbal, but anything if you don't."

Page filled the kettle and put it on to heat. "Let's go into the sitting room," she said. "It's more comfortable." *Even if it is equally tatty.*

Installed in the sitting room, Rose loosened the buttons of her suit jacket. A matching silk shirt fell in soft pleats from neck to waist. "Did you and Ian have a good time last night?"

Page's heart slipped away, and her stomach and everything else within her. "Ian told you we went out?"

Rose's hesitation, the vague deepening of her color, fascinated Page. "Well, no. Not exactly, that is. I kind of patched things together. Clemmie told me he'd asked for the number of Ruby's, then he wasn't at home. And, of course, Bob saw you in his office and found out about the arrangement for you to work for the firm. And believe it or not, my Bob has an eye for these things. He told me he thought Ian was really interested in you—personally I mean—and he was right, wasn't he?"

The heat in Page had little to do with Rose's words. While the woman talked, every second of last night's encounter replayed in living color. And again came Ian's promise: they'd have to do something about the way they felt sooner or later.

"Do you feel well, Page?"

"Of course." She nodded at Rose. "Ian did take me to Ruby's last night. It was lovely." The straightforward approach would be easiest in the long run.

"Ruby's?" Rose sighed. "So romantic. He must really think a lot of you. And Bob and I think he has good taste."

What exactly was this woman trying to accomplish? Page was convinced that Rose had a mission other than a polite, Sunday afternoon visit.

"You and Ian have known each other for some time now."

Page slowly brought her concentration back to Rose. "Several weeks," she said.

The kettle whistled and Page jumped up to assemble the best of her teacups and saucers. Fortunately her mother had taught her how to make tea correctly, and she warmed the pot with boiling water for a few moments. Even Rose's choice of Tanya's herbal tea, which Page detested, should taste better made this way.

She returned to the sitting room with a tray and poured. "I must admit I'm surprised to see you," she told Rose honestly. Looking down at her worn sweats she added, "I would have changed if I'd known you were coming."

"I know you would have," Rose said heartily. "And that's the main reason I didn't call. I thought we should meet as we are. No artifice."

Except the chinchilla and the smashing suit, Page thought, and immediately regretted her small-mindedness. What the woman wore was natural for her. If Rose Faber could reach out the hand of friendship, so could she.

Rose sipped Orange Pleasure tea with obvious approval and rested her head back on a blue armless chair that spilled stuffing from every seam. "Your apartment is charming," she said, "and Bob and I do so admire your inventiveness in business."

Page went on alert. The woman had said the same thing in various ways several times now. "Thank you," she said.

"You're going to be one of those women who become absolute powerhouses."

"Powerhouses?"

"In their communities, dear. It's always the women with vision who turn into leaders."

Page was becoming increasingly lost. "I don't see myself as ever having time to become a community leader." She stopped herself from adding that there was nothing she wanted less.

Rose smiled comfortably. "That'll change, you mark my words. There's nothing like a husband and children to put a different slant on everything a woman does. She stops caring so much about things she doesn't *have* to be bothered with anymore."

"What sort of things?" Page's grip on her saucer tightened.

"Oh, you know. Making money, or developing new friendships, all that stuff. Once there's a husband in the picture, his friends become yours and he takes on so many of the tiresome responsibilities we women were never cut out to handle."

Page was smitten with a sense of déjà vu. Weren't these the messages she'd grown up with, only slightly differently phrased?

"I do think we've managed to pass on our values to Ian." Rose's expression was serene and distant now. "Oh, he's had his little flings, but his head and heart are in the right place. He just has to find the right woman and he'll be the happiest man on earth."

An aura of unreality descended about Page. Rose Faber looked like a society matron from a *Town and Country* article who'd wandered into the wrong room. She kept on talking, but intermittently Page heard words like home, family, settled, values, provide...

"Don't you think so, dear?" Rose said, sitting forward.

Page had to respond. "I...oh, I expect so."

"Have you ever seen Ian with children?" The query was crooned in Rose's luscious voice. "You probably haven't had the opportunity. Lots of our friends have grandchildren, and if one of them is brought to visit us while Ian's over he just takes charge. I swear you'd think he'd been playing with babies and throwing balls to toddlers all his life. He has to be a natural, because of course he was an only child."

Beneath the chinchilla coat and mohair suit, Rose Faber had set out with the determined heart of a matchmaker. Page couldn't believe it, yet she couldn't deny the evidence. Ian was being presented to her as the perfect husband and father.

Rose sighed, evidently oblivious to the lengthy silences that greeted her little speeches. "Confidentially, Ian's admitted to me that he's ready to settle down and—this has to be strictly between you and me, Page—but he has hinted that he's becoming deeply attached to you. Isn't that lovely?" Her delighted laugh had a tinkling, girlish quality that set Page's teeth on edge.

"Really?" It was the best Page could do without telling the woman to stop meddling.

"Yes, yes. I can't tell you what it means to me to know that. And to his father. Ian's going to be one of those perfect fathers. Can't you just see him with his children?" Her eyes took on the appearance of one seeing a miraculous vision. "The woman who gets my Ian will be blessed. She'll never have to worry about another thing as long as she lives."

Page set down her cup, bowing her head to hide her face. She had to say something. "Ian's thirty-six, isn't he?" She didn't give Rose time to respond. "I'm surprised he hasn't, er, settled down before now if he's such a natural for the role."

"He's been waiting for that special person, Page. And until now she hasn't come into his life."

Page saw it all. The frustration Rose must have suffered watching her friends with their children tidily married and a batch of grandchildren tidily produced. And Ian was the odd man out, the one who hadn't slipped obediently into the expected pattern. For an instant she allowed Ian a little pity. Only for an instant. His mother was one smart lady. She'd categorized Ian's female companions to date and discovered some constants, the main one being that no woman had managed to get his wedding ring on their finger. But Rose, clever Rose, had sighted Page as something different and decided there was nothing to lose by closing in for the kill. First, much as she must abhor what Page did for a living, approval and admiration must be poured on to pave the way for what would follow: the carrot of an easy life dangled until the subject bit and held on.

Rose had made one fatal miscalculation... Page wasn't biting. What was supposed to sound to her like a dream was loaded with potential nightmare qualities, exactly the elements Page was determined to avoid.

Somehow she got through another half hour of Rose's "ode to Ian" without being rude, and when they parted it was on the note that Rose would look forward to their next meeting.

Page closed the door on her uninvited guest and tottered into her bedroom where she flopped, face down, onto the futon.

She closed her eyes, determined to sleep before it was time to go back on duty.

Ian could be in on it.

Now she was getting punchy. She maneuvered herself beneath the comforter and started a relaxation exercise.

What if Ian was sick of his parents harping on the subject of marriage and children and he'd decided to find a suitable candidate? Perhaps he thought she was suitable because she turned him on—no question there—and he couldn't believe she'd be fool enough to turn down an opportunity for a leg up the social ladder and a cushy place in his family's bosom, his kitchen, his nursery... and his bed. And then—and this she mustn't forget—she'd get a chance to become civically prominent.

She groaned and pulled the pillow over her head. There was no choice. Cool the relationship at once.

Her nose itched, and then all of her skin. Her *teeth* itched. Damn it, why did she have to want the man so badly?

"PAGE, wake up."

Her triplets were crying. She'd run out of disposable diapers and the car wouldn't start. "Go 'way."

"Page!"

The babies were useless on bicycles. All her clients were complaining about late deliveries. Ian said if they had more babies it would be easier because then she'd have more riders.

The warm softness was snatched from her head and light hit her eyelids.

"Page, will you wake up, darn it. It's after five. You've got to go to work."

"What?" She squinted up into Tanya's face and felt her brain slowly clear. The images faded into fragments, then disappeared. "What!" She leaped up, staggering a little, and looked at her watch. "Oh, no. I'm going to be late."

"I'm glad I came home," Tanya said. "You were mumbling and tossing, but you would probably have slept until tomorrow. You don't get enough rest."

Page stripped off the sweat suit, preparing to deliver a broadside on Tanya's nerve to talk about insufficient rest. Then she glanced at her roommate and stopped rushing around the room. "You look...different." Tanya's eyes had their old glow.

Smirk was the only description for the expression on Tanya's face. "You know what they say, kid. Love is the key."

"Yuck," Page said, incredulous. "I think I'm going to be sick."

It had been several days since the incident of the bruises and Page had seen Tanya on a number of occasions since. Thinking back now, a subtle change had been evident each time.

"You're just jealous," Tanya said. "You need to be more of a romantic, like I am."

Page thought of Ian. Then she very deliberately tried not to think of him. "I take it this means your love life has straightened out?"

"You've got it."

"I'm glad." She smiled and gave Tanya an impulsive hug. "Any man who had a chance to be loved by you and didn't take it would be mad."

Hadn't Rose said something like that, only about Ian?

BUSINESS WAS ESPECIALLY BRISK that evening. And Waldo's mood lifted as the night wore on—to the point where he insisted on paying Page more for each drop. She arrived home exhausted but satisfied and was met by a ringing telephone.

She answered without thinking. If she had she'd have expected to hear Ian and she might have chosen not to talk to him.

"Hi, sweetheart," he said.

A little twist, part longing, part the remembrance of her decision to be strong, tightened her throat. "Hello, Ian."

"That took a long time. Don't you feel like talking?"

She wished she didn't. "I just got home. My brain's probably on overload."

"That's one of the things I wanted to talk to you about."

"My brain?"

"No, this nighttime working. You've got a lot more work in the day now, sweetheart. And you'll get more if you want it. But it's time you gave up this night nonsense."

Just like that. Time for her to give it up. Then it would be time for her to give up the rest because Mrs. Ian Faber could hardly ride bicycles all over San Francisco delivering inter-company messages and packages.

"Did you hear what I said?"

"Yes. I'm not giving up any part of my business, Ian. I appreciate the extra work you've generated for me. It's been enough for me to be able to start thinking about more employees."

"So why—"

"But I'm *not* giving up a thing. Growth is going to be the deciding factor for me. The faster the better. I thought you understood that."

She heard him sigh. "I don't see how this one job can be worth what it does to your social life."

At least he was honest about the real reason for his concern. How could he intensify his campaign if theirs was to remain a Saturday-night-only courtship? "I'm satisfied with my social life."

"Are you?" He sounded hurt and Page felt regret.

"Maybe we've been concentrating too much on each other." The words were painful to say and she wished they weren't. "You don't need me to give you permission, but why don't you see other people? We don't have any hold on each other."

After a long time he said, "I see." And the rest of the message came without saying—he'd thought he did have some hold on her.

"Ian, I'm sorry to be short, but this has been a tough night. Could we talk some more about this another time?"

"If that's what you'd prefer."

"It is. I'll give you a call."

IAN RESISTED THE TEMPTATION to smack the receiver down. Instead he replaced it carefully in its cradle.

She was backing off. Why? He hadn't imagined her reaction to him last night. Without knowing the reason for her drawing back, he still believed she'd wanted them to make love and that she hadn't stopped wanting it.

So why the complete turnoff?

He got up from the couch in the salon and poured a stiff Scotch on the rocks. All night he'd waited until he was pretty sure she'd be home, anticipating that she'd be pleased to hear his voice. And while he'd waited to talk to her he'd done some thinking. Without reaching any final conclusions, he'd identified a subtle change in his feelings for Page. He did like her, a lot, but he was beginning to want her on a deeper level. That scared him, but he was ready to go on and take a chance at whatever might lie ahead.

Pushing her to give up night riding had been a mistake. That must be the answer. He already knew she hated being told what to do. The urge to call her back and apologize came and went. She definitely hadn't wanted to continue the conversation.

With the drink in hand, he wandered into his bedroom. He didn't turn on the light and felt his way to a love seat by the window.

Over there somewhere—he looked in the direction of Russian Hill—Page was probably already in bed. His own bed held no appeal. He wasn't tired. His needs were for something other than sleep, and he gritted his teeth against his body's answering leap at the thought.

He closed his eyes, willing quiet inside, but saw Page as she'd looked, semi-naked, her mouth soft and kissed…and on her face an expression that mirrored the desire he'd felt, felt now.

The Scotch made his nostrils flare but he welcomed the surge of warmth in his veins.

"QUIET. ALL OF YOU!" Page yelled over a lunchtime argument raging in the garage. "I said, be quiet."

"Tone it down, guys," the Zipper said, waving his arms like a baseball umpire signaling a successful steal. "The boss is trying to say something."

Gradually the din ebbed.

"Thank you," Page said. "Can we take this from the top?"

"I've had it," Ken said immediately and dropped to sit on the floor.

Page ignored him. For days business had been conducted with no interference from the phantom riders. But she'd been contacted midway through her morning ride with a request that she call Lilian. It appeared the truce was over and now she really had trouble.

"I just came from the hospital." Total silence let her know she finally had full attention. "Perkins has a mild concussion and a broken ankle, but he's going to be fine. They wouldn't let me ask him any questions, but I understand you know what happened, Buzz. Describe the guy and the bike involved, please."

Buzz popped a huge gum bubble and plastered her body to a wall. Between her hands she snapped a length of gold ribbon.

"Buzz. I'm waiting."

"I didn't see the guy."

Page frowned. "But the message I got said you witnessed the, er, accident."

Lilian came forward. Jemima had another cold and clung to the hem of her mother's sweater. "Buzz didn't see the guy, but she did see Perkins crash. He went up on a curb, hit a bike rack and did a forward somersault."

"He made a mistake, then," said Page. "Or someone got in his way. It was just an accident."

"The hell it was!"

At Ken's roar, Jemima started to cry, and the Zipper swept her into his arms. "Keep it down, Ken," he said, his eyes narrowed. "You're upsetting the kid."

Page waved for silence. "Ken," she said, "what point are you making?"

"The police took the bike away before Buzz could get a real good look at it, but she reckons the brake cable was yanked out." He rested his forehead on his arms as if he'd delivered final sentence.

"And what do the police say?" Hope flickered in Page. If the police were suspicious of foul play they might do something.

Buzz paced to the door and back. "They say what they always say. We're careless. We don't maintain the equipment. The bike was just plain mangled from the crash. In other words, nothing. But I know someone pulled that cable. It didn't look right."

"She could have something," the Zipper said quietly. "I'm not panicking, but I do think we'd better get into the habit of doing better checks."

Page nodded. "Okay. But you're gone, huh, Ken? You want out?"

"I'm thinking about it. Nothing's worth dying for."

Cold sweat shot out on Page's back. "Don't talk that way."

"You might not be so willing to brush it aside if someone tried to break your body permanently," Ken persisted. "And that's something else that's off about all this. Why are you the only one who hasn't been hit?"

"I don't know." Page wished she did. She certainly thought enough about it, and couldn't come up with a solution that made sense.

Jemima cried again, and the Zipper nuzzled her face into his neck. "Nobody's going to die," he said. "We're just going to work together—look out for each other."

"With one less rider," Ken commented, raising his eyes to Page's face. "How do you handle that one, boss lady?"

"Perkins won't be out for good," she said. "And I was going to hire some more people anyway. This just means I'll do it sooner.'' She glanced at Buzz who was still making cracking noises with the metallic ribbon. ''I wish you wouldn't do that, Buzz. You're making me more nervous than I already am.''

Buzz tossed the ribbon down, and Page noticed that it looked like one Tanya had worn a few times. She wondered where Buzz had found it, but Ken's voice boomed out again before she could ask.

Another half hour of bickering, and Page was back on the road. Lilian was contacting employment agencies and placing ads for new riders. With luck they'd be back to full complement, plus at least one, within a day or two.

At five she wheeled the Schwinn into the garage ready to take her break before going to work for Waldo.

Instead of the usual gaggle that heralded the end of the day, she was met by Lilian and the Zipper. Jemima was curled up on a small cot Page hadn't seen before.

''Page,'' the Zipper said. ''You'd better sit down.''

She closed her eyes. ''Not more problems.''

Lilian put an arm awkwardly around Page's shoulders. ''Nothing we can't work out if we stick together.''

Her head ached, and her shoulders. Her legs felt like lead. ''Just get it out.'' She checked an impulse to say she couldn't take any more. Giving up was a luxury she couldn't afford.

''Buzz had an accident and Ken quit.''

Chapter Ten

If nothing else, Chinatown was cheerful. Even in sheeting rain, the lights and fragrant smells were irresistible. Almost.

Page headed along Frank Street. She was delivering to a private address on Joice.

Her hair clung to her neck, and from time to time she wiped water from her eyes and face. This would stand out as the worst Wednesday of her life.

She made the drop at an apartment over a dingy variety store on Joice and contacted Waldo on her radio. "Move it," he said. "We're really cooking."

Without bothering to respond, she switched off and started to retrace her path. Coming out of Joice she swished through a deep puddle, blades of water shooting on either side of her bike.

She didn't sight the other rider until the spokes of his wheels glittered in a streetlight. Swathed in hooded oilskins, his head down, he didn't see her. Page slammed on the brakes, braced for collision and went into a skid.

"Watch out!" He wouldn't be able to hear her scream over the street noise.

Another cyclist did hear. He came fast from her left, miraculously passing inches in front of Page. "Idiot," he yelled.

Page came to a stop, the bike slewed, but her feet hit the ground firmly and held. Her heart beat in giant erratic bounds while she watched the irate interceptor, still shouting, ride out of sight.

Breathing deeply through her mouth to quiet her nerves, she scrubbed at her eyes and turned to deal with the other cyclist.

He'd gone. She fought down waves of sickness. Earlier Ken had asked why she hadn't been the victim of an attack. Well, she had now, or almost, she was sure of it.

She pushed off again and rode more slowly. If she could, she'd quit for the night. All her reflexes felt sluggish. She turned her thoughts to Buzz.

Buzz wasn't in the hospital, but she had sprained both wrists. When Page talked to her, the girl's determination to get back to work as soon as possible had come as a surprise. Rather than thinking of giving up, Buzz wasn't about to be beaten by a couple of "bum wrists." But there had been that same story. Failed brakes. And this time Buzz had a pretty watertight theory. She'd gone into an office to make a delivery. Right before that she'd used her brakes and they were fine. Afterward, on a downhill flight, they were gone. Buzz's contention was that someone had watched until he had a minute or two, when Buzz was away from her bike, to pull the cable loose but not completely free. It would look okay, but wouldn't hold when used.

Why was this happening? Where was the sense in victimizing a little outfit that was no real threat to anyone?

Farther down the street a group of people staggered from a lighted doorway onto the sidewalk. Page kept an eye on them as she approached. As so often happened, one man walked into the street without looking. She heard his loud laughter. "Rider on your left," she called, but still had to swerve to the opposite side of the road to avoid him.

The rain was even heavier. On nights like this, it wasn't too hard to agree with Ian's opinion of this facet of her business.

He hadn't called on Monday night, but on Tuesday she'd picked up the phone just as she'd been about to get into bed. "How about getting together Saturday night?" he'd asked. "I don't have any fantastic plans yet, but I'll come up with something."

She'd refused, and he hadn't tried to persuade her to change her mind. That shouldn't have rankled, but it did. She muttered under her breath, berating herself for being indecisive. If she'd decided the man was a complication she couldn't handle, she'd better find a way to stop mooning over him.

Maybe he'd call again tonight.

"Page Linstrom, wise up," she said aloud.

She started uphill again, her thighs and calves straining. With the slick streets came added tension, and she checked from side to side constantly, expecting trouble any moment. *Relax,* she told herself. *Be alert but loosen up.*

Ahead a traffic light turned bleary red. She was moving slowly, too slowly. When she returned to the deli, Waldo was likely to have one of his yelling attacks, and she wasn't sure she wouldn't yell right back.

At the junction, beneath the signal, she stopped and rested a foot on the pavement. She rarely got cold, but she was chilled now. Rain gear was something she avoided, always believing she should travel with as little extra clothing as possible holding her back. A hot shower as soon as she got home usually made her feel fine—though tonight she wasn't sure she wouldn't need a lot more than a shower to warm her.

Something shimmered to her right. The light turned green and she leaned on the pedals, pushing while she checked the side street she passed. Was the glimpse of metallic sheen caused by reflection on a wet blue slicker?

She shook her head, brushing again at her eyes. For an instant she'd got the impression of a cyclist holding himself and his machine close to the wall, his head hooded and held as out of sight as he could manage. Hiding? Watching?

Riding faster, she ducked her own head and pumped hard. Now she wasn't only cold and depressed, she was jumpy. The appearance of a bus helped. And a taxi. Gradually the foreboding dwindled, and she reached the deli.

Waldo hadn't been kidding when he said things were cooking. She set out from his shop again, this time carrying eight small orders in her basket and three more in a knapsack on her back. Her destination was the Nob Hill area. No long distances this time, and for that she was grateful.

While she pedaled, she mulled over what had happened and was in the process of happening to Pedal Pushers now. Lilian already had three possible riders lined up for interviews early the next morning. With luck they'd scrape through somehow. The main thing was to find replacements who knew the city.

Page blessed her good fortune that she made the first eight deliveries in record time. Switching and doubling back on small streets between Pine and Bush, she accomplished the transactions quickly and smoothly.

As she headed for an address close to Union Square, she recalled the best news of the day. The Zipper, with sweetly funny shyness, had told Page that he and Lilian had decided to "give it a try." Remembering her own serious suggestion that they not go into a relationship thinking it might not be permanent brought a smile to Page's lips. The picture of Lilian and the Zipper, Jemima in his arms, protesting that they *did* intend to be together permanently made the rain and cold lose their bite.

Another red light impeded her progress. Page swerved onto the sidewalk and sped into a small alley that would take her where she wanted to go as fast as the route by the main street.

A small lamp attached to a wall at the far end of the alley made a misty arch. She leaned down, pulling a Velcro tab on her shoe more snugly across her foot. Then she bent the other way to repeat the adjustment.

Silver threads. Spokes. Her forward thrust carried her on while she strained to see.

Page felt an upward clawing in her stomach. Someone was leaning against the wall, almost totally obscured except for that brief flash from the spokes of his bicycle wheels.

She applied the brakes. There was time to turn around. There had to be.

No time. She was almost beside him now. And the space was too narrow.

Speed was her only chance. Why had she slowed? What did he want—to kill her, rape her?

Page opened her mouth to scream. At the same time she opened up, pummeling the pedals, driving with legs that had no feeling.

She heard what he did before she identified what it was.

Metal, shrieking as it buckled, the acrid smell of jammed rubber. He was ramming something rigid into her wheel.

Sheen on blue oilskins. Low laugh.

Her feet stayed with the pedals. Then she hit, pitching, flying. The top of her helmet cracked on cobbles before the bike piled on top of her.

All the air went out of the night.

Page closed her eyes, scraped her hands beneath her to press her aching belly.

The stones were wet against her face.

Chapter Eleven

"Tell them to let me out of here," Page said.

"You're going to have to be patient. I'll get them to spring you when they're sure you're as okay as you think you are." Tanya sat beside her in a small hospital room. Curtains were drawn around the bed to give some privacy. Another patient lay only a couple of feet away.

Page tossed, drawing up her knees and turning on her side. "I'm bruised. My ribs hurt. But that's it, I tell you. I don't have time to lie here, Tanya. Make them understand that."

"They want to make sure you don't have any internal injuries. Please stay calm. If they see you're all upset they may keep you even longer."

Page glared and covered her eyes with the back of a hand. She did hurt all over. But she didn't need to be here. "They had all night to watch me. It's already eleven in the morning. I've got—"

"I know, I know. Did the police talk to you?"

"Twice. In the emergency room and about an hour before you got here."

"What did they say?"

She looked at Tanya again. "They asked bunches of questions and said they'd examined my bike. And yes, they agree that somebody probably jammed a crowbar or something into my wheel, then took off. But I needn't expect the guy to be found."

"Well, I guess that makes sense." Tanya played with the edge of a sheet. "How would you find someone like that in a city this big?"

"You sound like the cops," Page commented, exasperated. "A random attack. Probably never be repeated. And they weren't even interested in the fact that three of us have had crashes in two days. They think mine was probably something isolated and the other two were accidents. Accidents! Two bikes belonging to riders from the same firm lose brakes and it's an accident?"

"Did you argue about that?" Tanya asked.

"What do you think? Then they got all high-handed and talked about bicycle wars like we were a bunch of Hell's Angels. I tell you, Tanya, I just want out of here so I can get my business back on the road while I still *have* a business."

The squish of soft-soled shoes interrupted whatever Tanya might have said. "How are we doing?" The curtain swung aside and a nurse, thermometer in hand, approached Page.

"Nurse, I want—"

The thermometer was slipped beneath her tongue and a bony thumb applied beneath the chin. Her teeth snapped against glass. Page breathed heavily through her nose and caught Tanya's grin before it could be smothered.

"You're very popular, Ms. Linstrom," the tall, thin nurse said. Her name tag read S. Ribbenstraat. "You have two other visitors waiting outside, and there've been several telephone inquiries."

Once the thermometer was removed Page scooted up, shoving at her pillows and straightening the sheets. She'd show them how alert and well she felt and they'd be forced to release her. A plain white hospital gown did nothing for the image but she couldn't help that.

"We allow no more than two visitors at a time." S. Ribbenstraat spoke to Tanya. "Since the other two people are together, perhaps you'd like to change places with them for a while.''

Page cast a glance toward an acoustical-tiled ceiling. ''Anyone would think I was in critical condition.''

''I know.'' Nurse Ribbenstraat sounded human enough for Page to smile at her. ''Rules, rules and more rules. Some hospitals allow visitors to run in and out all the time, but we're not one of them, I'm afraid.''

''I'd better go home,'' Tanya said. ''Would you like me to call your folks?''

''No.'' Page sounded too emphatic. ''No,'' she repeated more gently. ''I talked to them a few days ago and they think everything's great with me. I'd rather keep it that way.'' All they'd do, Page thought, was repeat their opinion that a woman had no place trying to run a business alone in a big city.

''If you're sure,'' Tanya said. ''Call me as soon as you can leave. Okay?''

When Page nodded, Tanya leaned over to peck her cheek, then slid through the gap in the curtains, leaning back once to waggle her fingers.

Page smoothed her hair. She had been able to comb it early this morning and wash her face. Any other effort at beautification would have been a waste of time. The skin beneath her left eye was discolored, and her cheek was covered in scratches and little purple dents from grit.

''Page?''

Her mouth dropped open and her eyes widened. She tried to reverse her reaction, but knew it was too late. Lilian, dressed in a white blouse, gray woolen skirt and cardigan, came into the curtained enclosure. She wore hose and plain black pumps, and her hair was restrained by twin tortoise-shell combs.

''Um...Lilian,'' Page managed when she found her voice. ''How lovely of you to come to see me.'' In the eighteen months Lilian had worked for Page, she'd never appeared in anything other than jeans and sweatshirt, with tattered tennis shoes on her feet and her curly hair untamed.

"James, jr. is outside. He wanted me to ask if he could come in, too." Lilian bent closer. "He's trying to be cool, but I think he's scared by all this."

"He's not the only one," Page muttered. "Bring him in. And, Lilian, you look wonderful, but you didn't have to dress up for me."

Lilian's expression clearly suggested pity. "My mother brought us all up to wear our best to the doctor's. I don't remember much of what she used to say, but that makes sense."

Page didn't bother to ask why.

A couple of minutes later James preceded Lilian to the bedside. He stared hard at Page's face. "SOB," he said and blushed. "I mean, well...yeah, that's what I mean. Here." He dropped a bunch of brown chrysanthemums wrapped in cellophane on her stomach. "I don't like these much, but the grocery store didn't have anything else."

"Thank you, James." She was holding back, trying to be polite when she really wanted to bombard them, particularly Lilian, with questions.

"Sit down," she offered. "There're two chairs for the two visitors they allow at a time in here."

Lilian sat. James remained standing.

"I checked every bike in the place this morning," he said, and his grimy nails proved it. "All the new guys' machines, too. There isn't a screw out of place."

New guys?

"James is right," Lilian said, sliding forward on the chair. "We know the equipment is tip-top. And you'd be proud of our James. He gave everyone a lesson in spot checks. No rider leaves a drop location without making sure his machine is the way he left it."

Page held up a hand. Excitement swelled through her veins, but she had to take things slowly. "New guys? Did we get some more people already?"

Lilian laughed, shaking her head. "Gee, I'm sorry. The Zipper says when I talk I always start at the end and work back. There were three messages on the machine this morning. Two from employment agencies and one from a guy the Zipper spoke to at the Hotel Utah." She paused and clasped her hands in her lap. "We called the hospital and they said no visitors before nine, so we figured we'd go ahead and interview and try to get some riders on the road. Was that okay, Page?"

She wanted to jump from the bed. "Okay? Of course it's okay. You interviewed?"

"Yes."

"And you found a couple of people?"

"Five." Lilian flinched as if expecting a verbal blow.

James came a step closer, his face flushed. "They're all okay, Page. Honest. I was there, and the Zipper and Lilian grilled them like in one of those TV hearings. By eight-thirty they were all on the road. The Zipper's covering the radio while we're visiting you. He'll come later if you're still here."

"I don't intend to be—Ouch!" A pain shot between her ribs and she pressed a forearm to her side.

Lilian leaped to her feet. "What is it? Should I get the nurse?"

"No," Page whispered urgently. "They'll lock me away if I can't convince them there's nothing wrong with me."

"But there is," James said in his mature voice. "You've got to take it easy or you won't get better so fast."

Page wrinkled her nose at him. "Thanks, doctor."

"Page, James is right. We can keep going. You've got everything so well in place that it's a breeze. Or it is now that we've got new people. And Buzz called this morning, too. She says another week and she'll be ready to go again."

"Let's hope we'll have enough business to need this new army," Page said, not completely joking.

"We will," Lilian assured her. "You talked about someone to take on more night deliveries—and then there's that idea you had for expanding to Sausalito. We can handle it all. Wait and see. Another year and we'll be one of the biggest in town. I couldn't pass up any of those guys—there's a woman, mouthy but wise. I took them all because I know you're gonna need 'em."

Page couldn't help grinning. "Maybe we will. I sure hope so.... James! Why aren't you in school?"

He backed away. "I'm going now. Lilian called the school and said I had an appointment at the hospital." They all laughed.

An hour later Page was less euphoric than she had been when Lilian and James left. Professionally things looked rosy, but a brief visit from a doctor had punctured her bubble enough to cause a slow leak of enthusiasm. Her ribs were severely bruised, and there was a trace of bleeding from a kidney. She wouldn't be released for at least another two days, and definitely not until the doctor was satisfied there was no significant renal damage.

Nurse Ribbenstraat popped her head around the curtain, a sympathetic gleam in her eye. "The doctor told me about your urinalysis. Don't let it get you down. It's very common after the kind of fall you had, and by tomorrow your tests will probably be clear."

Page wasn't encouraged.

"There's a man here to see you. If you're too tired, I'll ask him to come back later."

Ian, Page thought. Then a cold place came into her heart. Ian wouldn't even know what had happened, and after the cool way she'd treated him lately he wasn't likely to come here.

"Shall I tell him you're tired?"

Page sighed. "No. I'll see him." It was probably the Zipper, and if anyone could cheer her up it was good old Zip.

Instead of the Zipper, Waldo Sands strode in, deposited a showy white azalea on her bedside table and pulled a chair close beside her. "You look like hell." He eyed her critically, peering at her face, lifting a hand to examine the scraped palm.

Page pulled the sheet up to her chin. "How did you know I was here?" As soon as she asked she knew it was a foolish question.

"When you didn't come back in or radio, I tried to reach you. Then customers started calling on orders that hadn't been delivered, so I got in touch with Tanya and she'd already been contacted by the police. You were lucky the next guy through that alley wasn't a wino with empty pockets."

Good old Waldo. Always the pragmatist. "It was a couple and they were great."

"I'm sure they were. Is your bike a total write-off?"

"From the way it sounds. My people will make sure I have the equipment I need by the time I'm ready to go. Which reminds me, Waldo. My knapsack's in the closet over there. I don't know what's in the deliveries, but something might be salvageable." She paused, remembering something else. "The envelopes. Oh, Waldo, I forgot about the money. I bet that guy took it."

He grimaced. "Don't give it another thought. How long will you be here?"

His nonchalance over the money surprised her. But then, Waldo Sands didn't need to worry about funds the way she did. "I'll have to stay at least a day or so. And I think they're leading up to saying I've got to lie low for a little while after that." She prayed he wouldn't say he couldn't keep the work available for her.

"Looking at you, I'm not surprised." He hitched at the knees of his pants and crossed his legs. His suit was of fine tan wool, his silk shirt the palest blue, his tie burgundy. The deli business must be booming, Page thought.

Waldo smoothed a manicured thumbnail as if deep in thought. "I feel badly about this."

Before she could regroup from surprise, Page's brows shot up. "You don't have to. Danger goes with the job." And she thought of Ian.

"You were working for me," Waldo said. "I've always been very pleased with your performance, and as soon as you're ready I want you back. I'm sure you don't have medical coverage, so I've arranged for all your bills to be sent to me."

Gratitude, and guilt for having misjudged him, sent tears brimming into her eyes. "Waldo, I—"

"You're grateful. Yes, I know. But as you'll already have worked out, I'm a selfish man and I don't let useful things go easily. You've been very good for me. Like I told you recently, if you want to put another rider on at some time I think we could expand our little night trips. That is—" he hesitated "—that is, if you haven't decided against continuing."

"No, I haven't." Page was emphatic. She held out a hand and he shook it. "It may take a week, two at the most, but then I'll be back at it. And, Waldo, thanks a million for thinking of the medical bills. I'll repay every dime, I promise. That'll take time, too, but you'll get it back."

He stood up. "We'll talk about it another time. Get well and get back to work."

At the door he stopped and turned. "Where did you say the knapsack was?"

She pointed to a narrow closet, and he removed the red pack. "We had some disappointed customers last night," he commented, wrinkling his nose at the crushed box he held up. The next thing he held up was a pile of payment envelopes. "Voilà, my dear. One less thing for you to worry about." He smiled and made for the door again.

He was wrong, Page thought. Those envelopes were one more thing to worry about. At least if they'd been missing, she could have considered theft as a possible motive for the attack.

The day crept by, punctuated by the delivery of little paper cups containing pills and regular checks of her vital signs. Rather than easing, the pain in her ribs got worse, and she learned this was to be expected, but that within a day or so it would be better. She was grateful no bones had been broken.

She slept for a while in the afternoon and later enjoyed a brief, lighthearted visit from the Zipper, who arrived in time to make horrified faces at her dinner.

Then the long evening set in. Earlier in the day the woman in the next bed had gone home, and Page was relieved to have some solitude.

She lost track of time. The lights in her room were turned off, and she lay watching figures pass outside her door. Occasionally a nurse came in to peer at her, but Page kept her eyes closed and feigned sleep.

The sound of the door clicking shut startled her out of a doze.

A faint and eerie glow from the window washed the room, silhouetting the tall figure of a man.

Page opened her mouth to scream, sat up and thrust her feet from the bed.

"Be quiet." Ian's voice, different again than she'd heard it before, but definitely his. He put a hand over her mouth as he spoke.

Page moaned. She hurt all over, and where his hand rested the skin felt raw.

"They wouldn't let me in here," he whispered. "Some mouthy bat said it was too late. I had to wait in a stairwell till I could sneak past."

She wanted to lie down.

"If I take my hand away you won't scream?"

She shook her head and sucked in a breath.

"I called when I thought you'd be home from work and your roommate answered. She told me what happened. Damn it, Page, why didn't you have someone get in touch with me?"

The pain in her side was intense now, and she couldn't turn to lie down.

"Say something, will you? Why didn't you tell me?"

"Ian," she murmured. "Help me, please."

"Oh, my God." He loomed over her. "What is it? What's happened to you?"

"Nothing. My ribs, that's all. I can't lift my legs to lie down. I want to lie down."

She heard him fumble and the lamp above the bed came on. "Oh, no. Look at you. I knew something like this would happen. Damn it all, why didn't you listen to me?"

"I hurt." She doubled over, close to tears.

"Sweetheart, I... Shall I lift you?" He sounded suddenly frightened.

Without waiting for an answer, he picked her up gently and placed her on her back. He was sliding her legs beneath the covers when the door opened and the overhead lights glared.

"What is going on in here? Ms. Linstrom, do you know this man?"

"Yes—"

"You must leave at once, sir. Our patients are sleeping."

Ian faced the small, wiry nurse who stood, hands on hips, in the middle of the room. "This patient isn't sleeping."

"We have rules—"

"This is my, um, fiancée. I just got back into town and found out she'd had an accident. We need to be alone, if you don't mind."

Page watched the woman's face and felt closer to laughter than she had in days. Ian had audacity, she'd give him that.

The nurse drew up to her full, short height. "That's all very well, sir. But this is irregular and I can't allow you to stay."

"Oh, nurse." Ian sank onto a chair and rubbed a hand over his hair until it stood endearingly on end. "If you only knew what a shock this has been. I'm sure you understand what I mean. I can tell a sensitive woman when I meet one. Would it be so bad if you pretended I wasn't here for half an hour or so, just until I can be sure Page is all right? Then I promise I'll go without another word." He smiled and the effect on the woman was predictable.

"Well . . . yes, I suppose that would be all right. But only half an hour, mind you. I'll be back to check."

The instant the door closed again, Ian stood over Page again and she stopped smiling.

"I repeat, why didn't you let me know about this?"

"I—"

"No." He gestured dismissively. "You don't have to try to explain. We both know the reason, don't we? You didn't want to admit that I've been right all along. A woman has no place in the business you're in. And I don't only mean at night."

Just like that. Page glared into his dark eyes. She'd learned the hazards of speaking first and thinking later. "Ian," she said very quietly, "your little manipulation with the nurse was amusing. Obviously you've had a lot of experience at putting women in their places. Don't try it with me."

He stuffed his hands into the pockets of his jeans and after a moment returned to the chair. Several times he said, "mmm," chewing on his lower lip while he thought.

Formulating the next offensive, Page decided. Then, with something close to anger, she acknowledged that he did really care for her and that she wanted him to, but not on his terms.

"What are your injuries?" He was curt, abrasive.

"Bruised ribs and a few scratches. I'll survive."

"How about the next time?"

"There won't be a next time."

He pushed his hips to the edge of the chair, stretching out his legs. His glare was aimed at his shoes. "You aren't thinking straight. Just because you're the product of an overbearing father, you feel you have to prove something by finding the hardest thing you can do."

Page snorted, disbelieving. "Can you hear yourself? Overbearing father? Boy, you could give lessons in that department. And you don't have any right. I didn't look for something hard. I looked for something challenging, which I might be able to get going without a lot of capital. Not having a bundle of money waiting like a magic carpet for you to ride on is something you wouldn't understand."

"Page—"

"Please. You've said your piece. You always do, no matter what anyone else feels. You're so used to being in charge you think you can take over wherever you are. Watch my lips, Ian. You have no say in what I do."

He covered his mouth and the hard light in his eyes turned anxious. "I know I don't, but I still wish you'd get out of this."

"You aren't listening." She sat up and winced. "This isn't a situation you can control. I have a living to make and this is how I intend to do it. Also, there are people who depend on me for their livelihood."

"Who, apart from you?"

Her patience snapped. "I have a staff of people who rely on the jobs they have with me. This accident is a setback, but that's all. As soon as I possibly can I'll be riding again. I'm not your mother, Ian. I don't need a man to make me feel whole. I don't want to get my kicks from telling a man how wonderful he is. Please, would you leave?"

He shot to his feet. Rage didn't suit him, and the vibes he sent out made Page sink low in her bed. "Who do I think I am? I think I'm someone who cares about you, you idiot. And I think I'm someone you care about—a lot. We've already established that, and I don't change my mind easily. And what the hell's the stuff about my mother and not needing a man supposed to mean?''

"Nothing." Despite Rose's interference, Page liked the woman. She didn't intend to come between mother and son.

"Don't give me that." Ian bent over the bed until his face was inches from hers. "You made a statement and I deserve an explanation."

Page thought as fast as she could with the clean scent of his breath on her cheek . . . and his mouth moving much too close to hers. "All I meant was that I make decisions and act on them based on my background and experience. So do you. Your mother is happy being a support system for your father and nothing more. I think that's great for her because she's happy that way. But it's not fine for me."

"I see." The twitching in his cheek betrayed the effort restraint was costing him. "Well, I haven't said I expect you to become a doormat for me, only that I don't like what you do. And I'm never going to change my mind about that."

Page closed her eyes, visualizing the loss of Faber's business.

A big hand, brushing back her hair, didn't relieve the anxiety, but it did touch something wanting in her heart.

"Is it so wrong for me to worry about you?" he said.

"It's flattering." There must be no backing down. "I'm very grateful for your friendship."

He withdrew his hand. The hardness was back in every line of his face. "You're welcome. And I suppose I have to respect your right to choose what's most important to you."

"Thank you."

Ian didn't look at her again. "I was a fool to hope you might feel the same way I did. And I really did think you might."

"And how was that?"

He spread his hands in the air. "Like we could have a chance at something worthwhile together."

"As in my becoming more important than a means to keep your bed warm."

"That was a rotten thing to say."

"I..." He was right, she thought. "Ian, I didn't mean—"

"Drop it," he said, and strode from the room.

How was she supposed to feel? Did he really think he was being fair? "Choose what's most important," he'd said, as if there could be no middle ground, no making room in her life for both him and her business.

Page pulled the sheet over her head. The overhead light was still on, and the cotton was luminous.

Ian had behaved as if there'd been some unspoken commitment between them. How did a woman deal with a thing like this? With wanting it all, the man *and* her independence.

"I'M FRUSTRATED, LILIAN. Do you blame me?"

Lilian made a sympathetic noise and set a cup of tea on the table beside Page's futon.

"How long have I been off work?"

"Only ten days. And you are working. Have some of this." Lilian pushed the cup closer.

"Paperwork is all I've done," Page grumbled, "and I get tired too easily. I want to get up to full steam—now."

"Give yourself a few more days," Lilian said in what Page thought of as her sickroom voice, low and croaky. "I've got to get back to the garage. Go through the stuff I brought up, and I'll be back later."

Left alone, Page looked at the pile of papers awaiting her and closed her eyes. She didn't feel like juggling numbers this morning.

The sound of the front door opening brought her eyes wide open again, and she sat up. Lilian must have forgotten to tell her something. Maybe there was a problem. Things had been going smoothly for Pedal Pushers recently, almost too smoothly, and she couldn't get rid of the premonition that peace wouldn't last.

Someone tapped on her bedroom door.

"Come in." She lay on top of the comforter in her favorite black sweats and elephant slippers, but she wasn't concerned. The only people who came to see her were used to her wardrobe.

"Are you decent?" Ian popped his head into the room and Page's blood left her veins.

"I'm always decent." Decent, but close to cardiac arrest at this moment. "Why don't you go into the sitting room. I'll be right out." When she'd recovered some composure and found something respectable to wear.

Undeterred, he came in, glanced around and, finding no chair that wasn't occupied with things Page didn't want to think about, sat cross-legged on the floor beside her. "Lilian let me in. She said you should be kept quiet because you're still recuperating."

He spoke as if there hadn't been a ten-day silence between them.

"I'm not an invalid," Page said. There was no elegant way to get up. "Another week and I'll be back to full output."

He smiled with the usual effect. "You sound like a generator."

She smiled back. The infuriating prickling came in her eyes. He was so wonderful to look at... and to be with. When he wasn't ordering her about. She tried to harden her heart. No doubt he'd be issuing those orders again any minute.

"I like your elephant feet," he said. "They have a certain... panache? No, that's not right. They give an impression of authority."

She sniffed. "That's what I think. I've considered having sneakers or cycling shoes made in the same style. Should impress the customers, don't you think?"

He bent forward. "Anything you do impresses me. I've spent the last nine days wishing it wasn't true. A couple of times I thought I might be getting close to persuading myself, but it won't work. I've got to have you in my life, Page."

The top of his head was within reach, and she ruffled his hair until he looked up. "How is it ever going to work out with you and me?" she asked him. "I don't want to sound selfish, but I'm afraid of getting hurt. Even now it's bad when you're not around. But at least we're still at a point where we can get out without being too emotional. If we keep going, it may not be that easy—not for me at least."

"We're not going to hurt each other."

"How can you be so sure?"

"I just am, that's all. And I'm sorry about the way I came on at the hospital," Ian said. "That was unforgivable, and I shouldn't have waited this long to apologize."

Sorry, but had he changed his mind about anything? "When you're a strong person it's hard to back down," Page said. "We're both strong. Have you thought about what that means?"

"That life with you will never be dull."

Page crossed her arms. He was so positive, and he automatically spoke as if their future lay together. She wasn't sure she was ready to believe that. Most of all she wanted the confusion to go away.

"Does your face still hurt?"

"No." A greenish tinge remained below her eye, but her cheek had healed completely.

"How about your ribs?"

"I'm not hurdling yet, but as long as I don't do anything too wild they feel fine."

He got to one knee and put a hand on each side of her on the mattress. "Then I'm going to kiss you. Very gently. Nothing wild—okay?"

Without waiting for permission, he settled his mouth on hers, and the sweetness of him made Page feel formless, a malleable thing beneath the persistent pressure, the parting of her lips.

He pulled back a little before he kissed her again more urgently, then withdrew altogether. When she opened her eyes he was sitting beside her on the futon, and there was no mistaking the tense set of passion in his face.

"I brought you something." His laugh was unconvincing. "Take a quick look and tell me what you think."

From the envelope he gave her, Page took a stack of photos. White beaches, palm trees, lush tropical settings and what looked like a small, white plantation house on a bluff overhanging a turquoise ocean.

"I think they're beautiful. I didn't know you were into photography."

"You don't know everything about me yet. But we'll try to take care of that. Do you like the setting in the pictures?"

"Fantastic," Page told him. "Where is it?"

"Hawaii. Maui. I stay in that house quite often."

She looked again at the shots. "Lucky you. I've always thought I'd enjoy Hawaii."

So far so good, Ian thought. But he wasn't kidding himself that the hardest part wasn't still to come. "It is lovely. And easy to get to—Maui, that is. They have direct flights out of San Francisco now, and in a few hours we can be there."

He watched her face for reaction, but she hadn't really heard what he'd said. She was studying the pictures.

"The drive up the road to Hana. That's where we'll have to go. It's pretty hairy. It's all switchbacks and one-way bridges. But you can smell mangoes and breadfruit, and it feels like the jungle.''

"Does it?'' She sounded wistful. A view of the house held her attention now. "It's hard to imagine. Like something out of the movies.''

"We could leave tonight.'' He stopped breathing.

"Oh, sure.'' She laughed. "I'm always doing things like popping off to Hawaii on a few hours' notice. You do like your little jokes.''

He was…he thought he might be falling in love with her. "I'm not known for my sense of humor,'' he said with mock seriousness. "In fact, most people are afraid of me.''

Page chuckled. "So I've heard in your mail room.'' She sobered. "The people who work for you say a lot of flattering things, like how they respect you. They also say you're one nice guy, Mr. Faber.''

He felt uncomfortable. "You mean members of my staff talk about me for no particular reason?''

Her blush relaxed him, and he leaned to kiss her brow. "You asked about me, didn't you?''

"Uh-huh. Does that make you mad?''

"Not as long as you don't do it again. In fact, I kind of like thinking you did that. The plane leaves at nine thirty-eight.''

She stared. "What plane?''

He crossed the fingers of the hand at his side. "The plane we're taking to Maui, so you can swim in the ocean and relax for a few days before you get completely back into work.''

She didn't speak for so long he felt panicky. "Say yes, Page. We'll have a great time and it'll be good for you. When's the last time you had a vacation?''

"I don't remember.''

"There you are, then. It's a date.''

"Oh, no.'' She scooted around him and stood. "I've got to get back to my paperwork.''

He got up and blocked her path to the door. "The paper-work will wait. Lilian said she'll get someone called James, jr. to give her a hand."

"You talked to Lilian about this?" Her voice rose to a squeak.

"Yes. I must say I like your employees. The Zipper's interesting. He told me he used to ride race horses, but he didn't like it because the horses had minds of their own. Bicycles only do what you make them do."

She groaned. "I can't believe you talked to my people about all this."

"Why? You talked to mine."

The parting of her lips, then the closing, let him know he was getting closer to his objective. She couldn't argue the last point.

"I can't go."

"You can if you want to."

"You don't understand that some people can't do what they want to do, do you?"

She was thinking of money as well as time. He went on, "Lilian said you can't ride for at least another week. She said she and James would take care of the books and that your roommate would be here to watch over the apartment. The only reason I can think of for your refusing to come is that you don't want to be with me."

"I don't have the right clothes," she mumbled. Nor could she afford to buy any. And despite Tanya's cheeriness lately, Page still worried about her and wasn't comfortable with the idea of leaving her completely alone.

Frustration made him flex his fingers. "We can get what you need there. We'll only be gone a few days." She was blushing, damn it. She must be thinking of the expense. "Oh, darn, trust me to forget the important thing. This vacation is my get-well present to you, so you can't refuse."

"I can." She frowned. "Things like this cost a lot, and I don't take expensive gifts from people."

Behind her frown trembled vulnerability and, he was sure, longing. Carefully, afraid she'd sprout prickles or smack him, he took her in his arms.

"I'm not people, sweetheart. I'm the guy who thinks you're something more than special. And if you don't let me do this I'm going to feel like the kid Santa Claus missed. You wouldn't want that, would you?"

She shook her head.

"Then it's settled. I'll pick you up around eight. Wear something light but with a coat on top. We'll leave the coat in the car. Bring a suitcase, and we'll get the extra things you need when we arrive in Maui."

He kissed her again, savoring the softness of her lips, then let her go. "Do we have a deal?"

"I guess so."

"Good. Rest a while if you want to. But be ready at eight." Inside he was terrified she'd try to back out, but he made himself grin. "By the way, the decor in here is something. I bet no one else ever thought of using bicycle parts as objets d'art."

Her laughter was what he'd wanted to hear.

Chapter Twelve

These were *South Pacific* beaches. Just like the ones in the movie. Page turned her head to say as much to Ian before she recalled that the beaches in the movie had indeed been Hawaiian.

Ian had felt her glance toward him. "Comfortable?" he asked.

"Mmm. It feels funny to be warm like this in November. But I love it."

"So you're not sorry you came?"

She almost hadn't come. "No." Right up to takeoff in San Francisco she'd believed she would back out. But they'd been here three days now, and Page was beginning to feel very much at home in the white house on the cliffs above them.

From time to time she thought of Pedal Pushers, worried that something might happen to another rider while she was too far away to take immediate action. But the peace here, the beauty of it all, managed to keep her concerns at bay.

"You need more sunscreen," Ian said. "I don't want you burning. Lie on your stomach."

"Yes, sir." Obediently she flattened her chaise and turned over.

The chaise gave with Ian's weight as he sat by her knees. "Did I say I think you should wear a bikini—or whatever this thing's called—all the time?"

She buried her face in her forearms and laughed. "You did—several times." The bikini was the most daring thing she'd ever bought. "The latest," the saleswoman in Lahaina had assured her of the tiny, flowered bottom and the bra, which was in fact two sections that adhered to her breasts.

Page would never forget Ian's expression the first time she'd joined him on the narrow beach below the house and taken off her wrap. Behind dark glasses his eyes were invisible, but she had no doubt where he was looking or that he liked what he saw.

"Aah. That's cold." A stream of sunscreen snaked across her back. But his hands were warm, and quickly slick.

He smoothed her body from neck to waist and down to the bikini bottom. Massaging in smaller circles, he covered her shoulders and arms, the backs of her legs. When he held her ankles and slathered the soles of her feet, she yelled.

"Important," he said, continuing until she wriggled. "If the bottoms of your feet get burned, I have to carry you everywhere, and gorgeous as you are, petite you aren't."

"Insulting—"

"Ah-ah. Don't say things you'll regret later. You need more here."

His fingers smoothed her sides and she shuddered, but he carried on, touching lightly the tender skin where the clusters of flowers didn't quite cover the fullness of her pale breasts.

He teased, nipped at her ear and bent over her until the hair on his chest met her bare back. Then he got up and waited until she rolled over onto her back and propped herself on her elbows. The sun was behind him, turning his already tanned body, the muscular arms and long, tensile legs, into a wavery dark form.

"On second thought I wouldn't want you to wear that all the time." The words were light but his voice thick.

Since their arrival on Maui he'd done this again and again—come close enough, touched or talked in a way that brought her desire for him tingling to life, only to draw away while she still ached. Was he really playing with her? Or did he keep reminding himself that he'd billed this trip as purely for her health? Page sighed and dropped flat on the chaise. Her health wouldn't tolerate many more exercises in frustration.

"You'd get cold. Probably catch pneumonia."

"What?" She shaded her eyes and squinted at him.

"Wearing the bikini all the time. You'd turn blue on that bike of yours in midwinter." He sat on the sand and picked up a stick.

"Very funny, Ian." His ability to turn sensuality on and off unnerved her.

He tapped her tummy with the stick. "Are you eating enough?"

"Yes, of course." His questions went off in the strangest directions sometimes. "Why would you ask a thing like that?"

"Oh, I was wondering if I should make some chicken soup or something. You've got the flattest stomach I've ever seen."

And then, between the aching moments of sexual tension there were these times when she felt more relaxed than she ever had. "I think you're suppressing fatherly instincts." She closed her eyes at once, remembering Rose Faber's visit. Some subjects had to be avoided.

Ian didn't answer at once. The stick continued its light tattoo on her belly. "Maybe I am a frustrated father. But that's not what I'm feeling right now, anything but. How are your ribs?"

Page's turn to be silent. His route to what he was really thinking might be tortuous, but it wasn't hard to follow.

"Page, do your ribs still bother you?"

"No. I feel like a whole human being again."

He cleared his throat. "You look like a very whole human being. Hey, how about driving the rest of the way up the Hana road?"

He bounced to his feet and hauled Page up.

"I guess we're going to Hana," she said, and smiled widely up at him. He seemed different here, carefree, irrepressible.

He only gave her time to find a pair of thongs and put on her wrap while he pulled shorts over his abbreviated swimsuit and shoved his feet into tennis shoes.

They'd flown into Kahului airport, where Ian had picked up a rental car for the long, twisting drive toward isolated Hana. The house—Page hadn't asked directly but she assumed it belonged to Ian—was twenty miles along the narrow, pockmarked highway. On their first full day, he had insisted they go west into the busy old whaling town of Lahaina with its cobbled streets crowded with tourists, its trendy bars and restaurants and a plethora of boutiques.

Page's necessary clothing had been bought, more than she thought necessary, but Ian, relaxed and happy and determined to shower her with things she didn't expect to wear again once she left Maui, kept suggesting and adding items. He'd refused to let her have the bill, but she intended to start paying him back as soon as they got home.

Yesterday and today had been spent relaxing, but Ian had let her know repeatedly how much he was looking forward to taking her to the end of the famous fifty-mile-long road to Hana. He hustled her into the car and shot from the driveway, only to slow to a crawl at once to negotiate the first of a hundred sharp curves.

"A person could get sick with all this winding back and forth," Page remarked as they bumped around a bend and dropped into yet another dip.

"You feel sick?" He glanced at her anxiously.

"No. Just making a comment."

The car windows were down and pungent scents wafted in. Shafts of sun pierced the dense trees and vines that enclosed the road like a tunnel.

Wet drops hit Page's arm, resting along the window rim. "It's raining again. This is the strangest place. Sun, rain, everything all mixed up together."

The car crested another rise, dropped again sharply to a bridge and Ian pulled onto a slim turnaround strip. "Let's get out."

"It's raining."

He stared at her. "So? Aren't you the woman who rides around San Francisco in midwinter wearing ballet tights?"

Mumbling that her work gear had nothing to do with ballet, Page climbed from the car. Immediately she was glad she had. Ian joined her and led the way along a tiny pathway beside a steep drop, which the bridge spanned. A few feet from the road they entered a fragrant grotto molded of giant, trailing philodendron leaves, spiky lauhala trees balanced on their tepees of straight air roots, ferns and myriad other specimens. Ian pointed out one after another, giving names she knew she'd forget.

"Listen," he said, holding up a finger.

Page tilted her head. A steady pitter-patter sounded, rain hitting the roof of foliage overhead. The air around them was moist and heavy with the scent of fruit and flowers, but no drops penetrated the green cave.

"Like it?" Ian's voice sounded funny again.

Page felt funny. "Yes." She swallowed, aware of how alone they were, how close. "Are these orchids?" Sprays of tiny, purple blossoms sprang from a mossy bed.

"Uh-huh."

"They just grow anywhere here?" While she outlined a flower Ian came to stand beside her.

"I've started needing you, Page."

She took a breath, held it, closed her eyes when she walked into his arms. "I know," she said against his warm chest. She needed him, too. He must know that.

"Don't go away from me again."

"I wasn't the one who went away," she said and held her bottom lip in her teeth, not wanting to spoil the moment.

"You're right." He loosened the belt of her wrap and pulled her close. "I was the one who went off in a sulk, wasn't I?"

"You were upset."

"So would you be if you walked into a hospital room and saw someone you . . . It was a shock to see you like that."

Someone you what? What had he almost said? "I should have let you know about the accident, but after our last telephone conversation I wasn't sure you'd want to know."

"You aren't always very smart."

"Thanks."

"I only meant that you should be able to read my signals better by now. You know how much you mean to me."

Her body was all exposed nerve ends. His hands were beneath the wrap, ranging over her back. Pressed to him she felt naked, wished that she was, that they both were.

Sun had faintly gilded the hair on his chest. She ran her fingers over it, looked at his tanned skin beneath her palms and kissed each spot she touched. He stood very still while she bent to brush her mouth across his flat stomach.

When she straightened he slowly opened his eyes. "We'd better not stay here," he said hoarsely.

Page smiled, watching his mouth before she guided his face down to hers. "Why?" she said and parted his lips with her tongue.

The noise he made came from deep in his throat, and she felt him quicken against her. He framed her face with his hands, and the control was no longer hers. The kiss he gave was urgent. Her legs shook and she clung to him, wanting to slip to the leaf-strewn ground and take him with her.

He lifted his head so abruptly she gasped. "Damn it." His chest rose and fell rapidly while he closed her wrap and hastily tied the belt.

Page caught his hand, ready to protest, when she heard what he must have heard. Voices.

"That's what I meant when I said we shouldn't stay here," Ian said, fashioning a smile and leading her back to the path. They exchanged nods with the two chattering couples they passed, reached the car and slumped into their seats.

"I feel like a teenager who got caught parking," Page said, scrunching down.

Ian leaned over and kissed the corner of her mouth. "Yeah, fun huh?"

"Depends on what you call fun."

"You sound irritable...and frustrated, maybe?"

She pulled up her knees and rested her face so that he couldn't see it. "Neither. Embarrassed, that's all. I got carried away, and that's not like me."

"Isn't it? That's too bad. I kind of enjoyed it."

He started the car.

Kind of enjoyed it? He *was* playing with her, putting her in situations where he could test her reaction to him. And she'd fallen completely into the trap again.

"Do you still feel like going all the way to the end of the road?"

Why did he ask? Because he expected her to insist on rushing back to the house where they could be sure of solitude? "Absolutely I still want to go. I wouldn't miss it now."

The last time they'd gotten really close she'd been the one to call a halt. She didn't think Ian was small-minded enough to deliberately turn the tables, but it was possible he'd decided to allow her to set the pace between them. Unfortunately she wasn't sure what she wanted the pace to be.

Many curves later they reached the Heavenly Hana Inn and stopped the car long enough to peer through its

Japanese screen gate, flanked by stone lions, to a luxuriant garden. The town of Hana was nothing more than a scant collection of aged but picturesque buildings. Page made appropriate noises of awe, but her mind was elsewhere. It was still elsewhere when they parked by a breakwater to watch the wild sea rush in, and when Ian pointed out what had been Charles Lindbergh's final home.

Two hours later they arrived back at the house and drove down the short, steep driveway.

"Do you want to live it up tonight?" Ian asked as he let them into the entryway with its shiny, red, koa floor and stark, white walls. "We could go into Lahaina or Kaanapali if you like. You haven't seen the hotels there. Quite something."

"That would take hours."

"We can go if you want to. I don't mind driving."

She felt irritable. "I do," she said, and walked past him.

The main room in the house had a fireplace, which looked much used—Page wondered why in this climate—and clusters of elegant bentwood furniture with downy cushions in shades of pink and gray and mauve. Beyond, through French doors, was a wide lanai, where the same colors had been used on the cushions of white cane chairs and chaises grouped around glass-topped cane tables.

Page went outside and dropped onto a chaise. She should shower and change, but she didn't feel like it yet.

Half an hour later she lost interest in the rushing, roiling surf, colored the palest lime green as the sun set. Ian hadn't joined her.

She shifted restlessly and felt annoyed with herself. Mature women shouldn't expect people to be nice to them when they were rude.

"Pupus!"

Ian had approached noiselessly on bare feet. He set down a tray bearing two tall glasses of something golden, each topped by a wedge of pineapple speared by a tiny red umbrella. The *pupus*, which he'd already explained was the local term for hors d'oeuvres, were macadamia nuts and a plate of tiny egg rolls.

"You're much too good to me." Page eyed the egg rolls. "I know you like to cook, but how did you whip those up so quickly?" Had he been up even earlier than she'd thought that morning?

"Miracles of convenience food, m'dear. You, too, can learn to love microwave fare. Feel any better?"

She rubbed at the arms of her chair. "I was pretty snippy. Sorry. I don't know what made me like that." At least she wasn't about to tell him.

He regarded her thoughtfully. "Have some of your *mai tai*. It'll relax you a bit. You're still convalescing in a way. The old nerves are bound to get pretty racked up by the kind of thing you went through."

They hadn't discussed the details of the accident, but she had no doubt that Lilian had filled him in. "You're probably right," she agreed. "I hope I never have another night like that."

"You won't . . ."

Page had lifted her glass. She paused with the rim against her lips, watching him. His features were taut. Then, gradually, they softened, but his chest expanded slowly and she heard him exhale. Without speaking he'd said it all. He hadn't changed his stand on Pedal Pushers one bit. He was only trying to time his next attack more diplomatically. She took several sips of the drink. It was excellent. Diplomacy should be her motto, too. Given time, if she didn't explode every time he did what came naturally to him, she'd win him over to her side. If she wanted to—and she was definitely beginning to think she might.

"Um, Page, remember telling me we operate from the base of our experience?"

"Yes."

"I can't seem to put mine completely away. But I want to. I don't want to cramp your style."

Not reminding him that he had no right to do so was hard. "We don't have to go into that. There isn't any need."

"Maybe not now. But there could be later on."

In other words he was beginning to see her as someone who might become important to him—very important. "It was nice of you to suggest going out tonight. I wasn't very gracious. But it's so lovely right here and we've got plenty of food." They'd bought supplies before coming to the house.

"You mean you're offering to cook me a gourmet meal?" He grinned, and she leaned to punch his arm lightly.

"Smart mouth. I meant we can throw something together and sit out here and enjoy the most beautiful place I've ever seen."

He parted his lips, then bowed his head before saying, "I've always thought of it that way, too, but it wasn't quite this beautiful before."

The territory was becoming dangerous again. Page got up. "If you don't mind I'd like to take a quick shower and put on one of those creations I'm not going to get to wear if I don't start changing four or five times a day."

"You'll get to wear them."

She'd reached the doors.

"We'll come back one day if you want to," he added.

Page sighed and went inside. Trips to idyllic settings were ordinary events to him. To Page this one time was a dream to be treasured, remembered, and probably never repeated.

The house was long, one storied, and two large bedrooms, each with its own lanai, faced the ocean. A third was smaller and had windows with a view through the palms that fringed the property on three sides.

Page showered and washed her hair quickly. She worked hard with her blow-dryer, brushing, shaking, until the heavy mass was shiny, falling straight but bouncy around her shoulders.

When she left her room and passed Ian's, his door stood open, and she heard running water. The shorts and swimsuit he'd worn lay on the floor where he must have dropped them on his way to the bathroom. She smiled before she headed for the kitchen. The small insights she was getting into his habits brought a certain intimacy and satisfaction. He wasn't totally organized. He also wasn't careful of such niceties as modesty. What if she'd walked by while he was flinging his clothes on the rug? Page's smile broadened. Of the two of them, she would probably have been more affected—much more affected.

While she worked in the kitchen, she learned something else about Ian. Like her brother and father, he took outrageously long showers. She'd found a wok, chopped vegetables, shelled and de-veined shrimp and assembled everything else she needed for the meal she planned before she heard the shower turned off.

After testing the air outside and finding it still deliciously warm, she set two places at one of the tables and took a single bird-of-paradise blossom from the sitting room to complete the arrangement.

She was standing back to admire her efforts when a pair of arms encircled her. "Mmm. You smell as good as you look," Ian said.

Turning in his arms, she hugged him back and pecked his cheek. "You smell pretty good yourself. And look pretty good." A khaki shirt, open at the throat and tucked into pleated cotton pants of the same color, gave him an island look that was fashionably casual. His hair was wet and his feet bare. Page studied his toes. "I see you dressed for dinner."

He put his hands on her shoulders and held her away. "Never mind me. Did you know that from where I'm standing that dress is transparent?"

Instinctively Page crossed her arms. "It is not."

But it was—or almost. Ian took his time following her outline inside the loose, white gauze dress that brushed the straps of flat, white sandals. Her hair, glossy and full, took on a burnishing from the flames of torches he'd lit before going to take his shower.

"Dinner's ready to go."

"I'll help." He followed her to the kitchen. Her usually smooth gait was jerky. He'd made her self-conscious. Odd that a woman who must know only too well the effect she had on men could still seem like an innocent sometimes.

They spoke little while they ate. Inconsequential comments about the food, which he hardly tasted, and the wine.

This wasn't working out as he'd hoped. He picked up his glass, then set it down without drinking. What exactly had he hoped for? That completely removed from everything and everyone involved in their day-to-day lives they'd find out what they truly felt for each other? Yes, that was it.

He stood up abruptly and walked to the steps at one end of the lanai. He had discovered what he felt—that he wanted Page with him for good. And he was pretty sure Page might want the same, but there were strings attached—on both sides.

"I'm going for a walk. Coming?"

She stood and picked up their plates. "I don't think so. I'm tired. I think I'll clean up these things and go to bed. You go ahead and I'll see you in the morning."

He considered helping with the dishes, but he thought she'd prefer to be alone.

The meandering route he took through the palms was familiar. He'd played in this garden above the sea as a child when his parents first bought the place, and had returned at least two or three times a year ever since. The house was the original structure, improved bit by bit over time. Once it had been the home of a sugar-plantation manager and his family. Ian recalled the black metal stove, replaced by a modern descendant now, that had been fueled by ironwood cut from casuarina trees on their own property.

Tonight the magic wasn't the same. He'd imagined all this with Page at his side, but something was planted solidly between them. Oh, the so-called chemistry was right—they both knew that very well—but going for a commitment between them presented a hazard because of the obstacle he couldn't accept and discard yet. He laughed, a short, mirthless sound that jarred him. He'd finally met a woman he could imagine spending the rest of his life with, and what held up the proceedings? A lousy bicycle, for God's sake. At least, that was the symbol of the obstacle, that and her crazy notion that she had to confront danger day in and day out to prove how independent she was.

This was their fourth night on Maui. Two more and they'd be San Francisco bound.

Ian propped a shoulder on a broad palm trunk and crossed his arms. He might as well face his immediate problem. For three nights he'd slept—if that's what it could be called—in a bed only feet from her. Each time he'd closed his eyes he'd imagined he heard her turning, breathing. He couldn't stand thinking of going back for more of the same.

The ocean fussed at the shore below, but he heard a different sound and turned. The white dress showed clearly as she picked her way over what was strange ground to her. Page had come in search of him.

His heart gave a thud. Had she seen him yet? Instinct stopped him from calling out or going to meet her. He wanted to watch her look for him...and find him.

"Ian, is that you?" She was still yards away, but she'd paused. He realized his light clothing must also show in the darkness.

"Yes. Over here. Watch out for roots."

He went to meet her and blessed the absent moon. Keeping a smile on his face was getting tougher by the second.

"Wow, it's dark." Her voice was breathy. "I thought I'd get lost out here."

She found his hand and he almost pulled away. Instead he twined their fingers together and held himself rigid.

"What's the matter?" She was sensitive. She hadn't missed his tension.

"Nothing. I thought you were going to bed."

She didn't reply immediately. Her grip on his fingers slackened and she removed her hand. "I'm sorry. I wasn't thinking. You want to be alone." She cleared her throat. "I'll go back."

"No!" He caught her wrist before she could turn away. "I don't want to be alone. That's the last thing I want."

"But you seem . . . you seem . . ."

"Don't go." He wanted to say so much, declare so much, but the words formed a maze in his head.

His chest felt tight. "Let's walk." He put his hands in his pockets and moved on. "Step where I step." With everything in him he wanted to hold her, to take her with him, but he didn't even trust himself to touch her.

He made his way to the place where a Japanese teahouse had been built between the palms. "Come in here," he said, climbing two steps and going inside. Benches lined latticed walls, which allowed the breeze to pass through.

Ian sat sideways on a bench, put his feet up and wrapped his arms around his legs. He rested his chin on his knees. There had never been a time when he felt less sure of how to deal with a situation.

For a moment he was afraid Page hadn't followed. He straightened and looked over his shoulder. She stood at the base of the steps to the teahouse. He couldn't see her face.

This was it. Either they confronted what was between them or they gave the whole thing up. "Page—"

"I know, I know. We've been fencing too long. I'm sick of it, too."

He breathed deeply, but his chest was still tight. "So what do we do about it?"

"Stop being scared, I guess."

"Scared?"

"Of letting go and taking a few risks."

"I don't think…" Hell, no he didn't think there were any great risks, because he believed she'd be happy as soon as they were together, really together. But she wasn't there yet and he had to give her time to catch up.

The moon had chosen that moment to appear. Silver gray crept from above to cast Page as a statue inside swirling gauze. She was waiting for him to go on talking.

"Sweetheart, I don't think we're going to risk anything if we decide to love each other."

He joined her and smoothed her hair back from her face.

"Is love something you decide to do?" she asked.

Her eyes glistened, and he thought he saw moisture on her cheeks. His thumbs confirmed the suspicion. "No, it's not." The tears were salty when he kissed her face. "I don't think we have any say in the thing at all. Darn it, *I* sure don't have any say at the moment."

"Hold me, Ian."

In his arms she felt small and shaky. She was vulnerable now, possibly more vulnerable than at any other time in her life. But so was he. The difference between them was that her weakening made him strong. Energy surged through him, and desire. She was fragile in some ways and he'd always remember and revere that in her, but she was also passionate and ready to share herself with him.

"Is it too cold for you out here?"

"No. I'm warm. You're not holding me tightly enough though."

He crushed her to him in a reflexive action and heard her make a small noise. "I'm sorry. Damn, I'm sorry. I forgot the ribs."

She giggled. "The ribs are fine. You winded me, that's all."

"Guess I don't know my own strength." With her still-damp face cradled in the hollow of his neck, he felt he could snap large trees if necessary. "I'm going to come right out and say something. Is that okay?"

She was unbuttoning his shirt and his stomach pulled in sharply. "Depends on what you intend to say," she murmured. Now she pulled the shirt free of his pants and kissed his jaw and neck again and again while she ran her fingers through the hair on his chest. When she raised her face her eyes were bright. "Say it," she ordered, putting her arms around his shoulders, "whatever it is."

"I'm in love with you."

"Kiss me."

He closed his eyes and did as she asked for a long time. Somewhere during the kiss his shirt fell to the ground. He knew that under the white dress, she wore a bra and panties of some pale color and it was time he saw what the color was. The edges of his mind dulled, but there was something else he knew he needed.

"Is there anything you'd like to say to me? Anything at all?"

"Like I love you, too? I do, Ian. Whether I want to or not, I do. And I sure didn't get to decide about it."

She slipped from his arms and pulled the dress over her head. Then she reached behind her back for the fastening of her bra.

"No," Ian said. "Let me look at you like that first." He touched the narrow bands of satin across her hips, slid his hands around to cup her bottom. "Peach, is that what this color is?"

Her laughter caught and faded. "Yes, does it matter?"

"Everything about you matters. I want to know all the things you like, including colors."

Keeping a forearm around her waist, he took off the rest of his clothes. When he was naked he urged her to him, and the smooth satin aroused him in a way only her flesh could improve on.

As if she read his thoughts she slipped the straps from her shoulders and leaned against him while she worked the bra to her waist, her breasts rubbing tantalizingly at him with every twist of her body.

He bent to kiss first one then the other nipple. She moaned and eased his head up until their mouths came together with fierce tenderness. When he reached for her hips again she was stepping out of the panties.

Soft grass covered the area where the teahouse had been built. He dropped slowly to his knees, passing his lips and tongue between her breasts and ribs until he reached her stomach. Her fingers were in his hair. He used his thumbs, his mouth, felt the trembling...

"Ian," was all she said before she pushed him to sit on the grass. Kneeling between his thighs, she kissed his brow, his nose, his mouth, all the time smoothing his body, every part of his body, with her hands, until at last she stilled, holding him.

For an instant passion flared unchecked, but at the center of the white heat came the sense that Page wasn't deciding what to do because she was a practiced lover.

The heat grew. He couldn't hold on. "Sweetheart, let me, okay?" He wasn't really asking permission to take over.

In a simple motion he moved her astride him. She closed around him, drawing him in until all conscious thought faded, and his being did what it had to do—be a man with this woman.

Page's head felt light. She still pulsed from the first release. Now it was happening again, this time as she'd longed for it to happen, with Ian filling her.

His movements grew stronger and stronger, and her own strength grew with each push. She braced her weight on a hand on each side of his shoulders. He covered her aching breasts.

Then it built once more, the searing that was sweet in its intensity, and she threw herself back against his raised knees.

He dropped his hands to his sides. She saw the gleam of sweat on his body and upturned jaw. Carefully, desperate to lie with him, she moved and was instantly enfolded and rolled to the grass.

"Thank you, my love," he said against her neck. "You are so wonderful."

She didn't know what to say. Heaviness seeped into her limbs and her eyes wanted to close.

Ian leaned over to peer into her face. "Sleepy, sweetheart?"

"Happy," she told him, and nuzzled his neck and jaw.

Above them, palm fronds clicked in the breeze. Later, when they'd returned to the house, that same flower-scented breeze wafted through the open windows of Ian's room to cool Page's heated skin.

BELOW THEM the ocean off the coast of Oahu stretched, sometimes emerald, sometimes turquoise, streaked with the gray shadows of hidden coral. On the return journey they'd had to change planes in Honolulu, but Page hadn't minded. In the six-hour layover Ian had taken her to Waikiki where she'd walked on the beach, made him take her photograph to prove she'd been there and announced she didn't need to return to anywhere in Hawaii but a lovely white house on the road to Hana, Maui.

They flew first class and Page had no doubt that Ian had never flown any other way. Without asking if she wanted any, he ordered a bottle of champagne as soon as the seatbelt sign went off.

The attendant filled their glasses, and Ian turned to Page. "We're flying back to the rest of our lives, so I think it's time we toasted a few things."

She smiled at him and lifted her glass, but felt apprehensive for the first time in days. "Well, I can start," she told him. "Here's to you."

He waited until she drank. "Thank you. Now I get to give a list. Here's to you, and us, and a great marriage and as many kids as we decide we can handle. And—" he put a finger on her mouth as she tried to speak "—last but not least to someone you wouldn't think of drinking to now— my mother, who is one smart lady."

He drank. Page didn't.

The elaborate arrangement of flowers on a serving table smelled cloying. "Why is your mother one smart lady?"

"I told her you'd probably never agree to go with me on this trip, but she kept insisting you would and she was right."

"It was your mother's idea for you to invite me to Maui?" In the past two days she'd forgotten Rose, forgotten almost everything but how good it felt to be with Ian.

"No-o, not exactly. I asked if they minded my using the house because I was thinking of inviting you to go, and she thought it was a great idea."

The air conditioning was too cold. And Page's brain seemed to be cooling, too. "The house isn't yours?"

"No, it belongs to my folks. I thought I told you that."

"You didn't."

His parents' house and he'd pushed her to join him there because his mother had encouraged him. A setup to further the marry-Ian-off campaign?

"We should set a date, Page. These things take time."

He hadn't even asked her to marry him. Not actually *asked* her.

"I think we'll open the rest of the house. You'll have a ball decorating."

Decorating. He was mapping out her life, and whatever plans she'd had before didn't enter into his calculations. A woman who was decorating and having as many babies as she and her husband could handle might have some trouble fitting in a business that usually left her four hours a day for sleep.

"You're quiet, sweetheart. What are you thinking about?"

She looked at him. Her declaration of love hadn't been a lie—she did love him, so much that at this moment it hurt.

"Page?"

"I was thinking that you'd better hold off on the wedding plans."

Chapter Thirteen

"Take things more slowly," she'd said. They were to back away from each other and spend time thinking about what they really wanted.

Ian stared into the refrigerator, forgot what he'd been looking for and slammed the door. In the three weeks since they'd returned from Maui he'd seen Page twice and talked to her on the phone a couple of times. On the two occasions when she'd agreed to meet him it had been for coffee between the end of her day shift and before the nap she needed to get ready for her damned evening shift. And he was sick of it.

He sat at the kitchen table and rested his brow on his forearms. One minute everything had been wonderful, perfect, a go from here to eternity. The next she'd turned cold fish on him.

As he had dozens of times before, he went over their conversations, hunted for the exact moment when he might have said something to turn her off. And he came back to the same one—on the plane when he'd mentioned that his mother thought the trip was a good idea.

But that made absolutely no sense. Page liked his mother—or at least, she didn't dislike her. And what difference did it make one way or the other? She wouldn't be marrying his mother.

Marriage. He got up and paced around the room. She had said she wanted to marry him, hadn't she?

Her business was the stumbling block. She didn't want to admit she could live without being responsible for her own fate—totally responsible, that was. He didn't want a wife without a mind of her own. Page's individuality and guts had been what first attracted him to her.

Well, hell, she could have her business. A bicycle should keep her really warm at night.

He checked his watch. Martin might still be at home and glad of some company. They'd patched up their differences over lunch, and some of the old rapport had returned.

Since he hadn't gotten around to installing a phone in the old kitchen, he'd have to go upstairs. He glowered at the ridiculous blue wallpaper. And he'd been dumb enough to think Page would want to help redecorate this place. He strode up to the salon. He'd actually talked to her about it. What a fool she must think him.

At the desk he found Martin's number and lifted the telephone receiver. Slowly he punched in digits, his skin growing clammy.

The ring droned in his ear, once, twice—ten times. She wasn't home. But of course she wasn't. Page was already out there in the dark and cold. He'd known it would be Page he tried to call even as he'd found Martin's number. He let the phone slip back into its cradle.

Didn't Page know what this was doing to him? Wasn't she suffering just as much? Half-hour dates for coffee every week or so wouldn't cut it for him, not when he knew, knew so very intimately, what they could have together.

A walk might help him straighten out his head. Dressed in a heavy, wool greatcoat but with his head bare, he set off. At the first corner he stopped beneath a streetlight. Misty rain sheeted down.

She was out here somewhere. His stomach turned as it did every time he thought that some other nut, or the same one, might be tailing her, waiting for another opportunity to attack.

He bowed his head and trudged on. She was her own woman. Page had made sure he understood that. His best bet was to work on accepting their relationship on her terms—at least for now.

"QUIET NIGHT," Waldo said, handing over two boxes. "Typical middle-of-the-week stuff."

Page did her best to smile before she set off. Tanya was behaving strangely again. She either had nothing to say or snapped monosyllabic answers to Page's remarks. Waldo Sands was undoubtedly the cause of Tanya's recurring troubles, and Page longed to say something to him about her friend. If there had ever been any doubt about Tanya's involvement with the man it no longer existed. Earlier in the evening, as Page approached the delicatessen, she'd seen her roommate get out of a taxi and enter the shop. When Page followed only seconds later there was no sign of Tanya.

Both of the orders Page carried now were for her own area, Russian Hill. She pedaled slowly. Since her return from Maui she'd noticed she tired more easily. The result of the accident, she supposed.

The rain was getting to her. She'd broken her rule tonight and put on oilskins. The restriction around the arms and legs irritated her.

Every light turned red as she approached. At an intersection she planted her feet, waiting, hardly seeing colors through eyes that saw things in a blur. The rain on the road to Hana hadn't gotten to her. But that had been warm rain . . . and Ian had been with her.

Green. She was off again. Being tired had nothing to do with the accident. There were no lingering side effects from a few bruises. The truth was that she was sick of being out here at night, worrying about who might be waiting in every doorway and alley she passed while she longed to be with Ian.

Instead of taking the shortest route, she detoured down Laguna past his house. No lights in the windows. He didn't go to bed this early so he must have gone out. Not that it was her business.

A few more blocks and she unloaded the second box. Unfortunately Waldo had radioed to say there was another order. It was past one and she wished she could go home. Instead she rode doggedly back to the deli.

Laguna and Green. Page read the address as soon as Waldo put the box in her hands.

"Something wrong?"

She looked at him unseeingly. "No, nothing."

"We haven't heard from Mr. Faber in a while. I thought we'd lost him."

"Evidently not quite," Page said, keeping her voice level. Inside she was jumpy, excited, apprehensive.

The box was heavy—more champagne?

She traveled fast until she was within a block of Ian's house. Then she stopped. Despite the hood pulled over her helmet, rain had driven in and the hair around her face was wet. With almost numb fingers she poked the strands back. He'd been angry the last time they spoke. According to him she was avoiding him, deliberately making him miserable. He didn't understand, he'd said. Yes, she was avoiding him, but she'd never consciously hurt him. Would he...? No, Ian wasn't a vindictive man, he wouldn't deliberately subject her to another scene like the one she'd encountered the night they met.

Page walked the bike the rest of the way. This had to be his way of getting to talk to her. She wanted to talk to him, too, but she was afraid of letting her emotional need for him influence decisions that mustn't be lightly made.

Lights were on in the house now. Hauling the bike up the front steps was harder than she remembered. She propped it against a pillar and knocked.

The door swung open. Ian stood just inside.

Page jumped.

"Hi," he said. "Rotten night."

"Yes. How are you?"

"Cold and wet . . . and lonely." He wore an overcoat and his hair was wet. His arms were crossed, his hands pushed inside the sleeves.

So was she, so very very lonely—so ready to forget everything but him. But she wasn't a fool. She'd seen what happened to a woman after a few years of being a non-person.

"I've got your order from Touch Tone." No exchange of words had ever been this awkward.

"I don't want it."

She'd lifted the box. "I didn't think you did."

"Can you come in?"

"I shouldn't. I'll probably be called out on another job."

"Is that the only delivery you've got now?"

Circles getting smaller. "Yes." Page held the box tighter. He wasn't closing the web about her without help. She wanted to be there.

"Well, you'll have to get your receipt, won't you? And it's warmer in here than it is out there."

Page stepped inside. "I'm dripping, Ian. I'd better not walk on any rugs."

He took the box from her and set it on the floor. "Sweetheart . . ." He bowed his head and she saw drops glisten in dark curls.

"Why are you so wet?" she asked. Suffocation must feel like this.

"I went for a walk. For two hours, or three, I don't remember. I was trying to stop thinking about you, and all I did was see you everywhere I looked." He kept his head bent and she touched a cold hand to his hair. Before she could withdraw, Ian trapped her fingers and held them. "This is no good, Page. You aren't happy, either. I can see you aren't."

But what could she do to heal the situation if she didn't know how to make him understand that she had needs separate from his and would always have those needs?

"Please stay and get warm."

She let him unsnap and unzip the oilskin jacket, and she turned while he pulled it from her arms. The helmet and pants she removed herself, then her sodden gloves. The radio was attached to the neck of her leotard, the silver one Ian liked. She went to press the button and call in, but he stopped her. "It's one-thirty and it's foul out there. Couldn't you ask whatever his name is to let you call it a night?"

"I still have to take the receipt back."

"Let me talk to him. I'll tell him I'll bring it by myself in the morning."

His meaning was implicit. He not only wanted her to stay a while, he was inviting her to spend the night.

Page signaled Waldo.

"Yeah?" He sounded tired.

"Would it be okay if I called it a night? I'll drop off the last receipt in the morning."

After a short, crackly pause Waldo said, "Sure, kid. We don't have anything else to go out. See you in the morning."

He switched off without waiting for a response. Page unhooked the radio. "If I'm going to stay for a bit I'll bring my bike in."

"I'll bring the thing in." She didn't miss the anger in his voice. How could they overcome their differences if he wouldn't give at all in her direction?

Page sat on the bottom step of the stairs and pulled off her muddy shoes. Then, with the bike making puddles on

Ian's Italian marble and her oilskins spread over the top of the machine to drain, she walked beside him up to the salon.

Once in the room he fell silent, sitting, still wearing the damp coat, on his beautiful leather couch.

Page waited awkwardly in the leotard and cycling tights, her feet bare since she'd taken off her socks.

She coughed.

Ian rested his head back on the couch and closed his eyes.

"Stay and get warm," he'd suggested. The atmosphere in this room was frigid.

The fire was laid. She picked up a box of matches from the hearth and lit the paper. The instant leap of flames was a relief, as much for the sound as the warmth.

She looked at Ian over her shoulder. His eyes remained closed. He'd retreated to his "your move" position. Page opened the door and walked up the hall until she found a bathroom. With two towels in hand she returned to the salon.

Ian was on his feet. "I thought you were running out on me again."

A great rush of anger powered her. "Knock it off, Ian. You're punishing me because you don't feel so good. Well, I don't feel so good either. Here." She tossed him a towel. "Get off the wet coat and dry your hair. And stop feeling sorry for yourself. Maybe then we can see if there's any point in trying to talk."

He stared, slowly taking off his coat. "Yes, ma'am. Anything you say."

As usual, her rage was short-lived. She couldn't help laughing at his comical surprise. "I've got a terrible temper, you know. I'm famous for my rages."

"How about your fibs?"

"You don't believe I've got a violent temper?"

"No. Dry your own hair."

She considered telling him to save his orders for subordinates. Instead she knelt in front of the fire and tossed her hair forward. "Smart people don't tramp around in the rain if they don't have to." The towel muffled her voice.

"Smart people don't *ride* around in the rain if they don't have to."

He was behind her.

"Ian, we've been over this so many times. This is part of my job. In time I hope I'll be able to do very little of the actual messenger duties myself, including any night jobs. But for now—"

"I know. For now I either accept things the way you want them or you'll walk out of my life."

Page stopped rubbing. She took off the towel and pushed her hair back. The fire was bright now and the smell of woodsmoke pungent.

"I'm not issuing ultimatums," she said. "And there's a lot more to discuss than how you feel—or don't feel—about Pedal Pushers."

He knelt beside her. "Discuss away."

She looked sideways at him and giggled. He grinned back. "Lovely pair, huh? Your hairstyle kind of suits you—primitive." He ruffled her tangled hair. "I probably look like a wild man."

"I like it." Unfortunately she liked him wet, dry, mussed up, tidy, awake, asleep—any way he came. She sat on the rug. "I think expectations are the question. Right or wrong, I feel you have certain expectations of me that I may not be able to handle."

"Like?"

"Oh, no." She shook her head. "I'm not making it that easy for you. You tell me what you see for the two of us in the future."

He sat beside her, his hip touching hers, and grasped his knees. "Okay," he said slowly. "From the beginning then. But afterward it's your turn."

"My turn will get mixed up with yours."

"Fine. Did you or did you not agree to marry me?"

Page sighed. He was one of those people who attacked in order to defend. "You didn't ask me."

"What?" A chilly finger and thumb yanked her chin around. "We spent days together as close as a man and woman can be. And I distinctly remember saying we had to—"

She jerked her face from his fingers. "It's coming back to you? That's right. You said we had to get on with wedding plans because they took time."

He wasn't quick enough to hide his exasperation. "Women," he said. "I didn't actually say: Ms. Linstrom, would you do me the honor of becoming my wife? That's it. You're something. Total emancipation until it comes to the old-fashioned stuff."

"Wrong." She did have a high boiling point, but it could be reached. "Absolutely wrong. Certainly I would expect you to ask me to marry you, but that's only a small part of what's going on here."

Their faces were inches apart. Page finished speaking with her lips slightly parted.

He'd seen many beautiful mouths, but none as beautiful as hers. Ian roused himself, moving his attention to her eyes. No relief from the spell there. "Page, will you please marry me?"

She closed her eyes, and he grabbed her before she could resist, kissed her with all the pent-up desire of three weeks' separation from a woman he'd come to need as much as he needed air.

When he raised his head they were both gasping. "That wasn't fair," she whispered. "Don't do that to me, please. We both know there's nothing wrong with our physical reactions to each other."

If he was supposed to feel guilty, something must be missing from his sense of right and wrong. "That silver outfit you wear feels good. It feels really good."

"Ian!"

There was no missing the warning. "Okay, okay. I asked you to marry me. What's the answer?"

"That we have a lot of ground to cover before I can answer."

If he suggested they continue their discussion in bed she'd undoubtedly walk out. Nevertheless, the notion made a memory of the chill he'd been feeling.

He stared into the fire. "Maybe I'm too uncomplicated, but I thought we'd made a commitment in Hawaii. But something changed by the time we left, didn't it?" At least she'd let him know they still had something to build on.

"I don't think anything changed," she said. "We didn't go beyond feelings, that's all. Good sex doesn't necessarily make a good marriage."

He winced. Her directness occasionally caught him off guard. "There's a lot more between us than sex. Not that it isn't a part of what's good for us. I'm glad it is."

"I'm not prepared to give up my work," she said, and he felt her tense beside him. "That means I wouldn't be able to be the kind of wife you want."

He didn't know exactly what to say. Her job did bother him, or rather some aspects of it. "I never said I expected you to give up your business for me. We'd both have to make some life-style changes, but marriage is bound to mean that."

"What changes would you make?"

"Well…" Now that he thought about it, he wouldn't have to change much. "I guess the main thing would be that home and family would take the place of most social activities I used to have. Not that I'll miss them." An understatement. "In fact I began to drop out of that scene some time ago."

Page rested her chin on a fist. He looked at her and bit the inside of his cheek. Gloomy was the only description for that look.

"Did I fail the test?"

"No. You wouldn't have to do anything else to make me happy. And coming home to you, being with you for part of every day would be bliss for me." She met his gaze squarely. "Do I fail the test?"

She was a puzzle. "I don't know what you're saying. As far as I can tell we want the same thing—to be together."

Her sigh was pure frustration. "You want me decorating your house and having your children and cooking meals and being a social success for you. To do all that I would have to give up everything else, and I'm not ready."

That was it. How could he be such a fool? "I . . . I don't expect you to do that."

"Yes, you—"

"No! Not immediately anyway." He must be careful. "You do like kids?"

"I love them. But not—"

"But not now. Fine. We'll wait until you're ready. As long as that doesn't mean I'm on social security before I get to hold our first baby."

"I don't want to wait too long, either." Her voice broke.

"So we don't have any more problems?" He reached for her, but she shrugged away.

"Don't try to go too fast, Ian. It's not that simple."

Ian got his own taste of frustration. "All right. Tell me where we go from here—in your opinion. I've got to be comfortable, too. You do understand that?"

She wiped the corner of each eye, but he made no attempt to touch her.

"I understand. This is how I think it goes. For the time being I continue exactly as I am. I may even get a bit busier for a while, because we've taken on new people and I'll have to do some street beating to drum up more customers."

He didn't like the idea of her knocking on doors. "Have you done much selling? It's tough."

"How do you think I got started? I'm not crazy about it, but I'm articulate and I make a good presentation."

"Maybe I should—"

"No, Ian. You shouldn't do anything, please."

"I was only thinking about a mailing."

"We already do mailings. Listen—" she faced him, and despite damp lashes her eyes shone "—things are clicking for me. I'm starting to see what looks like success way down the road somewhere. You've got to know how that feels." She paused, one hand rammed into her hair. "Maybe you don't know. It's got to be different when you go into an established business."

Her enthusiasm brought tenderness welling up in him. "I do know what you mean."

"Do you, Ian? When we get a new customer, I've been known to yell and jump up and down like a kid. I feel invincible."

"We do understand each other." He had to hold her. "We're more alike than you know."

"Maybe."

He put an arm around her waist and she rested her cheek against his neck.

"Sweetheart, I was wondering if there was something about my family, my mother perhaps, that bothers you. On the plane you seemed to freeze me out when I mentioned her."

She chewed a fingernail, something he'd never seen her do before.

"There is something," he said. "Has my mother talked to you?" He couldn't believe she'd go that far, desperate as she was for him to settle down. "Has she?"

"Your mother is a lovely lady. I like her."

"She *has*." He made to get up but Page swung around and held his shoulders.

"Rose came by to see me. She was charming, totally accepting of the fact that I'm very different from any of the people she's used to dealing with."

Irritation made keeping still a feat. "Was this before or after our trip?"

"It isn't important."

"It is to me."

She kissed his chin, but he wasn't about to be deflected. "Before or after?"

"Okay. Prior to the trip."

"About the time when you were giving me a hard time every time I called. Before your accident."

"Let's drop this."

Like hell. "Did she tell you what a wonderful husband I'd make...and father maybe?" Blood throbbed into his cheeks. A downward sweep of Page's lashes confirmed his worst fear. "Oh, no. And that's what made you turn off me."

"Don't be embarrassed." She smiled up at him and held his face in her hands. "Mothers like to do things for their children. And they want them settled. Particularly when they're as ancient as you."

He couldn't laugh. "Watch it with the ancient."

"Ian, we'll probably be the same with our children."

She'd slipped and now he did smile. "Our children? As in yours and mine?"

"Eventually. Probably." She let go of him and turned to the fire once more.

"When I mentioned my mother on the plane, you thought the vacation had been one more part of the plot to snare you, I suppose?"

"Let's just say I felt a bit manipulated."

So did he, but he wouldn't say so now. "Would you mind if I told my mother off?"

He was rewarded with a glare. "I'd never forgive you."

"Then I won't. Can we get back to where we were?" Logic was taking a back seat to what had been steadily building in his body and brain—desire.

"As long as we understand each other."

He was having difficulty thinking at all. "Understand?"

"We'll meet as often as possible and you'll accept that? You won't give me a hard time?"

"I'll never give you a hard time again." He nuzzled his face into her neck.

She moved her hair aside for him and pressed closer. "And we'll go slowly on the marriage thing?"

"Not too slowly." Her neck was so smooth and it smelled of a light perfume and wind and rain . . . and he was crazy about her.

"Mmm. We won't worry about details for a while."

Sounded good to him. Her mouth was soft and firm at the same time and tasted like mint. Did she chew gum? Irrelevant thoughts. She kissed him back with enough pressure to send them both into a heap on the rug.

The silver stuff clung, slippery, a second skin. Ian wanted to feel the real thing. Page had already undone his shirt and started her favorite kissing game over his chest and stomach.

"This thing you're wearing—help me." But she was too busy with his belt.

She shifted as he wriggled the ankle-length tights off.

"Okay. Time out." He pinned her beneath him. "Are you interested in my feelings?"

Her face was flushed. "I'm very interested."

"Good. I feel like a starving man faced with his first whole lobster. I want you out of this thing."

She stared, then covered her mouth and laughed.

"I'm glad you find this funny."

"Oh, no. Not funny, Ian. I'm insulted. I remind you of a lobster?"

"Don't tease me," he moaned.

Her laughter ceased abruptly and she sat up. "I'm not teasing. I don't ever want to tease you."

She eased the leotard from a shoulder, pulled out her arm, repeated the process until she was naked to the waist.

Ian's lungs refused to expand. He knelt beside her and tilted her head up to meet his kiss, gentle now, before he smoothed her body.

Leotards were a snap.

Chapter Fourteen

"They went *where*?"

James, jr. bounced Jemima in one arm and flourished a wrench with his spare hand. "I told you. Niagara Falls. They were catching a seven o'clock plane."

Page left her helmet strap hanging and sank onto Lilian's chair. "Why didn't they tell me?"

Red splotches popped out on James's face. Jemima wriggled and he put her down. "Don't touch anything," he ordered and was rewarded with a pout. "Zip said he and Lilian were too old to make a big fuss out of a thing like getting married. They decided to fly to Niagara Falls tonight, get married and be back in time for work on Monday morning."

"And you're in cahoots with them, you little crook."

"I'm helping, that's all," James said, sounding perturbed. "We all know you're working extra hard so you can...so you can..."

Jemima had arrived at Page's knee and she picked the little girl up. "Yes, James? So I can what?"

"Get married," he blurted and attacked parts of a dismantled bike with gusto.

Page rocked Jemima and kissed her shiny curls. "How is it that my employees know everything about me and I don't know the most important things about them?"

James yanked the wrench harder. "You do know about us."

"Answer my question. How do you know I'm thinking of getting married?"

The splotches became one total red face. "Lilian says that Mr. Faber calls all the time and sends flowers and stuff, and she says she can always find you at his house if you're not upstairs. And she says you'll probably marry him around New Year's."

It was Page's turn to blush. "A bunch of spies," she said, but without rancor. "And you could just be right. But I still wish Zip and Lilian hadn't sneaked off without telling me. I'd like to do something for them."

"You can. When they get back, tell them it's okay for Jemima to be here in the daytime."

The suggestion caught Page off guard. "She very often is. I've never complained."

"No. But they worry you don't really like it and Lilian wants the kid with her." He let out a whistling breath as if he'd done something difficult in saying his piece. "She's smart, y'know. Even if Lilian can't afford for her to go to preschool right now, that kid'll pick up a lot being with all of us."

Page hid her face in Jemima's hair. If they weren't careful the child would pick up more than she should. "I'll tell Zip and Lilian it's fine for her to be here," she said. The little one felt soft and smelled clean, a small-child smell that started an ache deep inside Page. One day... "James, how are you going to look after Jemima all weekend? What will your grandmother say?"

Mention of his grandmother always produced a blank expression. "Jemima'll be with me while I'm here in the garage. Buzz will take her at night. And I'm going to get her out for a walk every afternoon."

Page smiled. "You sound pretty organized." She couldn't think of a less-likely pair of baby-sitters than James Am-

well, jr. and Buzz, although she was now completely recovered from her accident. "But it's time she went to bed
now. You'd better call Buzz. I've got to get going."

Page set off, a warm sense of well-being fueling her. The
thought of Lilian and the Zipper making a home together
with Jemima brought an involuntary smile. And the business was really going well.

A month had passed since the start of her truce with Ian.
As James had suggested—and Lilian would have to be told
to stop monitoring private calls or keep her mouth closed—
they were planning a wedding around the New Year.

As with all nights now, this one went too slowly. While
she worked she kept her thoughts trained on the next day,
which was Saturday.

For several days fog had taken the place of rain. A misty
fog that rolled off the bay and slunk through the streets in
eerie streams.

Page wore a down-lined jumpsuit over her leotard and
tights. Ian's idea, and a good one since the suit was intended for cross-country skiing and was very light.

Friday was usually a busy night and this Friday was no
exception. By one-fifteen in the morning, twelve satisfied
customers had been dealt with and she'd been given enough
to do to keep her out until past her two o'clock cutoff. She
stopped at a phone and called her apartment. Tanya never
went to bed this early, and fortunately she was at home. Ian
now made a habit of getting some sleep and setting his alarm
so that he was awake to speak to Page at two. She didn't
want to disturb him early, but neither did she want him to
worry if she was late home. Tanya promised to give him a
message.

Another new dimension to Page's operation was a man
called Gary, one of the recently hired riders who had opted
to take on extra hours at night. He started at eleven, and
when Page had met him on her last return to Waldo's he'd

told her he was as busy as she was. The dream was finally becoming real.

Her radio blipped. "Hello, Waldo!"

A voice she didn't recognize answered. "He's stepped out. How many boxes do you have left?"

Page frowned. Waldo's radio was his private pet. "Two."

"Give me the addresses."

"One's for a place on Larkin, the other's Market. You want street numbers?"

"No. It's the Market one that's wrong. From what's written here I thought it might be. Somebody must have copied an address from the next column. Take it to Shipley. Instructions say there's a turnoff just before Rich. Keep your eyes open or you'll miss it. Some guy who lives in a studio apartment over a warehouse. You'll have to go through an abandoned junkyard."

"Sounds charming," Page said, but the dispatch had been terminated.

Twenty minutes later she pedaled slowly toward her last drop. This was a rough area of town, not one she'd ever been sent to before.

There were almost no streetlights. She passed one standard and glanced up. Broken glass reflected a glitter. Knocked out with a rock... or a bullet?

Street names were tough to locate. Fourth. She'd gone too far. An unpleasant thrust speared her stomach. The city was never this silent, particularly this section, from what she'd been told. The drunks and down-and-outs must be asleep... or tucked up in jail.

She wasn't sure exactly where she was, and by a dingy storefront she stopped to look for numbers. Gold paint peeled from glass above the door, and she bumped her bike onto the sidewalk for a closer look.

"Get the hell out!"

She reeled back, stumbling on her own wheels.

A lumpy heap rose, turning into a shambling figure that approached with weakly flailing arms. Page smelled liquor and sweat . . . and heard a stream of obscenities.

She leaped on the bike and rode on, sweat running down her own icy back.

"Man's place . . ." were the last words she heard as she hurtled around a corner and sighed her relief at the sight of the word Clementina on a sign. Only a couple of blocks away.

The dispatcher had been right. Missing the alley before Rich would have been easy. But Page's sharp eyes picked out a darker slit in a solid wall of darkness and she rode in. Her heart and lungs vied for her attention. They thudded and hurt in unison, and her throat burned. Ian was right. This could be madness.

She found the yard easily. The beating in her ears lessened and she breathed more easily. Not for long. Making out exactly what the junk consisted of was impossible, but it lay in hulking masses all around her. She couldn't see a warehouse.

This was one task she probably shouldn't try to complete. Waldo wouldn't expect her to go through anything this frightening.

Fear.

Page breathed through her mouth. Apart from the night of her attack she'd never felt afraid while she was doing her job—until now.

Her front wheel hit something and she braked hard. Careful where she trod, she dismounted and made her way on foot, peering ahead. There had to be a building here somewhere. She hated to give up. A flashlight would be a blessing. She'd never needed one before, but in future it would be standard equipment for any night-rider she employed.

"Hello?" She grimaced. The only person likely to hear that puny effort was herself.

Perhaps she should call Waldo and make sure of this. Her eyes were adjusting slowly. Rather than junk, the piles looked like tarp-covered boxes, or stacks.

A soft swipe against her legs almost stopped her heart completely. "What . . . ?" Another sweeping rush and a feline yowl, and she was left trembling but smiling. All the indigents in the area weren't two-footed.

There was no warehouse. No studio apartment. The yard was just that, a big storage yard. Now she felt too sick to go on or turn back. Something was very wrong.

Shaking so violently she could scarcely make her hands work, she leaned her bike against the nearest shrouded pile.

She unzipped her suit far enough to reach her radio. Instinctively, she crouched and bowed her head before starting to press the switch.

Her thumb never made contact.

The arm that shot around her throat and jerked her upright had metal things on it that crushed into her windpipe.

The white light that met her eyes blocked out the world.

SHE'D NEVER TOUCHED more than the edge of the existence that belonged to these people. Page walked through the receiving room at the police precinct house with the disjointed sensation that she'd entered a nightmare. Someone else's nightmare.

Her wrists hurt. The policeman who'd handcuffed her in the yard and reeled off a lot of words about her rights shoved her ahead of him between rows of men and women, some lolling with blank faces, some arguing, some crying.

"I'm a bicycle messenger," she tried again. Like all the other times, the officer wasn't interested.

"You'll get your chance," he said. "Be a good girl and don't make a fuss, and things will go easier for you."

Go easier. He'd talked a lot of nonsense about bets. She was supposed to know about it all, but she couldn't think straight.

In a cubicle enclosed by frosted glass she was pushed to sit on a shiny wooden chair and told to wait.

Minutes passed. Gray metal file cabinets. Gray shelves. Spilled papers. Chipped desk littered with Styrofoam cups and empty sandwich wrappers.

She wanted Ian.

The door opened. "Miss Page Linstrom?" A pudgy man with hammocks of fat beneath his eyes entered, reading her name from a sheet in his hands. He looked at her, saggy jowls wobbling. Not unkind, Page registered vaguely. Tired, bored, disinterested, nothing more. She was another stranger accused of... what?

"I'm Detective Sloane," the man said flatly. He opened the door again and yelled something. The policeman who had arrested her came in and took the handcuffs off her wrists before withdrawing again.

Sloane balanced on the edge of the scarred desk. "Says here you were picked up in a storage yard off Shipley. Care to save us all a lot of time and tell the whole story? Shorter the better. More names the better."

Feeling returned slowly to Page's fingers and she gripped the seat of the chair. Underneath it was satin smooth. How many other fingers had rested there, held on to something tangible while their owners sweated?

"Miss Linstrom, it'll be easier on you if you talk."

"I...I don't know what this is about." Her voice was high and squeaky. "I'm a bicycle messenger. I was trying to make a delivery."

"Hmm." He took a plastic packet from his pocket and emptied it on the desk. She recognized payment envelopes for Waldo, the ones the policeman had taken from her. "How long have you had this job?"

"Er—"

"Two years. We already know."

So why had he asked?

"Who is your contact?"

She felt faint. "I don't know what you're talking about. I want Ian."

"Is he your contact?"

Dimly she remembered scenes like this from movies. She wasn't supposed to answer questions until she understood what was going on. "Ian is my friend. I don't know why I'm here and I'm not talking to you till I do."

He got up and walked behind the desk, sat down and clasped his hands over his belly. "Lady, I don't think for one minute that you're as dumb as you'd like me to believe. We know what you've been doing and now we've caught you in the act. You were read your rights, so why not just come clean."

"There was something about a lawyer."

"Yeah, yeah." Still no anger, only resignation. "I thought you might be smart enough to finger whoever's making the big money out of this, that's all. Your lawyer would have been happy to walk in here and find half his work done for him. And we'd come off smelling like roses. But if you want it the hard way..." He picked up a phone on his desk. "Sloane here. Send a matron. I've got one for beauty portraits and prints."

Page shot forward in her chair. "What am I supposed to have done?"

He smiled and the effect wasn't reassuring. "You were given the charges when you were arrested, but I don't mind repeating them for you. Off-track betting is an offense in this state. You are a runner for an off-track betting organization."

Chapter Fifteen

How long had she been there? The cot she sat on was hard, covered by an olive-green blanket. For what seemed like days she'd remained motionless, listening to other prisoners coughing, swearing, shouting at passing guards.

Earlier they'd said she could be released if someone posted bail. She didn't have enough money of her own.

After she'd been booked, a woman had informed her of her right to make one telephone call. Her lawyer had been the suggested recipient. She didn't have a lawyer. One would be appointed for her if that's what she wanted. Her insistence that she didn't need one, that she wasn't guilty of anything, had caused a few unpleasant and knowing laughs.

The call she'd made was to Tanya. Ian had been her first thought, but she couldn't make herself dial his number. He'd told her so many times how much he hated the night work and shown his disapproval of her occupation in general. This fiasco would squelch any argument she'd ever made against his opinion.

Tanya had sounded distant, horrified. Page was not to worry, Tanya insisted, but nothing in her voice or what she said gave reason to expect help.

That had been hours ago. Page's watch had been taken away and put in a bag with her name and a number on it, but she still knew it must be midafternoon Saturday by now.

"Linstrom, get ready." A female guard, clipboard in hand, shouted into the cell without looking at Page.

Ready for what? She had nothing with her. A comb and toothbrush, a few basic needs had been provided, and she'd already done what she could for her appearance.

Sickness came in waves, and with it cold sweats. A tray of food, brought a long time ago, stood untouched on a chair.

The clack of heels returned. Page got up from the edge of the cot and stood with her fists clenched at her sides. She wouldn't think. Just go through the motions, do whatever they told her to do, wait for the hell to end.

Keys jangled and the door swung inward. "Move."

She moved. Into the corridor, through an electronically controlled door, reversing all the procedures she'd been put through early in the morning.

Her small possessions—watch, gloves, a gold chain she wore around her neck—were spilled onto a counter, and she was told to check them, then sign "on the line" to indicate that they had been returned.

Putting the chain on again was impossible. Her fingers refused to work the clasp. At last she was ready, back in the down suit, although she probably wouldn't need it, and with her helmet and gloves clutched in front of her.

"Right." The guard didn't smile or make eye contact. "You can go. I'm sure you've already been told not to leave the area and what any violation of bail restrictions would mean."

Page nodded. "Yes, thank you."

With the woman holding her arm she walked into a hall where the burst of noise and activity made her cringe.

Then her arm was released and she stood alone in the midst of chaos.

A different hand touched her lightly between the shoulders. "Are you okay?"

She looked up into Ian's face, and the tears she'd suppressed flowed unchecked. "I'm scared," she said, leaning against his chest and holding on. "I don't know what's happening to me."

He spread his fingers on her back. "It'll be okay."

"Ian, did they tell you what they think I've done?"

"Yes."

She raised her face. Fatigue grayed his features and dulled his eyes.

"Tanya called you?"

"Yes. Why didn't you?" He wore jeans and a parka and hadn't shaved.

"I knew what you'd say if I did." How long had he been waiting? "I wanted to talk to you, but—"

"We'll discuss it later. I want to get out of here." He eased her arms away.

The slight warmth that had seeped into her, the relief at the sight of him, ebbed away. There was something different about Ian and she didn't think she liked it.

They left the huge, gray stone building and crossed to a parking lot on the other side of the street. Ian opened the door of the Mercedes for her, shut her inside and walked around to slide behind the wheel.

He wasn't saying anything.

She should thank him for coming. And posting bail...he must have done that. He drove from the lot without glancing at her.

"Was it you who posted bail?" She touched his arm and felt muscle contract.

"Yes."

She removed her hand. "Thank you." The sick feeling overwhelmed her now. "They impounded my bike and radio. I don't understand—"

"Standard procedure, I imagine. They'd need to go over those things." His voice was level, but his knuckles showed white on the steering wheel.

What is it? Page longed to ask. *Why aren't you making me feel safe like you always do?*

Ian's chest felt as if giant hands compressed it. After Tanya Woodside's call he'd dashed down to the jail and demanded Page's release. There had been no mistaking the expressions on the faces of officers who listened until he'd finished railing: pity. They considered him a sucker for a beautiful woman who'd been living a double life for months. Then he'd been told the details of the arrest, the prior events. He didn't know exactly what to do next but there were questions of his own to ask—of people the police hadn't mentioned—and regardless of what happened he would never stop loving Page.

He was exhausted. No sleep. Only hours of waiting and wondering while he balanced attempts at logic with the facts he'd been presented.

"Ian?" She sounded as tired as he felt and something twisted inside him. "You don't believe I did what they said, do you?"

"How can you even ask me that?" he shouted, and when he looked at her tears shone in her eyes. "I'm sorry, Page. I'm uptight. Frantic. I don't know what to do first." How true. He'd been told there was evidence to incriminate Page but not what that evidence was. It had even been suggested that she could have engineered her own accident in an attempt to deflect any official interest in her illegal activities. He had never felt so impotent, or angry, or confused.

"Can we talk for a while?" Page asked.

He wanted to, but he didn't dare take the time. "I've got to ask some questions—try to make sense of all this. The sooner I get on it, the better."

She was quiet for a moment, then said, "I don't want to go home."

He closed his eyes fractionally. This was the hardest thing he'd ever done, to try to remain objective while all he wanted was to get her away from this mess—regardless of whether or not she'd done something wrong. Wrong? Hell, he must be cracking up. Page wasn't capable of what they'd accused her of doing.

"Ian, would it be all right if I waited at your place? I could call my staff from there and see how things are going."

For both of them he had to be strong. "I don't think that's a good idea. If the police want to talk to you they'll expect you to be at your own apartment. Get settled in there, and I'll talk to you as soon as I talk to someone who knows more about this sort of thing than I do."

Outside her apartment, Page watched Ian come around to open her door. She got out and stood in front of him.

"I'll come in and get you settled," he said.

He was anxious. Page sensed his tightly constrained nervousness, his desire to leave.

"No need," she said, needing him more than he'd ever know. "Do whatever you have to do."

His eyes showed uncertainty. "Are you sure you're all right?" he asked.

She made herself smile. "Sure." That he cared for her Page didn't doubt, but nothing in his life to this point could have prepared him for what he'd been through in the past few hours.

"Good," he said, backing away. "Talk to you later, okay?"

"Okay." But it wasn't. Couldn't he feel that?

Without waiting to see her inside, he walked swiftly to his side of the car and got in. Page stayed at the curb until the Mercedes merged with other traffic.

She went, not into the house, but to the garage and pushed open the door. That it wasn't locked surprised her. After what the police had said, she'd expected padlocks and chains to guard their precious evidence.

"Page!" Tanya, whom she'd never seen in the garage before, leaped up and rushed to fold her in a tight and shaky embrace. "Oh, Page, thank God you're back."

"I told those SOBs they were nuts." James came forward, more disheveled looking than usual. Behind him stood Buzz with Jemima on her shoulders.

"Page, Page," the child said around the thumb stuffed in her mouth.

"Shhh," Buzz said, jiggling. "Come and sit down, Page. Geez, we've been frantic around here."

Page ached with gratitude for these special people. With Tanya's arm still draped around her, she sat in the chair James set in the middle of the floor.

"What happened?" Buzz asked. She swung Jemima down, and Page promptly found her lap invaded by the sweet-smelling bundle.

She cuddled the child close and felt some of the tension slipping away. "You see before you a hardened criminal." The quip didn't have the right ring.

"Did they hurt you?" Tanya stayed close.

Page looked at her and noted that the pinched appearance had intensified. "They didn't hurt me—physically, that is. The damage happens up here." She pointed to her head. "Are you okay, Tanya?"

"Fine, yeah. Terrific. Tired, that's all. I couldn't sleep after you called." That made sense, but it didn't account for the new bruise on Tanya's temple.

Page decided to wait until they were alone to pursue that topic. "Thanks for calling Ian. I guess you did that?"

"I had to. I couldn't think where else to get the money, and I figured he'd want to go down there anyway." She glanced toward the door. "Didn't he bring you back?"

"Uh-huh. But he had to leave and check out some things." She thought about what Tanya had said, that she hadn't known where else to go for the bail money. More proof that there was no wealthy Woodside family she supposedly was always able to turn to.

James stood beside Page rubbing his bony hands together. "Do you know what those turkeys say?"

She felt the rage he was trying to hold in. "You mean the police?" Jemima had turned her face up to hers, and Page kissed a soft cheek. "What did they say that I haven't already heard?"

"How should I know?" Truculence didn't suit James. He shoved his hands in his pockets and paced to the window.

Buzz hunkered down in front of Page. "They came in here before James arrived this morning and found all kinds of money stashed around the place. Did they tell you that?"

They'd told her. She nodded.

"Page. I was here last night to pick up Jemima. James was here, too. We'd have seen bundles of notes packed in black boxes if they were here."

Page became very still. Black boxes? She spoke carefully, keeping her voice level. "The police didn't mention boxes to me. But, according to our men of the law, I'm very good at tucking away bucks. Rolled up and stuffed inside bicycle frames, they said."

James snorted. "There wasn't any money in any bicycle frames yesterday."

"How can you be sure?" She had to be sensible and ready for the contentions the police were bound to make.

He shrugged. "I just am, that's all. The weight would be different. The sound. I'd notice something."

"Yeah," Buzz agreed.

Tanya sat on the floor and crossed her legs. "James and Buzz know what they're talking about. And surely Ian will help you out. They'll listen to him. Pillars of society always carry more weight than the rest of us."

Page silently rocked Jemima. She couldn't second guess what Ian might decide to do. "We'll have to wait and see what happens. I know I haven't done anything wrong and that's the main thing. I've got to believe that there is justice." And she had to try making sense of something vague but insistent forming in her brain.

IN THE EARLY EVENING Ian called. He said he was still making inquiries and couldn't see Page tonight. He wanted her to sit tight until they could work everything out. Nothing would ever be so bad that they couldn't face it together. Was he saying he assumed her guilt but would stand by her?

Tanya, who had drawn a discreet distance away without leaving the sitting room, came to put an arm around Page as soon as she hung up the phone. "Is something wrong between you two?"

Page would have liked to be left alone to cry. "I don't know. And I'm not sure I care."

"You don't mean that. Give Ian a break. He must be shocked like the rest of us are."

But the rest of them had shown their support with something more precious than money—their faith in her.

She turned to Tanya. "Forget about me for a minute. What did you do to your face? You've got a bruise."

Tanya touched her temple. "I don't know," she said, but color rose in her cheeks. "I guess I bumped it without noticing."

The doorbell stopped Page from replying that Tanya must have *felt* the blow—just as she'd felt her fall a few weeks earlier.

Their visitors—or rather Page's visitors—were two policemen.

A middle-aged officer pushed in front of a younger man and stood on the doorstep with his feet spread. "Page Linstrom?"

She nodded. A little sound let her know Tanya was behind her left shoulder.

"Detective Sloane wants you down at the station."

She found her voice. "Why?"

He shrugged and the other man leaned forward. "A few questions, ma'am. We should get going."

"Couldn't you ask me the questions here?" The inside of her throat hurt and she could barely swallow.

"That wouldn't be convenient," she was promptly told. She knew arguing would be useless.

Detective Sloane, looking even more tired than the night before, was already installed behind his ugly desk when Page entered his office.

"Sit down." He waved to the slippery chair. "Sorry to bring you in again. We need to clear up a few more points."

At no time before had she been given a chance to plead her innocence, and she didn't expect any change in policy now. But she was going to try to make this policeman listen anyway.

"The man who called me on my radio last night . . ." She paused until Sloane looked up. "The one who told me to go to a different place. Do you know who he was?"

"No. But I'm sure you do."

She drew in a shaky breath and pressed on. "I never heard his voice before. Waldo usually gives me my instructions. Talk to him, he'll tell you." She'd tried to call Waldo herself earlier but there'd been no answer.

Sloane laughed shortly. "I'm sure Mr. Sands would tell me if I asked him. We aren't concerned with him now, only with the outfit you were working for."

"I don't know what you're talking about," Page muttered.

Sloane shuffled papers and mumbled, then burped and didn't apologize.

"Sure you do. You ready to give us some names?"

The helplessness intensified. "What names am I supposed to give you?"

"Okay. A quick synopsis to help your memory. We got a tipoff last night, and the information we received checked out. The caller said you'd be making a drop in that yard and you were there. Our mistake was not waiting long enough to get whoever was supposed to take that box from you."

"Box?"

"Don't be coy with me. The box you were supposedly delivering. We found more of them at your garage. They were useful, weren't they?"

"You're not making sense."

"No, of course not." He gave her a thin smile. "You didn't use those deli boxes to pick up bets and deliver pay-offs, did you? What made someone turn you in? How long have you been stockpiling money in that garage of yours? Is that what happened? Did you steal from your head hon-cho until he got mad enough to take you off the street? Are you sure it isn't time to let whoever your boss is take some of the heat? We'll give you all the protection you need if that's the hang-up."

He was mixing her up. "I'm a bicycle messenger," she said, feeling like a parrot. "I've got my own company and I work all day, as well as at night. Waldo Sands is just one of my customers. I don't know what happened last night, or how there came to be money in the bikes or in those boxes—"

"And in the box you were about to deliver at the storage yard. And in the envelopes you hadn't yet emptied of incoming bets."

Page stared. "In the envelopes?"

"Surprise, surprise." He sounded bored. "Yeah, in the envelopes. Not that you knew about it, of course."

"Sure I did. Payments for goods."

He laughed unpleasantly. "Lady, there aren't goods in any deli that bring the kind of bucks you were carrying. You want to talk about it now?"

She only stared.

Many more abortive questions followed before she was treated to another unwelcome ride in a police car. Back to her apartment.

Page sat behind the two officers, so wide awake she doubted she would ever sleep again. The whole thing was coming clear to her now.

Page pressed a fist against the cold window and rested her brow on top. She had it. All of it—or almost all. Although they didn't say as much, the police understood the basics too, but expected to get at more evidence. She was supposed to supply that evidence. That's where they'd slipped up in their calculations, because she wasn't guilty of any crime. But she would be able to give them some of what they needed.

Page rolled her head against her fist. Why had it taken so long to remember about that box?

Before she could go back to Detective Sloane to tell him what she'd figured out she must talk to at least two people.

One of them had set her up last night.

Chapter Sixteen

"You know they've arrested Waldo Sands?"

Ian exchanged glances with his father and looked back at Walt Isaacs. "I didn't know. What does that mean?"

The lawyer sank lower in his chair, tipped back and crossed his feet on his desk. "It means that unless the guy says your lady friend's innocent you'd better buy a commuter pass to the local pen."

"Ian," Bob Faber said as Ian leaped to his feet, "we've got to stay calm if we're going to help Page."

"I don't like the way he talks about her." Ian leveled a finger at Isaacs. "I'm here because we were told you're the best in town. I expect you to be on our side."

Isaacs studied his fingernails. His jeans were the designer variety and his blue sweater was cashmere, but even slouched in his chair he exuded slick, all-pro city lawyer and Ian didn't like him.

When he spoke he stared at Ian with hard blue eyes. "Ready to get down to this? If you are we'll talk. Otherwise I've got better things to do. In case you haven't noticed, this is Sunday and the reason I'm here is because you hounded my household staff half the night and I didn't want you to keep it up today."

Bob Faber's hand shot out to grip Ian's arm. "Sit down, son. We know you're doing us a favor, Isaacs, but I expect your bill to reflect that. Where do we go from here? Or should I say, where do we start?''

Isaacs swung his feet down and opened a folder in front of him. It contained a single sheet of paper. He read quickly and pushed the folder aside. ''She isn't in custody?''

''No.'' Ian hated this cold bastard. If he hadn't come so highly recommended he'd tell the man to get lost.

''That's strange. She should be.''

''What the hell do you mean?''

''Ian.'' Bob Faber's voice held a note of pleading. ''Cooperate. Hear the man out.''

''I don't know why she isn't behind bars,'' Isaacs continued, unperturbed. ''What I'd like to suggest up-front is that we go for a plea bargain. It's her best shot.''

''The hell—''

''Ian! For God's sake. Start thinking with your head.'' His father's thin face turned red. ''We're upset, but we can't do a thing for Page if we don't keep our heads.''

''Right,'' Ian said tightly and subsided into a chair. ''I apologize, Isaacs.''

''Forget it. The police are being tight-lipped. But from what I got from a source of mine, she looks guilty as hell. She had money on her and they found more in her garage. The story is that she's working for a big-time operation in competition with Sands. She's a plant.''

''Knock off the present tense,'' Ian said, then shrugged. ''Go on.''

''Yeah. Okay. She's supposed to be a plant whose function was to feed back information about Sands's activities. The police believe she double-crossed whoever she was working for and they turned her in as a way of getting rid of her and taking Waldo Sands out at the same time.''

''Crap,'' Ian said through clenched teeth.

His father cleared his throat. ''I agree with Ian. If all this is true why hasn't she, er, fingered her boss?''

Isaacs's laugh chilled Ian. "This is big time, guys, big crime for big bucks that's likely to pull in a bundle of names we'll all recognize."

"I figured out that much," Ian commented.

"Good. I guess you've also heard of honor among thieves. Forget that one. Try fear among thieves. She's not singing because she wants to stay alive. She knows they'll take her out if she opens her mouth."

Ian massaged his temples. "I don't believe a word of this."

This time Isaacs didn't laugh. "You'd better hope we get a judge who doesn't believe a word of it."

WHEN WOULD THE POLICE show again? Page made her way slowly back to her bedroom. She'd been there most of the day. Wind rattled the window and she jumped. Her nerves were shot. She had to talk to Ian before she was picked up again. Where was he? Last night his phone had been steadily busy and today he wasn't answering. She didn't have the energy to go looking for him. The clock in the sitting room chimed six. How much longer did she have?

She stretched out on the futon without putting on the light. Each time she got up she felt dizzy, and the fear that she might really be sick grew. There was no time for illness now.

The phone rang and she reached for it, hardly able to breathe.

"Page? This is Ian." He didn't wait to be sure who had answered. "We'd better get together."

"Yes." But she couldn't ride to his house, not feeling as she did.

"If I come to your place can we have some privacy, or is your roommate around?"

The urgency was there, the suggestion that he felt panicky. "Tanya isn't here." A headache joined Page's other symptoms.

"I'll be right over."

He hung up. Page slowly did the same and put on the lamp beside her bed.

IAN RAN DOWNSTAIRS and outside, pulling on his raincoat as he went. The young evening snapped about his ears as he opened the car door. No dampness softened the air, and he felt winter's tightening grip.

The drive to her apartment took minutes. He parked in front, leaped the steps in one bound and rang her bell. Then he turned his back. A darkening sky touched trees and rooftops. Each breath he took carried brittle air into his restricted lungs. Please let him find the right words...and have enough strength for himself, and Page, if necessary.

The lock rattled behind him and his resolve wavered.

Hinges creaked.

"Page. Oh, hell, Page."

Ian walked inside and pulled her into his arms. He crushed her to him, kissing her hair, her closed eyes, her cheeks. At first she responded, then as abruptly, she pushed him from her and went into the kitchen.

He called her name and heard her say, "We've got to talk."

"I know," he shouted, waving his arms, his carefully hoarded control fleeing completely. "So talk. But for God's sake make me understand what's happening." That wasn't what he'd intended to say, or at least, not in that way.

He followed her into the kitchen. She wasn't there. More slowly he entered the hall leading to the rest of the apartment. "Where are you?"

"Sitting room," she said clearly and he found her huddled on a shabby blue couch in a cluttered boxlike room.

He leaned against the wall just inside the door and crossed one foot over the other. His careless comment had already made this harder than he'd feared. "I love you, Page. I'll always love you."

"I know. But you also think I'm a criminal. I'm not."

The pounding in his chest eased, but only slightly. "The police have some strong evidence. We have to come up with a way to combat that."

She wore jeans and a blue sweater. Her face was pale and there were dark shadows under her eyes. They'd both been through too much.

"There is a way to combat it," Page said. "First we have to be honest with each other."

"What do you mean?"

"I know the whole story now. I worked it out."

He saw her look at her socks. They were mismatched, and she hitched her jeans farther down. He walked to stand in front of her.

"You mean you can prove your innocence?" The thrill of hope seemed unreal.

"I didn't do anything wrong, Ian. Obviously you wouldn't have any way of being sure of that, given the way we met, but honestly, until Friday night I don't think I'd ever as much as thought about betting. Why should I? It's not something that's ever touched me before."

"Go on."

Page pushed back her hair and kept her fingers against her scalp. Her legs ached, and her arms. When Ian went home she'd take her temperature.

"Page, speak to me."

She took a deep breath. "Something the police said last night—or something they didn't say—made everything clear. There *is* no unknown betting operation I'm working for, or anyone else in this case, although the authorities think there is. Those envelopes of Waldo's for his so-called deli clients are the way he collected and paid on bets. I was just a pawn who carried them around. On Friday something went wrong. There have to be a lot of rival operations and one of them managed to get a call through to me. They sent me to that yard and tipped off the police. Then they planted money in my garage. All very tidy. First Waldo used me as a runner. Then one of his competitors used me to eliminate him."

"What was it the police didn't say?"

"That Waldo is in custody. And he has to be, or they'd be searching for him, because he isn't at his place. When I asked them to talk to him they pretended they weren't interested. That didn't make sense."

She laughed without mirth. "They believe I'm a kind of double agent, a crook with her feet in two camps. And their theory is right except I didn't know a thing about it. Now by suggesting the only way I can stay out of prison is to implicate these people I'm supposed to know, they hope to get more information out of me. They'll take me in as soon as they're tired of waiting for me to make a move. This all seems like something that only happens to other people."

Just voicing it all brought wobbly excitement, the start of relief. She knew her theory was right.

"Okay," Ian said. "So why didn't you tell this theory of yours to the police and defend yourself?"

She got up and rested her hands on his chest. "You were frightened when I was arrested."

He looked into her eyes. "Wouldn't you have been if the position were reversed?"

"No. I'd have believed it was a mistake and expected everything to be cleared up."

"I did. But I was still frantic when nothing positive happened."

Her mouth dried out. "We met when I was making a delivery for Waldo. Your name was on the envelope. Ian, were you one of Waldo's clients? It doesn't matter to me if you've placed a few bets here and there. But it's going to come out if I tell the whole story from beginning to end. A lot of names are going to come out."

At first she thought he was taking her in his arms. Instead he gripped her shoulders and put her away from him. "You . . . you think I'd let you suffer to protect myself?"

"Ian, I—"

"I love you. I want to marry you. And I've been through hell over this. Where are you coming from? Can't you see what it's like for me? I saw a lawyer today, and he thinks the evidence against you is solid. You're going to have to prove you weren't involved with Waldo or someone like him. You can't use holding back out of loyalty to me as an excuse for not giving whatever evidence you've got."

She was crying now. "I couldn't risk hurting you."

"I haven't done anything."

She gulped and the tears stopped. "I believe you if you say so. But neither have I."

"You were caught with evidence that suggests otherwise."

"You sound like a policeman."

He moved away. "I know I'm not involved with this. I've spent all afternoon interviewing some of my 'friends' and I found out what I needed to. If you'd thought hard enough about that first night you came to my place you might have remembered a comment that the order had been placed in my name. I didn't place it. I'd never heard of Touch Tone Gourmet before."

"One of the others called Waldo? Of course. I do remember now. So one of them was a betting client of his?"

"Does it matter to us? The police will get around to that. But it doesn't alter the fact that you were employed by Sands, and at this point you're under suspicion."

"I'll do something about that."

"Do it now. I'll come with you."

She could hardly see him through a blur of tears. "Thank you. But you have to trust me. There's one more thing I have to do first."

"What?"

"I can't tell you."

He pushed a hand into his hair. "That sounds like another way of saying you can't trust me. Or you won't. I don't buy that, Page. If you've got everything under control and you're in the clear, why not finish this now?"

"I'm tired," she told him. "I think I need to be alone for a while." Only an hour ago she'd longed to see him. What was he making her feel now? Did he doubt her innocence even though he insisted otherwise?

Ian's face set in rigid lines. "You don't want me here?"

"I didn't say that."

"Oh, but I think you did and maybe you're right." He went to the sitting-room door. "I'll look forward to hearing how things work out for you. Let me know if you decide I can do something to help."

"Ian!" She leaped to her feet to follow him, but stopped when she heard the front door close. The car's engine sounded as a muffled roar before tires squealed and the noise quickly faded.

Page walked back down the hall. Holding her eyes wide open seemed to help the dizziness. She stumbled and caught herself against the wall. When she reached her bedroom she took the phone off the hook. Ian was unlikely to call and there was no one else she wanted to talk to. She thought she would vomit soon.

Early the next morning after drinking tea—the only thing that sounded good to her—she checked in at the garage and found the morning routine clicking.

"You doing okay?" the Zipper asked on his way out. He and Lilian had returned the night before.

"Sure," she lied, waving as he left.

Jemima sat on Lilian's knee while she worked the radio. "Hi, Page," Lilian said and continued filling in dockets. "Things are hopping around here."

"And you're coping okay?"

Lilian glanced up and moved her mouthpiece aside. "I'm coping fine. Zip's mad enough to take on the whole San Francisco police department but I'm coping with that—not that I blame him. You look like hell."

Page grimaced. "I know. That's how I feel, too."

"Did you hear any more from the police?"

"Nope." She was surprised they hadn't come to get her by now. Not that she cared much now that she felt estranged from Ian. "I think I may have the flu. Will the place fall down if I go upstairs again? I'll try to make it in again this afternoon."

"It'll be fine." Lilian frowned, and Page saw her chest expand. "I don't think you've got the flu. Once this stuff with the cops is sorted out you'll be okay. Go get some rest."

Page smiled and trudged down the alley beside the house, then around to the front steps. Lilian wasn't to know that she'd never feel completely okay again. Oh, she'd heal, but nothing would ever be the same.

She went into the apartment, closed the door behind her and locked it. No need to postpone the inevitable any longer. She put on the chain.

"Are you locking me in?"

Tanya's words pounded into Page like a blow. She spun around. "I thought you were still out."

"And you were making sure you'd know when I got back?" Tanya's hair hung in uncombed tangles around her pale face. She wore a long coat over a brown, checked shirt and jeans.

"What makes you say that?" Page's heart beat harder.

Tanya walked, tennis shoes scuffing, into the kitchen, with Page close behind.

"I got back a little while ago. I was going to try to get away without seeing you." Tanya indicated a suitcase and a large duffel bag near the door leading to the rest of the apartment. "You know, don't you?"

"Love makes people do crazy things," Page said softly. "I don't think you wanted to hurt me."

"But I did. I hurt you a lot." She sniffed and looked at the ceiling. "I loved him so much, Page, so much."

Page pulled out a chair and sat down. "Why Waldo? Of all the men you could choose, why pick one...?" What was she saying? Wasn't she the one who'd told Ian you couldn't decide who to love?

"I didn't love him at first." Tanya hunched in a corner. "See, I don't have a rich family waiting to hand out bucks like I told you I did."

Page made a sympathetic noise, but she didn't say that she'd figured out for herself that the wealthy Woodsides were a myth.

"Waldo gave me things. He gave me everything. And he treated me like someone special."

"You are special. When did you know what he was into?" She was going to get through this with Tanya and help her make some decisions. After that she'd start picking up her own scattered pieces.

Tanya slid down onto the floor. "I knew a long time ago. He used to brag about it...all his money. I was a safe pair of ears, because he'd bought me."

Page visualized the box of money in Tanya's drawer. "When did Waldo start hitting you?"

A small noise came from Tanya's throat.

"Why would you keep going back for more of the same? You could have walked away."

"Walked away to what? I know what having nothing feels like, and I couldn't face it again. Wrong, I know. Weak, I know. But that's the way it was."

"What made you...frame me?"

Tanya covered her eyes. "I'm sorry, Page. He didn't want me anymore. I was supposed to get lost while he took up with someone else. He gave me a bunch of money as a pay-off and told me to take a walk."

"But you wouldn't stay away."

"I couldn't. On Friday I went to him again. He was with her—the new woman. He hit me in front of her."

"Then you came back here. And when I called to let you know I was still out and would be late you decided to get back at him through me." She was tired, but there was no stopping now.

"I thought the police would go straight for Waldo and find out you were for real."

"They had Waldo figured, Tanya. But I was framed tight enough for them to believe I was in it, too." Page took a crumpled wad of gold ribbon from her pocket. "When did you drop this in the garage? On one of your secret visits to check my movements in the job book?"

"Page—"

"The other night you contacted a rival outfit and gave them my call number?"

"Yes," Tanya whispered.

"The call number was easy to get from Waldo's, right?"

"Yes. I got it a long time ago."

"And it didn't matter that I would end up in jail and scared to death?"

Tanya hugged herself. "I wasn't thinking anymore. I'd tried to warn Waldo that I meant business weeks ago with those accidents—"

"With those 'accidents' my riders had?" She sighed, wanting desperately for this to be over. "You never talked to Ken about my problems because you didn't have to. You already knew because you'd given your rival outfit information about us and then you saw what happened. My God, Tanya, they put both Perkins and me in the hospital. No wonder Waldo was so quick to pay my medical bills. He really needed me back at work and thinking nice thoughts about him. Boy, did you make a patsy out of him."

"He asked for it. But I didn't expect you to get hurt." Tanya lifted her chin and her eyes were filled with tears. "I never thought anything would really happen to you—or anyone. The man I was dealing with said he only wanted to slow Waldo down by frightening him.''

One more thing. ''If you didn't intend me to be seriously implicated why did you plant money in the garage?''

''I couldn't think straight anymore.'' Tanya covered her eyes. ''I just wanted him to get what he deserves. He never believed I'd do anything to hurt him. He could always bring me to heel, he said.''

Page thought of something else. ''When I was in hospital I wondered why the envelopes hadn't been taken from my backpack when I was attacked. Now I know. Your friends didn't need them.''

Tanya had stopped listening. ''Waldo said I was a loser. He said I was useless and should creep away somewhere.''

And she would have crept away if Page hadn't caught her. ''If you want to run I won't stop you,'' she told Tanya. ''But I am calling the police, and they'll find you.''

''Call them. I'm not going anywhere.''

''I won't press personal charges against you,'' Page said. ''You'll have to answer for some things, but at least this way you'll eventually get to start over again.''

''In jail?''

''Maybe not. I know a police detective who likes to make deals.''

WHAT A DIFFERENCE A DAY MAKES. Wasn't that the way the song went?

Page propped herself against a wall in Union Square and watched a man in a clown costume making animals from skinny balloons.

''And an elephant for the boy with red hair,'' the man said, crouching in front of a freckle-faced toddler to offer a pink masterpiece with a foot-long trunk.

Two women accompanied several children, who watched the clown with the single-minded intensity Page had so often seen in the very young.

In her hand she held a rolled copy of a newspaper. She opened it again, turned to an inside page and read an insignificant article most people would miss: San Francisco had one less off-track betting outfit. Her own name wasn't mentioned. She was "an informed source." There had been arrests and would be more.

And an hour ago on this Monday in late December she'd spoken with another informed source. A doctor.

In about seven months Page would become a mother.

Chapter Seventeen

This was only the second time Page had visited Ian's suite at Faber and Faber. She walked from the elevator to his secretary's empty desk.

An oak-framed clock on the wall showed four-thirty. Ian was in the building. Page had checked the parking garage and found his car in its marked slot. She would wait until his secretary returned and ask to see him.

The pills the doctor had given her earlier in the day for nausea worked. She'd taken the first one as soon as she'd gotten back home to change for work and felt better already—physically. Once she'd seen Ian and told him what he had a right to know it would be business as usual for her.

The intercom on the secretary's desk buzzed, buzzed again, and again. Page looked at the control panel. The signal came from Ian's office. He must be in there and not know, or remember, that his secretary was away from her desk.

There wouldn't be a better or an easier time to say what she'd come to say.

He didn't look up when she entered his office. "Clemmie, what the hell's with you today? I rang half a dozen times. Take this stuff and get someone to run it down to the art department. Then I want you to keep trying that number I gave you till there's an answer."

Page closed the door. "Hello, Ian."

His head jerked up, but he remained crouched over the papers on his desk. "Page! I've been trying to call you. Your phone's been busy since last night."

"I took my phone off the hook."

"All night and all day?" He sat back, a pencil braced between the fingers of both hands. "I went over this morning and got no answer. And that watchdog of yours in the garage said she didn't know where you were."

She wouldn't be pushed around by him just because he'd had some sort of guilt attack about the things he'd said to her. "Lilian didn't know where I was."

"And she didn't tell you I was searching for you?"

"She hasn't seen me yet," Page said, and sighed. Buzz had been covering the radio when she went to the garage for her bike. "And she won't hear from me until I leave here and report in, not that you have to concern yourself with any of this. You must be very busy, so I'll make this short."

"Please—" he got up and skirted his desk to stand in front of her "—sit down. We were idiots last night."

She gave a grim laugh. "We seem to have a talent for saying the wrong things to each other."

He looked tired, so tired. "I did try to call last night, but like I said, I couldn't get through. I figured you were asleep so I didn't try to come over. Then today I still couldn't reach you. I read—"

"The paper." She completed his sentence. "I didn't come about that," she told him.

"Let me get you some coffee?"

The pulse in his throat was visible and strong. If she put a hand on his chest she'd feel the same beat. How was it that he didn't have to touch her for her to feel that he had? "No coffee, thanks. Ian, I'm pregnant. This morning a doctor told me I should deliver in about seven months."

She made herself look at his face. His lips were slightly parted. He stared back at her, but she couldn't read the expression in his dark, dark eyes.

"I'm not sorry," she went on. "Don't ever think that. And don't think I'm here because I expect help." She paused, and he continued to stare. "Getting pregnant may not have been very smart, but I do like children. I'm going to love this one, and I'm not a kid myself anymore, so it's time I started a family if I'm going to have one.

"The thing is that I kind of assumed I might not be ovulating because I'm so active I don't have many periods. So I'd put it out of my mind and that's why it happened."

He was utterly immobile and silent.

Page took a deep breath to finish her piece. "I'll have the baby and return to work as soon as possible. You haven't made any secret of how keen you are on children, and that's why I'm telling you this. I would have anyway, because I don't believe in depriving another human being of his or her rights. You have a right to know, and if you want to see the baby, or be a part of its life, we'll work it out.

"That's all I wanted you to know."

She backed away. He opened his mouth wider, and muscles worked in his jaw, but he still didn't speak.

Page found the doorhandle behind her and slipped from the room. By the time she reached the street she was running and fastening the chin strap of her helmet at the same time.

She was also crying. When was she going to accept the message that love was not only something you couldn't decide, it also didn't go away when you wished it would?

WHERE WAS SHE? How had she gotten away so fast? How could he have let her get away at all?

Ian dashed to the street. No sign of a red leotard and tights or white helmet . . . or a bike that resembled a pile of junk.

Rushing back into the building he ignored greetings from colleagues and employees and snatched up the phone on the information desk.

"Pedal—"

"Ian Faber here." He interrupted Lilian. "I don't know what instructions your boss has given you about letting me have information, but I want to know where she's headed and I want to know now."

He heard the dispatcher swallow. "Um, Mr. Faber, will you hold?"

She clicked off on him before he could reply, and he gripped the receiver in both hands, rolled to the balls of his feet and bounced. How could he have stood there like a statue while she gave him the most important news he'd received in his life? Shock. The only plausible excuse was that she'd thrown him into shock.

"You still there, Mr. Faber?"

"Yeah, yeah."

"Ms. Linstrom just called in for her next drop."

"You didn't tell her I—"

"No, I didn't tell her you were on the line. She's headed for Jeffry Sidds on Drumm. That's—"

"I know where it is, Lilian. Thanks." He hung up and shot from the building. Drumm was close and he'd do better on foot than in his car.

He wasn't in such terrific shape. Two blocks of running flat out, and his breathing sounded like something out of a scene in an Alfred Hitchcock movie.

When he passed Slattery he peered ahead, searching for anything bright red—and he saw it. Shiny red, and a bicycle, but it immediately slipped from sight. Just about where Drumm would be.

Women in New York wore tennis shoes to work and carried heels, or whatever else they wanted to use indoors. The trend had spread throughout the country's major cities.

Who said men in slippery leather-soled shoes were better off than a woman in high heels?

He skidded to a stop at the end of Drumm Street, just in time to see Page walk slowly from a building and mount the bike again.

"Page!''

His yell was lost in the hubbub.

She pushed off, head down, gaining speed.

Ian ran full tilt. His lungs screamed for relief.

He saw her make a left at Halleck Street. Now his shirt stuck to his body, and he yanked his tie down until he could work the button at his neck free.

"Page.'' Around the corner, and he barreled into her as she climbed off the bike, an envelope in hand. "Thank God. I couldn't keep this up much longer.''

She was, he realized, holding him while he trembled and fought for breath. "Ian, are you all right?''

He rallied, lifted his chin and ran a finger around the inside of his loosened collar. "Great shape,'' he said, fashioning a smile that couldn't possibly look as phony as it felt. "Need...'' He still hadn't caught his breath. "Need to talk to you, that's all.''

She let her hands fall from his arms, and he felt he'd lost something desperately important.

"I'm sorry if I dropped a bomb on you,'' she said, apparently reading the address on the envelope. "There didn't seem to be a better way to deal with, um, it. You really don't have to worry. I'm very much in charge.''

He bridled. "The hell you are. Not on your own.''

Page took a step backward and the uncertainty he'd seen on other occasions came into her eyes. "I know what I'm doing,'' she said. "And I'm a capable woman.''

Ian's breathing had returned to normal. People brushed past, hurrying on their appointed daily tasks, but he ignored them, reaching for and gently taking Page's arms in his hands. He eased her nearer. "I know how capable you are. But could you let me be capable for a change?"

Her marvelous blue eyes darkened, and she didn't stop him from taking off the crash helmet and tossing it into the basket on her bike.

"Everyone needs to be capable sometimes." Her voice had that breathy quality he was so crazy about. "But, Ian, don't worry about me or about doing the right thing. I'm really happy about this baby and I wouldn't change a thing. We'll be all right, really we will."

He couldn't remember the last time he'd cried, but he felt very close right now. "You sure will be all right."

"I know...I knew you'd start worrying about your child. That's something I can accept. I would, too."

"Please, could we stop this. I said we'd both been foolish, and if you'd given me a chance I'd have said what I've been trying to say to you since last night."

She bowed her head. "Say it."

"Okay, okay. I shouldn't have flown off the handle at you the way I did yesterday. I was stressed out."

"And now the truth is out in the papers you're over that nagging little doubt you had about me?"

"Damn it, Page, I..." He let out a soundless whistle. "Sorry. I keep doing that, don't I? But you keep driving me to it. I hadn't even read the paper when I was trying to reach you last night. As you'd notice, if you stopped to think, the news only broke late this morning."

He was right, and she was tired and beginning to feel weak again. "You talked about how much evidence the police had against me."

"I know. And I didn't handle it well. But I was terrified they had you cornered and would lock you away. I came to you last night ready to work out a plan of attack. Then I overreacted when you asked if I'd been betting. I'm sorry. I was wrong."

"So was I. But that doesn't alter the fact that I'm not into shotgun marriages."

"Oh, Page." She didn't stop him from drawing her to him. "Couldn't you stop being superwoman just for once. I sure don't feel super-strong right now, and I'm happy for you to know it. What I feel is... I feel a million feet high and happier than I'll ever be able to explain. And I'm not only interested in the baby. It's the baby and you as a package that drives me wild. A package attached to me. Don't you feel that? Don't you know what I feel? It's got to be the same for you as for me."

There was a moment's pause, a moment when he saw her mouth tremble. Then she placed a hand on each of his shoulders and looked into his face. He felt people bump into them but didn't care.

"You've got to think carefully," she said. "Is what you're feeling now something to do with guilt? If it is, Ian, then it's misplaced."

She had the bluest eyes he'd ever seen. He hoped the baby would be a girl with the same color eyes. When she curled her fingers around his lapel, staring downward, he realized he'd put a hand on her abdomen. He laughed self-consciously and hugged her again.

"Sorry if I'm familiar. But I do have a vested interest, you know. There's no guilt in this, Page. I think I started loving you the night we met."

She didn't appear to be listening closely. Her face settled against his neck and he locked his knees. This wasn't the moment to crumple to the sidewalk.

"Page, did you hear what I said?"

"Yes."

"Will you please marry me?"

Page registered another bump from a passerby and moved closer to Ian. "I don't know. I don't know about anything. Do you understand yet that I won't give up my business?"

He looked fantastic, a slight sheen on his brow, his collar loose, his hair curling in the light fall of San Francisco's misty rain.

"I understand," he said. "But you come home to me. Today, you come home to me. And every day."

"You're reacting, not thinking. It's the baby."

He shook her, but gently. "No, it's not only that and you know it. We covered all this ground before, then got side-tracked. Think back to where we were with each other a week ago." He brought his face very close. "I can't live without you because I don't want to. But there are one or two things that ought to be said." One dark arched brow rose higher than the other.

"Name 'em," she said.

"No more late-night deliveries of champagne and truffle pâté." His lingering kiss made a quiet place around them until he raised his head. "And you'll agree that as a pregnant woman, maniacal bicycle riding is out."

"I have a question or two first," Page said.

"Make them fast." His impatience showed and it amused her.

"You want us to get married?"

"I already said that."

"Okay. That's fine. And I promise to be kind to your parents and try to make you proud. But you won't expect me to play bridge every day or serve on committees for the rest of my life, will you?"

His fingers were making holes in her arms. "I don't want you to be anything but yourself. I don't want you to change. But we will have some compromises to face, you know that?"

"I know that."

He passed his tongue over his lips, frowning. "Does that mean you will marry me?"

"Yes."

He shook his head, smiling, and folded her close. "Thanks a lot for the enthusiasm. You are such an incurable romantic."

POSTSCRIPT: Three years after their marriage, Page and Ian Faber have two children, a boy Robert—named for Ian's father—and a girl, Zara, now nine months.

In addition to Jemima, Lilian and the Zipper have a two-year-old boy, Mark.

Pedal Pushers continues to operate under Lilian and the Zipper's management with Page's careful guidance and never diminishing interest.

Page and Rose Faber are close friends although Rose has given up on persuading Page to own a fur.

Tanya Woodside plea-bargained and received a suspended sentence for her part in Waldo Sands's operation. She is now happily married to a professor of economics at a Californian university and studies computer graphics.

Harlequin Superromance

Here are the longer, more involving stories you have been waiting for... Superromance.

Modern, believable novels of love, full of the complex joys and heartaches of real people.

Intriguing conflicts based on today's constantly changing life-styles.

Four new titles every month.
Available wherever paperbacks are sold.

SUPER-1

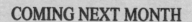

COMING NEXT MONTH

Taylor House

by Leigh Anne Williams

One house... two sisters... three generations

**Harlequin American Romance introduces
the TAYLOR HOUSE trilogy in October 1988**

The Taylor family of Greensdale, Massachusetts, had always
been "the family on the hill." Grammy Taylor and her two
daughters, Katherine and Lydia, were admired more than they
were known and loved. But the passing of the matriarch
brought with it a unique test for the two sisters—could they
save Taylor House... and save the town?

—Meet Katherine, who is determined to bring her dream to
 life.
—Meet Lydia, who hopes to keep that dream alive.
—And meet Clarissa, Katherine's daughter, whose wish is to
 carry on the traditions of Taylor House for a new generation.

A story of family, home and love in a New England village.

Don't miss the stories of these three women in the October, November and December
Harlequin American Romances for 1988:
#265 *Katherine's Dream*, #269 *Lydia's Hope* and #273 *Clarissa's Wish*

TAYLR-1